G000124907

The

Lost Finch

By

MJ Birkett

First Published in Great Britain in 2022

Paperback ISBN 978-1-8384489-9-8

MJ Birkett Publishing: Salisbury
mark@mjbirkett.com

For Mum

Part 1 — Scarlet

Chapter 1 — Baby Scarlet, 4 weeks old (1980s, Gadsby Street)

Francis Finch rested her bike against the depot wall and nipped into the warehouse to pick items: sachets of tea, sugar, and cereal. Toilet-rolls, toothpaste, and bubble-bath. Everything the old biddies needed. She dumped the items in her basket and set off.

'Thanks for covering Gina's shift,' the gaffer said, staring at her legs as she cycled away, pressing the pedals fast.

The town drifted by and her body warmed, fighting against the brisk chill. First stop. She wiped the sweat from her forehead while pushing her bike between two terraced houses. A cut-through lane.

She mounted the bike against the brick wall, jamming the handle into the drainpipe. She knocked, but let herself in without waiting for an invitation. 'Hello, Mrs Elliot? It's Francis Finch. Gina's still off sick, so you've got me again. I've got your items. Mrs Elliot?'

Fran placed the shopping on the kitchen counter and meandered into the house. 'Mrs Elliot?'

'Oh, hello dear. Sorry, I wasn't paying attention. Look at this precious baby,' Mrs Elliot said, rocking a tiny newborn from the comfort of her armchair. One month old. Fran smelt its warm flesh before she saw its scrunched-up face, and as its features came into view, she radiated the largest smile, inducing colour into her pale cheeks. 'These are my neighbours, Joe and Sally.'

'Nice to meet you,' Fran said, lowering herself beside the armchair, ready to coo the newborn. Mrs Elliot lifted the baby, gesturing for Fran to take her. 'If you're sure?' Politeness.

Mrs Elliot and her neighbours insisted Fran have a cuddle. The baby passed over.

'Oh, you are a little sweetheart. Aren't you? Yes, you are. Yes, you are,' Fran said, the infant gripping her finger with its entire hand. She leant into her forehead and inhaled. New baby smell. 'You must be so proud. She's gorgeous.'

'She is. But sadly, she's not ours,' Sally McGuinness said, sitting in the armchair opposite and reaching for a cashew nut from the little bowl resting on the coffee table.

'Joe and Sally are foster carers. They look after unwanted little babies until the council finds them a proper home,' Mrs Elliot said, attempting to stand. 'Do you want a cup of tea, Francis, dear?'

'That's my job,' Fran said, her trance with the baby breaking as she remembered she was at work. 'I've left your items on the counter. Let me make you a cup of tea and pop them away.'

'Sit down.'

Mrs Elliot patted Fran on the back and shuttled past in her old lady slippers. 'I'll sort it. Not dead yet. And besides, you've got your hands full. Sit down, duck. Enjoy the baby.'

Mrs Elliot flopped her hand at the sofa. 'Take a break while you can. You're rushed off your feet.'

Fran would usually protest, insist on making the tea while Mrs Elliot argued back. The charade would continue for a few rounds, and then Mrs Elliot would surrender. Fran provided company as well as delivering bits and pieces. But with the tiny baby in her arms, professionalism melted. She sank into the sofa beside Joe and abandoned her sense of duty.

'You don't think of babies in foster care. People imagine teenagers. Children. Do you get many?' Fran said.

Sally had filled her mouth with cashew nuts. Her hand covered her mouth, and she animated chomping to excuse the lack of immediate response. Joe stepped in. 'Not too many babies. Mostly young children and teenagers, as you say, but we've had three or four. Over the years.'

'Four!'

The cashews were gone, freeing Sally McGuinness to speak. 'I remember each. I know I'm not their mum, but each baby is unique. Unforgettable. Well, to a mother-figure, anyway. Joe's brilliant, but they're all the same to him.'

She leant forward to squeeze his knee and kiss his cheek, an advantage to there not being much room between the floral sofa and armchair.

'It's true. Nappies. Lots of nappies. Even more milk,' Joe said, reaching out his hand to let the baby resting in Fran's arms squeeze his finger. She thought him a kind man.

'Do you find it hard to let them go?'

'Never pleasant, but there's compensatory joy. With babies, you know there will be a happy ending,' Sally McGuinness said, grinning. 'She's taken to you.'

She admired the natural way Fran handled the baby. 'She's been a crier. More so than usual,' she added, cupping her hand in the bowl of cashews and scooping another bundle.

' "Happy ending?" ' Fran said, repeating Sally's phrase while flooding the baby with more smiles and silly nods.

'There are plenty eager to adopt an innocent baby. It's almost certain she'll end up with a loving couple who'll spoil her rotten. The older kids, though. They break your heart. People think they're too troubled. They go from home to home. Town to town. I think her mum—' Sally switched from generalisations and spoke about the infant in Fran's arms. '—She must have known at some intuitive level it was better to act quickly.'

Sally placed another cashew into her mouth, sucking out a little of its sweetness before she crunched.

'Did you know her mum?' Fran asked.

'Not personally,' Sally said with the single cashew in her mouth. 'Teenager—' she moved another cashew nut toward her mouth. '— Nurses said she already had a baby, and they hadn't bonded. Apparently, she thought it'd be better to give this one over before it got too late. Tragic really. Poor girl.'

Fran's arms steeled around the bundle of warmth on her lap. 'Do you know where the girl's from?' She said.

'Here. They avoid transferring babies too far away for their first few weeks in case circumstances change. The policy is to allow the mothers to take them back if they reconsider. But from experience, it rarely happens.'

Sally continued chatting away, but Fran entered a trance.

'Your tea, love,' Mrs Elliot said, re-entering the room and placing two cups of tea in lilac mugs on the coffee table. She stood in front of the small gas fire boxed to the wall. Fran barely noticed her presence. Her mind blocked the immediate sense of the room. Its flowery furniture, shaggy carpet and chintzy ornaments. Sally's chatter blurred into background noise, emanating from somewhere much further away. Mrs Elliot's colourful cardigan dulled into low resolution charcoal. Her heart repeated a strapline. *She is your niece.*

'Are you ok, love?'

The room quietened as Sally, Joe, and Mrs Elliot picked up something was wrong. They each stared at Fran. Sally nudged Joe's knee with her own. He drew forward and reached out to withdraw the baby, which triggered Fran to lock her arms. It led to an awkward altercation. Joe's forearm pressed on her wrists, but Fran did not loosen. Mrs Elliot gasped.

'Francis, love!' she said, her upper body bending over the coffee table. Her hands waving in Fran's face. Fran was a lovely, rational lady. This wasn't her. 'Francis, dear!'

Mrs Elliot increased the volume of her voice as Joe attempted to remove the baby again. 'Francis, come on now, dear. Mr McGuinness needs her back. Francis!'

'Please, let me hold her. Just a little longer.'

Fran's grip remained hard, but a softness crept into her voice. It eased Sally and Joe's anxiety. A little.

'We're just a tad worried, love. You're distracted,' Sally said, releasing the couple of cashew nuts from her hand onto the coffee table, and then raising her palms to signal Joe could ease up, at least a little.

He leant into the sofa, not relaxed but posturing as if he were.

'I'm sorry for scaring you, but I won't hurt her. I'm not like that,' Fran said, keeping her eyes on the baby.

'Oh, love. I didn't think for a second you would hurt her,' Sally said, even though she didn't believe it. She had experience of diffusing these situations. Assert trust. De-stress the person. Help them transition into a rational headspace and get them to comply with small reasonable requests. She continued to speak, keeping a conversation brewing. 'We're just a bit worried that she'll be scared if you grip too tightly. What is it, love? What's happened? You can tell us.'

Fran's arms eased, and the baby wrapped her little fingers around her thumb. She burped, causing a tiny splutter of milk to surface. Fran dabbed her sleeve on the baby's mouth and her entire body warmed as if she had thawed from a miserable outing. Her senses returned. She ignored Mrs Elliot's bemused stare and looked at Sally McGuinness. 'She's my niece.'

Sally avoided the impulse to look at her husband, feeling it was important to maintain eye contact with Fran. She examined her face, believing there was truth there. Mrs Elliot's attention departed. She went inward, searching for her memories of who and where Francis Finch fit. Her hand gushed to her mouth as the pieces slotted together, like the end of an Agatha Christie novel (she had a stack on the dining table). 'Oh gosh dear, you're Fae's daughter — from the Co-op. Her youngest, Evelyn, isn't it? She had a baby a year back? She's had another?'

Fran responded without removing her gaze from the baby's eyes. 'We can't let her go again. We didn't want our Lyn to give her up.'

Eventually, she searched the room for feedback. Sally sighed and gave Fran what she was looking for.

'Look, if she is your niece, you'll have rights. Obviously, I'll need to ring the social and go through the details, but when all is said and done, if you're willing to accept guardianship, you can. She can go with you. May sound a tad harsh, but the state views it as one less problem for them.'

Fran squeezed tighter. She expected a fight, one with the odds stacked against her. Not an offer to bring the baby home.

'Just like that? I can take her now. Just like that?'

It was absurd. Unbelievable. Authorities didn't work like this.

Sally McGuinness pounced into action, a deep pragmatism and sense of service activating and overriding her own desires and needs. 'Let me ring Reeta from the social, tell her what's happened and confirm everybody is who we think they are — and of course, it won't be "just like that". They'll need to visit your house and talk to everybody. But yes. It's unlikely two babies were born at the same hospital, on the same day, to an already teenage mum. So chances are she is your niece. And assuming you don't live in a drug den or hostile environment—'

'—We don't!'

'Then yes. She'll go with you.'

Sally McGuinness walked across the room. She had to keep moving. Keep acting. 'I'll nip around to use the phone; get the process started.'

Fran convinced herself the baby was her niece. The tiny fingers gripped her thumb, and she just knew she was a Finch.

Mrs Elliot sank into her chair and made her reservations clear. 'Oh dear, but what about poor Evelyn? What'll she say?'

Fran ignored her. She watched Sally McGuinness wrap around the front garden and disappear into her house. In her absence, Joe assumed her peacekeeping role. He rephrased Mrs Elliot's questions with a simpler one of his own. 'Do you live with your sister?'

He laid his hands on his thigh.

'Will that matter?' Fran questioned back, stiff.

Mrs Elliot wedged herself back into the discussion. 'Dear, if she gave the baby up...?'

She perched closer to the edge of the armchair as she spoke. Fran, again, ignored her. 'Mr McGuinness, will it matter?' She repeated, her pulse quickening. She felt as if she were treading a rope-bridge across a nasty cavern.

'Not really. If a willing relative accepts guardianship, the social will—'

'—I will accept guardianship,' Fran said, needing to breathe, but refusing to do so until she had crossed the bridge. She was one step closer. One step closer to taking her niece, but it still felt too precarious to let her guard down.

Mrs Elliot, alarmed at the speed of movement, tried to slow things down. 'But what about Evelyn? It must have been a tough decision for her to make, and now you're taking it away!'

Her hands gripped together, and her body rocked a little to offset the emotion. She wasn't comfortable intervening.

'She won't have to do anything. Me and Ma will—'

'—Dear, come-on now. It's not about that. The girl is her mother, and she made a tough decision to do best by the child.'

Fran pivoted upward with the baby clutched in her arms. She turned her back on Mrs Elliot and planted small kisses on the newborn's soft cheeks. The affection balanced her dual emotional state of resentment toward Mrs Elliot and absolute devotion toward the baby and just about restrained her impulse to fight. Also, the stillness provided space for her to register genuine hope. Mrs Elliot wouldn't be trying so hard to convince her not to take the baby if there wasn't a serious chance of it happening. 'What would you do?' Fran asked, expecting only one answer from the old lady.

'Duck, it isn't about me. Or you.'

The tension in Mrs Elliot's shoulders loosened a little, and her bosom lifted. She breathed into her old lungs. Whereas Fran stiffened and her neck tensed. Mrs Elliot continued. 'Dear, it isn't our decision. It's Evelyn's. She obviously thought this was best.'

Fran strode to the window, baby still in hand. She rocked and planted more kisses; this time on her forehead. 'I don't even know your name,' she said aloud, noticing a tiny scar at the back of her tiny ear. She leant in to kiss the lobe and whispered, 'let's call you Scarlet. Scarlet Finch.'

'Her name is Annabelle,' Mrs Elliot said, having not heard Fran's whisper and having not been able to lip read with Fran's back still turned to her. 'Annabelle,' she repeated.

Fran twisted to face Mrs Elliot squarely, boring every ounce of strength she possessed. 'Her name is Scarlet.'

Mrs Elliot sighed but nodded as Sally McGuinness appeared in the front garden. She gave a selfless smile from the other side of the glass, which Fran caught as she twisted. She could tell from Sally's face it was good news. Scarlet was coming home.

Fran scooted around Mrs Elliot's coffee table with Scarlet still gripped in her arms. She was ecstatic, but told herself to wait. She shouldn't believe what was happening until she had definitive confirmation. But it felt like Christmas Eve. She had no serious doubt Santa was coming. Just an inability to tolerate the wait. Fran knew Scarlet was coming home.

'I'll collect my bike this afternoon,' she said. Statement, not request.

But Mrs Elliot couldn't let the conversation drop. 'Are you sure this is right, Francis? Why don't you go home and discuss it with your Ma and young Evelyn first?'

She shuttled to blockade the exit.

'—Besides, it's a long walk.'

Her arms folded across her self-knitted cardigan. The door blocked.

'It's fine,' Fran said, wedging herself into the small gap between Mrs Elliot and the wall, forcing the old lady to shift and stiffen.

Sally McGuinness came along the corridor and settled the tension. She told Fran it was good news. Mrs Elliot shifted out of the way.

'We have a car. Joe can drive us,' she said, resting her hand on Mrs Elliot's arm. A gesture to say she appreciated the effort. But that it was also over. Futile to persist with trying to stop an inevitable course of action.

Fran halted her advance along the wallpaper and Mrs Elliot moved back to give her room while Sally McGuinness continued to lubricate their standoff. 'Joe, why don't you take Fran to the car while I pop and collect Annabelle's things?'

Fran's impulse was to snap Scarlet's real name, but she clamped her tongue. Mrs Elliot recognised the restraint. She appreciated Fran's fierce maternal instinct and accepted, as Sally had already done, the baby was going home. That it was right.

Mrs Elliot relaxed her cardigan-covered arms and capitulated. She moved away from the exit and said what Fran held back. 'The baby's real name is Scarlet.'

It was her way of giving approval; of telling Fran she understood what she was fighting for; and that, despite her conservatism and grave reservations regarding the way it was being done, she agreed with what she was doing.

Sally McGuinness nodded with another selfless smile, accepting the name change without a flicker of protest or sense of loss even though she felt a deep pain at seeing the child she'd mothered for the last few weeks renamed on the spot as if she were some branded product. No longer hers. But she knew it wasn't about her. 'Of course,' she said. 'I'll collect Scarlet's things.'

Her tone was compassionate.

'Joe,' she said, letting her husband know she was ready. He led their collective exit.

Outside, he opened the car door of the rusty-orange Ford and Fran climbed in, Scarlet locked in her arms. Mrs Elliot leant against the porch wall, watching them sitting still in the car. Sally collected bottles of milk, clothing, and a few toys. With the things, she climbed into the backseat and waved goodbye to Mrs Elliot. The car spluttered into life, and Mrs Elliot waved back. She watched them and the car disappear before going inside.

Five minutes later, they pulled onto the pavement outside Fran's house. Curtains twitched in the terraced windows as neighbours wondered who the fancy car belonged to and what it was doing on their predominantly carless street. Rose, the neighbour, grabbed her shopping trolly on the pretext of heading to the Co-op. She stepped onto the street. 'Hello, dear. Who's this beautiful little darling?'

She shuffled forward to coo at the baby. 'Oh, she's adorable. Yes, you are. Yes, you are,' she said, leaning forward to peck and then brush the baby's cheek.

Sally straightened her back after curving out of the car. With bags in hand, she joined Fran and Rose. 'Hello, Mrs Finch. I'm Sally McGuinness—'

'—That's only Rose, the neighbour,' Fran said, dismissing the lady and her trolly. She clambered to the door, fishing for keys, but Ma opened it from the inside.

Rose waved hello/goodbye at Sally and the baby, then continued wheeling along the path to distance herself, but not so much she wouldn't be able to hear any ensuing commotion.

'What's going on? I thought you'd gone to work,' Ma said, looking confused, even though she had a firm idea of what was happening. Behind her, June came thrashing along the corridor, smelling drama. She slid around Ma to inspect the fuss first hand.

'Fran?' June said to her sister, springing onto the pavement from the doorstep. 'What's going on?'

Unlike Ma, she wanted an answer.

'Meet Scarlet,' Fran said, radiating joy as if she were holding a puppy with a singular purpose in the world. Spread happiness.

June was unimpressed that the fuss was about a baby. 'Who the fuck's Scarlet?'

Ma mustered her entire might to not slap her daughter's legs. Angry at June's language. 'Don't swear in the middle of the street,' she said, causing June's muscles to tighten. There was an unusual fire in her breath, and she seldom told them off for real. Let alone in front of strangers. What was going on?

From the upper window of next door, Winston and Ivan's brutish faces appeared. They hung out to see the car. Though seeing June, they seized the opportunity to fire a few nasties. 'Another sprog? Can't be yours, June! Nobody touch that,' Winston said, sniggering to his little brother, who also laughed, even if it was less enthusiastic. Less visceral.

'Fuck off, Waverley, you nonce!' June replied, knowing how much Winston hated it. She spat on the pavement beneath his window and then stuck her middle finger at him, smiling.

Winston fired another missile; this time to Fran, who he mostly ignored. 'Frank Boucher finally give you one then, Francie?'

Mrs Winstanley, their mother, opened the front door and stepped onto the street. She looked at her boys from below and told them to go inside. 'I'm sorry, love,' she said, turning to Ma. 'You know what men can be like.'

'Don't worry, Iris. You know we don't pay no attention to them,' Ma said, reassuring Iris it wasn't her fault for the way Winston and Ivan had turned out.

'Mrs Finch, shall we go inside?' Sally McGuinness said, stepping toward the house.

Ma moved aside. 'Of course, come-in.'

Fran and Sally slid past. Ma sucked herself into the coats to make space. More psychological than real. A gesture to imply room. Their bodies brushed against each other as they crossed. Fran's face beamed with joy as she carried Scarlet inside. Once she and Sally cleared the door, Ma peeled off the coats and stepped onto the doorstep. She whispered, 'You too, June.'

But Iris and her boy-men heard.

'Yeah, get inside before they catch you, nut-job!' Winston said.

'Fuck off, Waverley!'

June stuck her middle finger at Winston again, and he did the same back. Ignoring him, she went inside, slamming the door harder than she meant to, eliciting another scowl from Ma, who even leant forward to tap her thigh. And although it had no force, June sobered at the contact. Ma was not physical. The tap was tantamount to a slap in other households.

Ma shuffled into the kitchen, heading on autopilot for the kettle. 'Can I make you a cup of tea?'

'That would be lovely,' Mrs McGuinness said, leaning against the twenty-year-old kitchen cupboards.

Ma hovered the kettle in the sink and then looked at her slippers while the tap filled it with water. She braced herself for the conversation.

'You know who Scarlet is, don't you Mrs Finch?' Sally said.

Ma broke the gaze toward her slippers and pulled the kettle away before it overflowed. 'Who gave her that name?'

Fran spoke up. Proud. 'I did.'

She sat at the tiny table wedged into the crowded kitchen. Not enough room to sit at. Though they did. She gazed at Scarlet's sky-blue irises.

Ma brought herself to ask the question. 'Why's she here?'

She plonked the overfilled kettle onto the base and then dragged her body along the edge of the work-surface. She opened the back door. Aerated the kitchen, but not so much for the neighbours to hear their conversation.

Fran switched to incredulity. 'It's her home, Ma! Why else would she be here?'

It was the most natural truth to her, and she couldn't understand their lack of instantaneous joy.

Ma lit a cigarette and stared at the red light on the kettle. She blew her cigarette smoke while listening to the mechanisms choking in the machine, then returned to the sink where she stared out the window. The garden needed mowing. She took another long drag, exhaled, and then asked the only thing she needed to know. 'Mrs McGuinness, is it permanent?'

Sally McGuinness answered Ma while smiling at Fran, who had barely removed her eyes from Scarlet the entire time. 'It is if you're willing to take her.'

'Of course we are! I've already said this,' Fran said, causing Scarlet to squirm at her uncontrolled burst of energy.

Ma turned and rested her back on the counter. 'It's just—'

'—Ma! This is her home.'

'I know it is—' she said, picking up a tea towel and clenching it with both hands. '—But what if Evelyn doesn't want her?'

June bent down and examined Scarlet's face. 'This is her baby?'

They ignored her stupid question.

'Ma, we can look after her, even if—' Fran said.

'—I'm not worried about us looking after her.'

It was rare for Ma to interrupt. She twisted her body back to the kitchen window and continued speaking with her back turned to them. '—Will they allow us to keep her even if Evelyn doesn't want it?'

Mrs McGuinness knew she was the representative of Ma's "they".

'Yes—' she said, landing a nuke strike in Ma's heart, whose legs dilapidated. Whose muscles turned to jelly in one swoop. Strength melted. Struggled to keep upright. '—Just show the social you are a responsible caregiver. Both willing and able to provide a safe home. There is no more to it. They will pop over to check and confirm details but believe me, I've been in many homes and they'll have no problem here.'

Ma swept across the kitchen and lifted Scarlet from Fran's arms, planting kiss after kiss, and wetting every inch of her delicate dry skin and soft hair. Scarlet sank into Ma's grandma-bosom, and released several joyful squeaks beneath a symphony of cooing and coddling. 'Hello, you. Hello, you. My precious little angel.'

Her words rolled into a slow chant, which whirlpooled the little thing into a mystical sandstorm of love. Ma nodded along as Sally McGuinness spoke through details, but she didn't listen properly; neither did Fran. June was the only one paying attention. She didn't see the fascination or hype with the baby, and though she kept it quiet, she doubted whether they were doing the right thing.

After a good forty minutes, Sally McGuinness left. A social worker had confirmed the baby's identity on the phone, and another would visit the home later that afternoon. It was done. Outside, Joe McGuinness leant against his car, smoking cigarettes. Ivan and Winston bombarded him with questions about the car's intricate workings and performance. He answered, even though he really just wanted to smoke his cigarettes in peace. As his wife came out, he squashed a half-smoked one into the pavement, freeing his hands. He gave her a long, loving hug. They got into the car and drove home alone. Quiet and a little sad. Another baby moving on to live without them; another baby with this chapter—them—erased from its life.

In the living room, Ma and Fran fussed and cooed Scarlet, but June sat on the sofa, fidgeting. Her feet dug into the cushions; her hands wrapped around her shins; and her chin pressed into her kneecaps. 'What about Evelyn?' She said, unable to remain silent any longer.

Fran responded in a bored, unimpressed tone. 'What about her?'

She knelt on the floor beside Ma's chair and played with Scarlet while she sat on Ma's lap. She bobbed Scarlet's tiny fists up and down.

June found herself in the unusual situation of defending her younger sister. 'She gave her up, and you've gone against her decision. I'm not sure it's right.'

'—She's our niece!' Fran said, certitude spitting across the room.

June submitted to its intended shame. Her cheeks rouged beside her chin-supporting kneecaps. She chewed her lip and decided it was better to leave the conversation where it was. Maybe Fran was right? She watched her playing with the baby and reconsidered. Nothing. The seed of doubt only grew in her gut until it felt like early appendicitis. It wasn't right. But this wasn't her area, and she would not get involved. She lumbered off the sofa and sulked out of the room. A silent protest.

Hours rolled by with Fran and Ma enchanting Scarlet into her new home. They got Evelyn's first born, Lilly, to crawl toward her baby sister. To stare and become mesmerised by something so similar. Only a year between them. Evelyn was pregnant with Scarlet within six months of giving birth to Lilly.

June, upstairs, grew restless. She ventured into the attic, searching for things she cleared away when Lilly arrived. She resented giving up what little space she had, but did it without complaint. Or much. This time, though, she would defend her territory. Would fight. The baby wasn't having any more of her space. Fran could sacrifice. And what better way to make the point than reclaiming old belongings?

She took an old chair from Ma's bedroom and positioned it beneath the attic hatch. After removing her boots, she climbed onto the chair, stretched her fingertips to the square wooden block, and pushed until it popped open. She lifted her feet onto the banister while pressing her palms into the wall. Her slim waist limited the banister's moans, but it squeaked and swayed. She'd not lifted herself into the attic in years. And although she had always been tall, more able to get up than her sisters, she didn't really like the attic's dark and dusty enclosed space. As soon as whatever box or bin-liner Ma passed up, she'd toss it away and get out.

Now, though, she had a torch. A fancy Maglight nicked from Ivan's car. They'd never owned one before, and Ma wouldn't risk them using candlelight in case it caused a fire. June hadn't stolen it because she wanted a torch for the attic. She stole it because it belonged to him. Hoped he might come asking her about it. Any opportunity to chat. No matter how trivial. She stole his stuff whenever the opportunity arose. She loved him. Loved his things.

For the first time, June saw the attic lit up. Much vaster than she'd imagined. Awe inducing. She'd felt nothing like that at church christenings or weddings. The illuminated beams and short brick walls dividing the terraces' attics mesmerised her. Feeling confident, she stood upright, knowing she wouldn't bash her head. She'd been afraid of spiders and bugs scuttling into her hair, but now she could see there was nothing to fear. Indeed, there was hope and opportunity. The walled boundaries ended halfway to the roof. Passable. She tiptoed to it and shined the torch over. A little bundle of bags and boxes illuminated around the neighbour's hatch. Rose's stuff. She twisted to shine the torchlight on the opposite wall, preying it was equally passable.

Jackpot.

June trod the planks over to it. To Ivan's wall. She shined the torch, and it illuminated a similar cluster of boxes and bin-liners around the hatch. His stuff. Access to his bedroom. Access to him. She felt like a character in the Goonies discovering one-eyed Willy's treasure.

She gripped the torch with her teeth, slimed over the wall—avoiding contact with the beams—and lowered herself onto Ivan's planks. Her shins pressed into Ivan's dust. She crawled beside Ivan's dark, seaweed-looking oceans of insulating wool bordering both sides of her body. A few of the boards creaked, but her petite frame prevented too much noise. At the stockpile around the hatch, she began loosening several of his bags.

'June, what're you doing?' Ma said, her voice filling the attic with a God-like omnipresence. It almost caused June to drop the torch and create a thud on Ivan's hatch. With it still gripped in her teeth, she scuttled back over the wall, but hid it before dropping her head into the hatch. She saw their upstairs corridor, but no Ma. Paranoid. She lowered her voice. Not wanting it to carry.

'What? Nothing. Just getting a few bits.'

Her head dangled out of the hatch. She could not afford for anybody to share her newfound secret. If Ma, Fran, Winston or Ivan discovered the attics joined, they might do something about it. She had to protect her treasure. Her hair drooped over her face, making her look like a demonic doll.

'Don't fetch anything unnecessary. We have to make extra space for Scarlet. In fact, we should put things up there,' Ma said.

June lost the zeal to defend space in the bedroom. Adventures of getting into Ivan's bedroom occupied her imagination. She could look and touch his underwear. Smell his socks. Examine his dirty magazines and see the type of women he masturbated over. She could rub his toothbrush over her own teeth and taste his saliva. Her soul energised with missionary purpose. Giving-up a bit of space was of flea-sized significance compared to all this. Irritating. Whereas Ivan's house offered June a divine experience. Unregulated access to the man she adored. Or at least his things.

'Don't come down yet. I'll hand you a few more things,' Ma said, seizing the opportunity. It was usually such a hassle, but June didn't argue in her state of ecstasy. Her head still flopped out of the hatch while her imagination throbbed with excitement, blood gushing into it and eliciting dangerous levels of fantasy-inducing oxygen. *Socks. Pants. Dirty*

T-shirts. Socks. Pants. His toothbrush. Socks. Pants. Crusty used tissue paper. Passion upon passion.

Ma pushed a bin liner of old clothes and items into June's hair. 'Put those up while I grab a few more bits.'

June pulled herself from the junkie honey-prison, harbouring dormant within every addict's soul. She took the bag and placed it onto the plank, the path bridging fantasy and reality. For now, the bag of crap would protect her secret. Ma passed another couple up. A barricade. A cluster of crap blocking the way to the magic wall. Reinforcements to protect her little secret.

June slid out of the Hatch. Her feet landed on the banister, less elegant than a ballerina's descent. She fixed the lid and then returned the chair to Ma's bedroom. Afterward, she closed her own bedroom door, lay down, and dreamed of Ivan. When would he and his family leave the house?

Meanwhile, Evelyn and her squaddie-date had returned to Birmingham New Street to take the train home. They stopped beside the shopwindow of H. Samuel where he jested about wedding rings. 'That one'd suit ya.'

The squaddie pointed to the most expensive ring on the display.

'Who says I want to get married?'

Evelyn's girlish blush betrayed the womanly act she was going for.

'Ya say'in ya wouldn't want me babies?'

He sounded out whether she really liked him, whether she wanted to go on another date, but his soft boyish tone and flushing cheeks betrayed the intended bravado. He misread the deepening rouge of her cheeks for innocence and coyness when really she was just embarrassed. She had avoided her motherhood status; was determined to remain quiet about it. He would find out eventually. Of course he would. But it wouldn't be because of her inability to swallow a few emotions. She would not cause his fading interest. She would not cut short their romance.

Evelyn forced reality into her gut. Let bacteria eat it for lunch. Though she knew it would only satisfy their hunger for so long. Reality always returns. She knew her life would be difficult. Contain a lot of hard feelings.

'Come-on, ya must want kids one day, eh?'

Evelyn slid against the glass of the window display. Jewellery dazzled. Gold wedding rings. Diamante necklaces. Brass bracelets. Silver earrings. 'That's pretty,' she said, stopping to point at a barbell.

The squaddie took her hands from behind. He wasn't interested in the jewellery. He was interested in her. His body spooned into her back and his lips kissed the back of her neck. 'I really like ya, babs.'

Evelyn felt the moisture in his words. He then twisted her around and pulled their bodies together, face-to-face, with the window-display supporting her back. 'Yas a keeper,' he said before planting his bulbous lips on hers, tasting the top layer of her cherry lipstick. The shake of trains pulling onto platforms beneath the shopping centre channelled up her body. Welcome tremors.

Afterward, she stared without restraint at his eyes. She wondered who he was beneath the barrack boy banter and the smooth talk. He misread her contemplation for romantic enchantment, telling himself she felt a divine love that elevated her from the here and now. A boyish grin broke out across his face, energised by the throb of validation her misidentified love triggered in him. His lips stretched until he looked like a football hooligan with a Chelsea smile. 'Come-on,' he said, propelling their joined hands into a swing that sliced the air, back and forth until the ticket barriers forced them to separate.

He re-gripped her hand on the platform and continued holding it as they boarded the train and then waded along the aisle looking for seats. His palm was hot, and his fingers forced Evelyn's fingers to space more than was comfortable, but she liked the idea of him possessing and protecting her. Perhaps he would stick around if the feeling strengthened?

'I'll walk ya home,' he said once the train arrived in Nuneaton station.

'You don't need to.'

Now she was coy.

Outside the station, they meandered to the ring-road. Hand-in-hand, they sounded out their next steps.

'I want to, babs—' he said, referring to the walk home and stepping toward Attleborough where Evelyn lived. She smiled at his insistence. '—Besides, we need to agree on our next date.'

As they cut through the churchyard, squaddie John described Manchester, promising to take her next weekend. Once they reached home, he leant in for a longer kiss. His eyes were closed, but Evelyn kept hers open. She stared at the bushy brow above his closed eyelids, tasted the salt and vinegar lingering on his lips from the packet of crisps they'd shared on the train, and wondered what he would think if he learnt she had a kid. Kids.

The kiss ended, and their eyes met. She touched the fur of his eyebrow. He smiled. 'Ya really are gorgeous, ya know that, right?'

She removed her hands from his face, summoned an appropriate flush of modesty, and diverted the conversation from her appearance. 'I better get in before June comes and poaches you.'

The key entered the lock, but Fran opened the door from inside. Evelyn's big sister stood on the flowery carpet holding Scarlet, the baby Evelyn had given up for adoption. Fran smiled like a victorious captain returned home from a self-started war; the sound of war drums beating in the distance. The squaddie presumed it was the same kid June held when he called for her that morning. Evelyn knew immediately it was not.

'It's Scarlet!' Fran said, expecting Evelyn to be joyous.

Evelyn's lungs took too much air. They felt like cups overflowing with too much water. She couldn't breathe, but she had to. A pragmatism kicked in. She hurried a goodbye, attempting to rid Brummie John from the ensuing argument (and to prevent the revelation of her motherhood). One problem at a time. But before she could get him away, June rushed down the stairs, amplifying the drama, and Ma ambled toward the door with her own gleeful, expectant grin. 'Can you give me a minute to say goodbye?'

A dispassionate coldness steeled Evelyn's plea to her sisters and Ma.

Fran became outraged. 'Evelyn, it's Scarlet! Your baby. She's more important than some worthless squaddie; just tell him to piss off, and come meet her properly.'

Evelyn exploded.

'Who do you think gave birth?'

Her fingers dug into her own skull as Brummie John looked like an abused dog kicked by its owner. Even June experienced a hot-flush of unfamiliar yet throbbing compassion. Her heart reached out to her little sister.

Silence brewed anger like a broth turning bad. Spoiling by the second. The sisters suspected one another of foul play. Their minds raced. Each over-calculating their next move. But it was futile. Raw emotion and chaos erupted. The sisters fired accusations and insults, spearing one another with javelins of half-truth, and allowing their passions to surge.

'I meant her away,' Evelyn said, ablaze as the embers of the earth's crust. Her eyes crackled and blasted awful sincerity. Ma's tears mixed with her mascara and ran like soot down her face, as did June's. The neighbours pressed hands into their chests as they stood against jarred open doors. Yet no tears welled in Fran. She remained aggressive and pitiless. Unapologetic in her fight.

She hurled ice-blue, evangelical stalagmites at her ungrateful baby sister. 'She's your daughter, you selfish cow! I can't believe you would wish her away. What sort of mother would ever do that?'

She saw Evelyn as obstinate, a spoilt brat who refused to acknowledge, let alone appreciate, what her family had done for her.

'I want her to have a better life!'

Evelyn's ferocity energised in response to Fran's attack. Her words were strong, not meek, like a fire eating its way to the higher floors of a burning building. There was no compassion or let-up in either Evelyn or Fran's stance. They both spoke with absolution and terrifying condemnation of what the other had done. They charged the atmosphere with a nasty storm cloud.

'You had no right.'

Fran extended her arm and pushed baby Scarlet across to Evelyn. Into the smoke. Her little limbs lingered over the doorstep like an immigrant with feet in different lands. Caught between borders. Mom and aunt. Scarlet's tiny eyes squinted and her soft exposed arms tucked into themselves. But Evelyn's fury expanded into the force of a black-hole, causing Fran to pull her back into the safe orbit of her domain. 'Well, it's tough. She's staying with us. You're her mum and you'll thank me one day for what I've done, even if you're too damn selfish to see it now.'

Fran spoke with absolution. Her missionary words pierced Evelyn's darkness, but made other parts more resolute.

Evelyn responded with an iron voice. 'I love her. I will always love her. But I cannot be her mother. She deserves better. She can't stay. You can't have her. She isn't some doll, Fran!'

'—Don't be so self-pitying!'

From behind, Brummie John reached for Evelyn's hand. She evaded it and stepped forward to take Scarlet from her self-righteous sister. Evelyn softened as she looked down into her daughter's vulnerable face, but hardened as she shifted back up to continue the fight. Lava swirled around her pupils. 'Give her back,' she said, taking one last hug.

John's fingers brushed the back of Evelyn's wrist.

Fran felt her providential power melting, as if God was leaving her crusade, abandoning her righteous mission. It wouldn't do. She fought harder. Against God himself if need be. She released a fierce bolt of desperation. 'You know she's 15. You're touching up a minor, you dirty bastard.'

Vindication eased the heat of Evelyn's fire despite the nasty attack on John. Fran was suffering, resorting to cheap attacks because she was losing the moral high ground. Evelyn wouldn't blink if John slipped away, never to be seen again. Piercing her older sister's self-righteous hubris was worth ten thousand Johns. But by a miracle, John stuck. He stepped closer, pressed himself against Evelyn's back. His chest supported the back of her breast bones. His solidity absorbed and safeguarded her further heating. She held her position. 'You're wrong Fran. You've crossed a line, and you know it.'

Evelyn's shoulders loosened a fraction further. 'She has to go back.'

But Fran, in true evangelical fashion, could not surrender. It was not an option. 'You can't stop her staying.'

Evelyn mistook it as an expression of hopelessness, but Fran meant what she said. She stared at Scarlet and her heart broke as it continued to beat. But neither the break nor the beat distorted her feeling of certainty. Fran persisted.

'You can't make us. We have the right to keep her.'

Like a judge slamming his gavel, Evelyn felt a strange premonition, an ominous future awaiting them all.

A cry broke the stalemate as Lilly's cry leaked from the living room into the corridor. Ma went rushing for Evelyn's firstborn. She returned with Lilly in her arm, and Fran used it to launch her ultimate weapon. 'Squaddie, meet Lilly. Evelyn's eldest.'

Evelyn felt the tension in Brummie John's arms, now wrapped around her waist. But it was another miracle. His flesh remained attached to hers. He felt well over his head. He did. But for whatever reason or virtue, he stayed put. Strong. Gripped to Evelyn, and the more Fran attacked her, the firmer he stuck.

Evelyn, though, had reached her limit. More heat and she'd become Chernobyl. She pushed Scarlet to Fran and moved away from the doorstep. The baby winced as it flew from mom to aunt. 'She has to go back.'

Evelyn's voice was now more sombre than angry.

Fran scootched Scarlet into a firmer grip and dismissed her sister's declaration. 'We have the right—she's going nowhere.'

But again, Evelyn misread Fran's remarks for desperation. She turned away from her baby and sister, and John pulled her head into his chest.

Fran, smelling the weakness, mobilised herself for victory. 'I mean it. We have rights. The social are on their way and they'll confirm everything if you don't believe us. The foster carer has been on and off the phone all morning. She's said they'll grant full permission for us to raise her even if you don't want it; you selfish cow.'

Brummie John found his voice.

'That can't be right.'

Buoyed by his intervention, June found the courage to voice her own opinion. She stepped past Fran and the baby onto the street to stand closer to her little sister and the squaddie. 'Fran, if Evelyn—'

Fran shut her down.

'—it's done June. She's staying, and that's that.'

'Then I'm going,' Evelyn said, depleted of energy and fight. She twisted to face her older sister, and even though she knew begging would have no effect, she tried it as a last resort. As expected, Fran declined to proffer any form of mercy or compromise. Like a hard-faced empress, her ice-blue eyes froze over, her back stiffened and her voice turned cruel. She treated Evelyn as if she were vermin. Returning Scarlet to foster care was an abomination worthy of old testament justice.

'—That's your choice,' Fran said, adjudicating the matter.

Ma whimpered from behind with baby-Lilly in her hands. 'Where are you going to go?'

Evelyn didn't know, and she didn't hide it. 'I don't know, but it won't be here, Ma. Not like this.'

Brummie John's arms remained stuck on Evelyn's. Fran, noticing, couldn't refrain from kicking her when she was down. She didn't believe he would take her in, and still outraged by Evelyn's selfishness, she snided at the prospect of her staying with him. 'Is your squaddie going to take you into the barracks?'

'—I've got places I can stay,' Evelyn said, lying.

Fran took the advantage and turned away. 'Ma, will pack your things,' she said, glancing over her shoulder to add, 'John can collect them for you.'

It was her last word. She withdrew into the house, Scarlet in arm. Ma lingered on the doorstep, her lips whimpering.

'Please, Evelyn, just come in. We'll work it out.'

Ma's plea was sincere, but lacking in expectation. Evelyn hurt too much to return, and at some level, Ma knew. She recognised the sacrifice in her daughter; giving the baby away was not selfish. But Ma could not think that way. Her own impulse to provide for Scarlet's needs—to be the one to love her no matter what, regardless of whether it was selfish—meant she could not support Evelyn's nobler aims.

'Come in, June,' Ma said, gripping the door handle. The conversation was over.

June leapt to hug her little sister with the most forceful squeeze she had ever mustered for anybody within the family. Evelyn felt her ribs contract. June's arms finally unwrapped, and she went inside. Ma closed the door. Her eyes wet. Her heart heavy.

On the street, Brummie John hugged Evelyn tight. The neighbours scuttled behind their own shutting doors and sliding nets and the moon edged itself into view.

Chapter 2 — Baby Scarlet, 0 weeks old (1980s, Hospital)

Thick light seeped into the bedroom, waking Fran, June and baby Lilly. Evelyn awoke hours ago, tossing but not turning in bed because of her giant bump. Her contractions had intensified by dawn to the point she needed to speak up. But like the nine months of her second pregnancy, she endured the suffering, saying as little as possible, preferring circumstance to force her to talk.

Across the wall, Ma wedged her back against the headrest and puffed her first cigarette, flicking the burnt ends into the ashtray. Full of nicotine and tar, she rose, collected her work uniform, and then put on tights.

In the sister's blue and gold wallpapered bedroom, Aunty Fran saw to baby Lilly. Her fingers brushed Lilly's soft cheeks, and she cooed into the cot before lifting her out. Lilly sank into aunty Fran's warm arms, and as if in wings, glided across the room toward her mom. Fran perched on Evelyn's bed and baby-talked in a way that her sentiment extended to her little sister as much as it did to baby Lilly. 'Morning, sunshine. Who's a little darling?'

'Fran?' Evelyn said, but she muffled her words into the second pillow clutched to her chin and chest. Fran didn't hear. Her attention remained on Lilly. She blew a gentle raspberry into her cheeks.

Evelyn tried to get her sister's attention again. Louder. 'Fran?'

But Fran continued to coo the baby against the backdrop of her sister's calls. 'Who's a beautiful princess?'

'—Fran, it's coming!' Evelyn said, making herself heard.

Aunty Fran shifted Lilly into a tight hold of one arm while stroking Evelyn's fringe away from her forehead. 'Are you sure?'

Evelyn's eyelids clamped hard as her face shunted forward and then dropped back onto the pillow. She was sure.

'June, wake-up!' Fran said. 'Lyn needs to go to the hospital. Get Ma, will you?' She meant the question as an order.

'Now?' June said, groggy and only half awake.

'—Now.'

June forced herself upright. She stretched her head back against the purple headboard and pulled her scrunched nightie sleeves away from her armpits. She looked at Evelyn. 'Are you sure, sure, Lyn?'

'She's sure,' Fran said, snapping. 'Get Ivan to bring his car around.'

Ivan started work after them, but June wasn't sure whether he would get up this early to help. She ran her tongue over her front teeth and considered if it was worth asking. She wanted to avoid jeopardising any reciprocal interest by appearing too needy. June pushed her fingers upward, brushing against the blanket of freckles on her cheeks. She had to ask, even if it counted against her. It was the right thing to do. 'I'll knock him up.'

'Tell Ma, on your way out,' Fran said, as June lumbered out of bed.

June banged the wall and shouted to Ma before pulling her boots from beneath the bed and putting them on. 'Ma! Lyn's having the baby.'

Lilly, still in aunty Fran's arm, squirmed at June's shouting, causing Fran to scowl in her direction. 'You could have popped next door and not screamed through the wall.'

June didn't acknowledge Fran's reprehension. She thudded Ma's bedroom door with her fist before darting for the staircase, which she trampled in her nightie and vintage boots. If she was going to ask for Ivan's help, she would at least manufacture a bit more drama to make the situation more important than she considered it to be.

In the blue and gold bedroom, Evelyn's grunts became explosive as her contractions toughened. She was desperate to stay quiet, but she couldn't contain the pain. It leaked and spurted like water from a punctured pipe. One thought ran, trampled, over her mind. Don't make Ma come. She wasn't afraid. She was angry. Ma hadn't spoken about the new baby for the entire pregnancy. An elephant wasn't in the room; it was in every room. The unacknowledged foetus pushing them apart. Why should she be involved now?

Aunty Fran, still holding baby Lilly, nipped to the bathroom to gather towels. Evelyn, lying in bed, split her mind. Half focused on the fear of giving birth. The other half on Ma coming through to witness. She listened to the wall. Pictured Ma putting on her uniform, rolling her tights. Puffing her cigarette then resting it on the ashtray. Why hasn't she said anything?

Memories penetrated Evelyn like reversed gravity, while the aches in her back made her want to pee. She remembered herself at primary school, standing frozen behind a chair mounted on child-sized tables. Wee trickled down her leg and formed a small puddle of soured gold around her shoes.

The front door banged, bringing Evelyn back to the present. 'She's gone', Evelyn said, murmuring to herself so that Fran could not hear. She assumed Ma had gone, but it was Ivan and June. Ma hadn't left. Evelyn listened to them rush up the staircase, June's owl nightie swooshing and her knee-high leather boots crunching each step. Following Fran's lead, Ivan helped lift Evelyn out of bed. She barely noticed him as another contraction seized her attention, which at least distracted her from the disorientating anxiety over what was coming next.

Fran continued clutching Evelyn's hand even though her own arm ached from holding baby Lilly on one side. She needed to switch hands, but letting go felt cruel. With Ivan, she encouraged Evelyn to move.

Evelyn limped across the bedroom, wearing the black nighty with horrid flowers woven into the fabric. It was dirty and tatty. She wore the disgusting thing for months, not because it was the only thing that fit - she had clothes - but because she'd become strangely attached to it. They trudged down the staircase together. Ma watched from the banister, whimpering and feeling useless.

They stumbled to Ivan's red Cortina, which he parked on the wider pavement around the corner. Evelyn had never been in a car. More were around, but nobody she knew could afford one, including Ivan. He borrowed it (without permission) from the garage and called it a work car, as if he were a business executive from Birmingham. Evelyn, with plenty of help, folded into the Cortina. It was her first car journey. Though not her first trip to the maternity ward.

The duration and intensity of the contractions lengthened and strengthened. Evelyn opened her eyes as the pain built and clamped. A cycle of opening and closing. Seeing and not seeing. The views of the town fractured into mosaic pieces. She willed the blackouts to ease the pain of the contractions. They didn't.

The terraces, schools, and warehouses leading to the hospital blurred as the car zipped through streets she had known her entire life. If she was not about to give birth, the unfamiliar and exhilarating speeds would have mesmerised her. But her mind could not focus. It mothballed itself. Closed itself to outside business and yearned for dark emptiness. The capacity to think and worry waned. What was the point? The baby growing inside seized what little attention she could muster. Evelyn stopped caring about Ma not being there. She stopped caring about the lack of acknowledgement. She can stand behind that counter and serve cigarettes while I have this baby. Or at least she stopped caring as much.

At the hospital, Evelyn stumbled across the foyer, hooked between Fran and June's arms. The nurses shrieked. Not expecting Evelyn, given she'd had no antenatal care. They found a bed quickly though. Made room and looked after her.

And luckily, the birth was simple. Evelyn and the baby were healthy. The doctors did not hang around and the nurses and auxiliaries stepped in, replacing scary forceps with blankets.

After Evelyn sat in the ward and held Scarlet. Gazed at her tiny body. Joy radiated across her face like a deep red petal whose blooming occurred in compressed minutes, rather than days. However, the joy wilted at an equally unnatural speed. The baby was taken. Scarlet. Gone.

Evelyn sat alone on the ward, beside the other mothers, entranced with their newborns. She looked around and saw them squeezed into tired, fleshy, protective arms. But like the dirty flowers on the black dress, her soul faded. Worn and torn, the joyous red on her face discoloured into sore purple bruises. She was alone, fatigued, and empty. Ma wasn't there. June and Fran weren't there. Scarlet wasn't there. Alone.

Chapter 3 — Adult Scarlet (2000s, Cemetery)

Early morning sunshine fused with the fading orange glow of street lamps. Scarlet darted along the empty pavements in the haze. Somewhere, her friends lay on cheap mattresses sweating out alcohol and drugs, their bodies knackered. Scarlet resolved to do better. She wasn't about to join AA or commit to life long sobriety, but she promised herself more.

She ran through the pedestrian tunnel connecting the cul-de-sacs on either side of the railway, holding her breath to avoid the smell of piss. Her feet paced. She disliked using the tunnel alone in busy periods, and she hated using it at this eerie hour, when some lingering sexual predator unfulfilled from the night might be around to ambush her. She returned to a brisk walk as she exited, and then a stroll as she approached the cemetery. Lilly rested there.

Scarlet enjoyed visiting her late sister at dawn. The place was quiet and beautiful. Trickles of light sprinkled onto the grass between hundreds of headstones, and nobody was around to disrupt it. Calmness presided. And there was also a distinct absence of bouquets: no garish flowers or rustling cellophane wrapping on the graves attempting to conquer or disguise the inherent death bound into the place. Scarlet could be sad.

The cemetery's iron gates needed oiling. Scarlet pressed through and walked toward the orange sun, which lifted higher and stretched wider by the minute. She could still stare at it without hurting her eyes. Further into the cemetery, the warming marshlands beyond also came into view. Birds fluttered and squawked, the only noise apart from the gate and passing trains.

Scarlet knelt on the grass in front of Lilly's headstone and greeted her sister, knowing nobody could listen to her speak aloud. Bum followed knees onto the grass and both legs twisted to the same side.

'We don't have a word for death-days,' Scarlet said. 'We should be grateful: there would be cards and flowers everywhere! Ma still loves a card. Everybody in town does.' Scarlet smiled and paused the conversation for a moment. Her stare broke from the headstone and she glanced briefly at the ground.

'I wish you could see me, Lilly.' She returned her gaze to the grave as if Lilly sat on the headstone. 'I've stopped taking the crap. You'd be proud. It was hard, but I've done it. I knew I could—just needed to want it. Visiting has helped. A lot.' Scarlett brushed a lock of hair behind her ear and continued. 'The sun looks like an Ibiza moon, the sort that romantic couples watch while holding hands on the rocks. Did you ever go to Spain?' Scarlet wondered whether Lilly had ever travelled on a plane. She hadn't known enough about her life.

'Of course you did,' she answered her own question. 'You had days when you'd wake up in Paris, eat lunch in New York, and dance the evening away in LA... just like every girl from Nuneaton.' Scarlet winced. 'I'm funny now, too.' She rubbed the stud on her earlobe and then tucked the same lock of hair.

'I thought about how close you came to prison. You told me you woke up in a cell already wearing clothes because you'd become too scared to undress the night before. You said the cells reminded you of a dirty carpark. I think of that every time I cut through Sainsbury's now - although Nick's got plenty of grim stories involving that place.' Scarlet grinned. 'The gays in this town are pure filth. You would have loved them.' She glanced at the ground, then straightened her posture. The sun asserted itself into a higher position.

'What a weird comparison — a dirty carpark. Who makes that connection?' Scarlet said, smiling and sharing her admiration for Lilly. 'My big sister does. She who despite facing a year in prison and weeks of cold turkey, put her big girl pants on, and continued responding to the world with poetry.'

Scarlet rubbed her stud again. 'I know I'm sentimentalising. You were terrified; scared-to-death of waking up in a cell, but I have a point. You fucked-up, Lilly. But you never completely gave up. I have to remember you that way.'

A lump rolled against the skin of Scarlet's throat, and a tear dripped down her cheek. 'I thought I'd last longer before getting so emotional,' she said, tasting the salt in the tear which had rolled onto her lip.

'Sorry, I couldn't help. I'm ashamed sometimes to think how you remained so good-humoured around me and Nick when Ma had her bad days. You made out everything would be fine. Was fine... But your body, Lilly.' Scarlet switched between memories of her late sister bravely comforting her and their little brother, to memories of her sickly anorexic body provoking such terror and trauma in them as younger siblings. Damage outweighed protection.

'Your body shook like you had flu, and your legs, Lilly.' Scarlet covered her mouth and restrained sobs from overpowering and shutting down the flow of memories. 'Your legs,' Scarlet repeated, speaking into her palm. A tear rolled onto her thumb. 'Your legs were so thin. They looked like Granny's.' She spluttered a choke-like laugh as she remembered them playing dress-up as little girls. 'Do you remember getting our legs slapped by Ma for raiding Gran's wardrobe?'

Scarlet removed her hand and let the tears become joyful. 'Ma was most annoyed we'd dressed Nick up. What did he look like in those tights and curtain dresses, cigarette drooping from the side of his mouth?' She recalled more happy memories of Lilly and Nick. Them doing things they shouldn't have been. Eventually, the laughter simmered, and the seriousness returned.

'You closed your eyes in the cell and listened to the other women. You said they had Jamaican accents. I tried so hard to picture their faces, realising you would do the same. But I couldn't see anything. No matter how hard I tried, I couldn't see anyone. Just darkness. Though the stabbing thought of you going to prison filled the void fast enough.

Proper prison. You were going to prison if the hearing went bad. It was terrifying: the not knowing.'

Scarlet rubbed her stomach and nipped the question she wanted to ask in the bud. She moved onto another memory. 'You wanted to be a journalist when we were kids. I took one of your dresses once, but when you saw me, you just said that I could have it because "journalists don't wear dresses". You amazed me. I expected an earful — not for you to give me the dress.' Scarlet thought about the red, yellow and green stripes running the entire way down the frock. 'God. It was ugly. I understand why you did it now.'

After a brief pause, Scarlet leant back, her hands pressing into the grass behind her torso. 'One of the female guards let you nip into another cell; you met one of the Jamaican girls — she had a London accent — and she leant you a small black mirror. It didn't have a handle. You said you had to cup your hand around the edge and tilt it toward the window for the light. Of all the things, isn't it funny what we remember?'

Scarlet pictured herself swirling in the ugly coloured dress Lilly had donated. She watched her younger self looking in the mirror; her examining the pair of blue-green eyes staring back. The same blue-green eyes that would widen into sink holes in adolescence. A gust blew, and Scarlet rubbed her arms. She willed herself away from dwelling on mistakes and refocused on Lilly.

'You sorted your hair for the hearing. I didn't understand why you'd done that. What difference would your hair make to the judge? God, I was naïve. Anyway, I'm glad you told me about that Jamaican woman's little black mirror. It's another thing that helps me remember.'

Scarlet turned away as her cheeks flushed with a tinge of confessional shame. 'It used to make me mad: I'd get angry about needing an ugly dress or a random black mirror without a handle to remember you. I'd feel ashamed for needing things; give myself a hard time for not thinking about you unaided—' Scarlet said, slowing her speech and returning to look at the headstone.

'Now I'm grateful for every scrap of story I have; for any random object that takes me to you.' Scarlet stroked her stomach again. It was becoming something she did on autopilot.

'—It's getting harder.' The shame in Scarlet's cheeks budded. 'I have to go.' Her trousers absorbed the damp dew from the blades of grass. She didn't want to mind, but the wet linen irritated her skin and she needed to move.

'They took you, Lilly - the guards – after that. You said they led you outside, to a police van parked in a courtyard. I'd never considered the practicalities of getting from a cell to court before you told me that. I steered away from the details; from considering how things happen. Not my place.'

Scarlet twisted her legs to the other side, shifting the weight from one bum cheek to the other. 'It was raining, and the sky was dark. The guard was complaining about missing breakfast. Again, one of those stupid details I'm now thankful for: a slobby, overweight guard ignoring his alarm clock and moaning about a never-eaten bacon and egg muffin. One more image connecting me to you; of remembering how attentive you were,' Scarlet said, and then hesitated. She willed herself to not go there, to no avail. 'Sis—Lilly—Why did you do it?'

A small dose of anger crept into Scarlet. Directed at Lilly; for leaving. But then it rerouted to herself. Scarlet knew she couldn't get an answer. Even if Lilly returned from the cold earth itself, she could not answer that question. There wasn't an answer. Not a good one. Stupidity? A cry for attention? Weakness? Infatuation? Foolishness? There were too many answers. None exclusive. Lilly had done it, and she could not undo it. The heroin deserves a good chunk of blame, but it wasn't the entire story. There was more to what happened.

Scarlet learnt not to cry at this part. Lilly's ending is cold and empty - beyond sad. Not tear-inducing. She reserved sentiment and cried to childhood memories. She knew no words or way of remembering the end.

'I'm going. For good — but I'm afraid of forgetting you,' she said, sobbing in a way she hadn't for years, that sort of heart-aching, first-love lost, teenager sob. She felt she was losing Lilly again.

Scarlet's shins pressed into the grass, and gravity pulled her tears to the grass. She leant forward and kissed the stone. 'I love you,' she said, then stumbled upward onto her feet, rubbing her stomach and the headstone. 'We won't forget you. I promise.'

Scarlet pulled a gold-plated necklace from her pocket. 'It's Gran's. Not worth much, but special, sentimental. I'm leaving it here. With you.'

Scarlet tugged the strainer from the base of the headstone. Nobody left flowers anymore, so it was stiff. The gold-plated necklace fell into the dark hole and then the strainer went back in, squashing the necklace into the earth. Scarlet stood and kissed the headstone a final time. She then turned and never looked back.

Chapter 4 — Baby Scarlet, 1 week old (1980s, Gadsby Street)

'You've lost a lot of weight,' Gran said, snapping at Evelyn.

Ma evaded the topic and walked into the kitchen. Her girls followed.

Gran continued to squark from her armchair. 'Well, at least you're not wearing that tatty old dress anymore. Still can't understand what your obsession was,' she said. Them being in another room didn't faze or disrupt her monologues. 'Fae, you need to make Evelyn take better care of the baby.'

Ma unravelled the wrapping from several bunches of fresh flowers on the worktop. She filled a vase with tap-water and arranged the flowers, taking stems from each pile one at a time.

'Oh Fae, you didn't need to buy that many. Two bunches would have done fine,' Gran said, twisting in her armchair and continuing to speak from the living room, which also functioned as her bedroom.

Fran lifted Evelyn's fist-born from the pram, a hand-me-down from Aunty Filomena, who wasn't a real aunt. She carried Lilly through, re-joining Gran, perching on the bed, and bobbing the baby, up and down, on her knee. Gran disapproved. 'That baby needs its mum, Francis. You can't keep tending to her, otherwise they won't bond.'

The bobbing shifted from knee to thigh and invigorated. Fran took little notice of Gran. Only Ma listened properly, albeit from a distance. She was still in the kitchen, facing the garden, faffing with the flowers. Arranging and re-arranging.

Gran persisted. 'Evelyn, come-on, take your baby. She needs to feel your arms, not your sisters.'

Evelyn remained glued to Ma in the kitchen. Like Fran, she listened but didn't take proper notice of Gran's bark. It was as if she spoke another language. One she could technically understand, but not respond, feel or react to.

Ma turned from the sink. 'Lyn, go sit in the living room with Gran.'

Evelyn felt Ma's words like a banging drumstick inscribing letters on her heart. She walked between Lilly, bouncing on Fran's lap, and Gran's jerked face, tutting in the armchair. Ma followed with the vase, filled with beautiful flowers, and a box of chocolate eclairs. She placed them on the side table and then sat in the armchair wedged beside the bed. 'June brings some plates through.'

Gran hadn't forgotten about the baby. 'Fae, come-on now tell Evelyn that she needs to tend the baby herself.'

Ma lifted out the armchair she had just sunk into and reached for Lilly. Fran passed her across and as soon as Lilly landed, Ma began blowing raspberries into her cheeks. She sank back into the chair, smothering Lilly with kisses. June brought the plates through and distributed the four chocolate eclairs. Ma didn't have one.

The sugar and carbohydrates didn't thwart Gran's stiff resolve, but it provoked a ceasefire. 'It ain't right Fae, the baby needs its mum, but I shan't say no more.'

June sat on the curtain-patterned two-seater and everyone ate their eclairs. Ma cooed Lilly and asked the others how they tasted. Mouthfuls of cream and Choux pastry halted their approving. Fran performed a peekaboo for Lilly between each of her bites, and Ma squirted more raspberries to prolong the chuckling.

Gran licked the last of the cream from her plate. 'That was lovely Fae, but you needn't get any next week.'

She repeated herself every Saturday before switching focus to the week's news. 'The Americans are giving the death penalty to that killer clown murdering all those boys.'

She dabbed the newspaper, resting on another side table.

'What killer clown?' June asked, her face animated amid the backdrop of the curtained sofa.

Gran elaborated. 'That fruit loop going around murdering all those young boys on a ranch somewhere – Chicago.'

'Those Americans aren't all there,' Ma said. 'We wouldn't get anything like that here. Would we, Lilly? No, we wouldn't. No, we wouldn't.'

Ma blew further raspberries into her cheeks, eliciting more chuckles. Fran performed another peekaboo from the bed.

'Where'd you hear about that killer clown, Gran?' June asked, evading Ma's attempt to steer the conversation into milder currents.

'That new programme on the Television—what's it called, Fae? I forget the name. Newsnight!' Gran answered before Ma could say she didn't know, and then steer the conversation to local gossip. 'Mind you, I don't enjoy watching it before bed. Murdering clowns, shootings and earthquakes—' Gran shook her head. 'And that's with having a bit of cheese, too.'

'Did you like that new cheddar?' Ma asked.

'Shootings? Who got shot?' June fired her questions before Gran could start waffling about the new cheddar for fifteen minutes.

'That Beatle fellow. I never much listened to their stuff though.'

June sank back into the overly busy two-seater sofa and the animation in her face fizzled out. John Lennon's shooting was old news. Boring.

'What's cheese got to do with killer clowns?' June asked, with lower expectations of intrigue.

'Don't you know anything, girl?' Gran said, snapping rhetorically. June was twenty-one, but Gran still made her feel like a small child. Ma blew another raspberry and Fran another peekaboo.

Gran eventually moved on to answer June's question. 'Cheese gives you nightmares if you eat it before bed. A load of nonsense, of course. Old-wives' tales to stop you getting fat by eating too much before bed. Speaking of which, Evelyn dear, you have lost a lot of weight—what diet have you been on?'

Evelyn sat on the floor beside Ma's chair. Her legs pitched upward, covering her stomach, and supporting her chin, which perched on the summit of the kneecaps. She shrugged. Evelyn avoided speaking to gran whenever it was possible.

'Ma, does cheese really give you nightmares if you eat it before bed?' June asked.

'I think so.'

Gran resolved the matter. 'If you're trying to lose weight like your sister, I'd avoid eating the cheese for that reason alone.'

None of the Finches were fat. In fact, June was rake thin. She did not need to lose weight. None of them did.

'June doesn't need to lose any weight,' Ma said, clarifying to the room rather than Gran directly.

'We can all stand to lose a bit of weight.'

Gran had to have the last word. But her comments were more ignorant than malicious. Despite her wearing thick-rimmed red glasses, she couldn't see well. She read library books with a magnifying class.

'Ma, does it really give you nightmares?'

June was not interested in weight. She hardly thought about appearances.

'Child, what is it with you and nightmares?' Gran snapped again. 'Nobody really knows. If you're that scared about weight gain, don't eat it just in case.'

Later that evening, as everybody got ready for bed, June snuck downstairs, guiding herself into the kitchen by brushing the walls with her fingertips. She left the fridge door open for light while she sliced six chunky pieces of cheddar. She wanted nightmares. Her teeth pierced the cheese, but she swallowed before breaking it down; overriding her gag reflex, she forced it down her oesophagus.

She climbed into bed beside Fran, who was already asleep, as were Evelyn and Lilly in the bed and cot opposite. Beneath shut eyelids, June tried to imagine the killer clown from America. The words kept repeating in her head. Killer Clown. Killer Clown.

But she woke the following morning, either not having had a nightmare or not remembering it. Either way, the cheese didn't and wouldn't work.

'What's wrong with you?' Fran asked. She already had Lilly in her arm.

'Nothing,' June replied, dipping her head under the bed to snatch her boots. 'I'm going round Ivan's.'

'He won't be up yet and men are beasts on Sunday mornings. Leave it alone for a while.'

'We're supposed to be going to Birmingham. He promised.'

'Well, give him a few hours. Let the whisky work its way out.'

Fran pulled a T-shirt over Lilly's tiny head and arms while the boots fell from June's hands and collapsed back on the floor. June pulled the duvet over her body, but sat up, resting her head against the purple headboard. 'I tried eating cheese last night,' she said, confessing.

'You want to put on weight?' Fran asked.

'No.'

'No?' Fran straightened Lilly's T-shirt, blew a raspberry into her face, and then lifted her in repeated swings and swoops, cooing at their face-to-face contact. 'Brrrr,' she said, her lips vibrating like a motor.

June's legs pitched, forcing the duvet into a mountain shape. She folded her arms. 'I wanted nightmares.'

Fran stopped the swings and settled Lilly into a wedge between her arms and her bosom. 'Why?'

'I wanted to know if it worked.'

Fran moved over and perched on Evelyn's bed. She rocked Lilly back and forth in a gentle, rhythmic arm swing. Evelyn was awake, listening to her sisters, but she kept her eyes shut.

'Don't you want to know why?' June said, sulking at Fran's lack of interest.

'Sure.' Fran served the white lie on autopilot.

'I want to give Ivan nightmares.'

Fran twisted Lilly and smelt her nappy. She had no interest or time for June's cheese-nightmare obsession, and even her feigned interest was waning.

'Oh, forget it. You don't care.'

June tossed aside the duvet and stomped out of the bedroom. The bathroom door slammed.

'She's a madam. Yes, she is.' Fran cooed the baby. 'We didn't mean to upset aunty June, did we? No, we didn't,' she continued, mumbling to Lilly in a silly cartoonish voice. 'No, we did not. We did not mean to make Aunty June all crazy, did we?'

'Nobody made June crazy—she was born that way,' Evelyn said, her head still glued to the pillow.

'And now your mummy is awake too, isn't she? Yes, she is.'

'Ivan isn't interested in her,' Evelyn said, rolling her body to face Fran and Lilly.

'We're not getting involved, are we Lilly? No, we're not.'

Fran placed Lilly on the floor and reached for a fresh nappy, wiping cloth and talcum powder.

'Me neither. I was only saying.'

Evelyn yawned while stretching her toes and fingertips at both ends of the duvet.

The bathroom door swung open and the floorboards along the hallway amplified June's thumping feet for the entire house to hear. 'I'm going to wake him. He promised. He can get up and take me. Hungover or not. He promised.'

Evelyn rolled her face back into the pillow and Fran changed Lilly's nappy. They were making it clear they weren't getting involved.

The staircase withstood June's stomping, but the wallpaper behind the front door received a nasty dent as she flung the handle into it. Outside, she stormed across to Ivan's.

'Watch it, love. You nearly took me out!' Rose said, the old lady from next door. She stepped back onto the pavement after dipping onto the road.

June banged Ivan's door three times with the flat of her palm, and her neck tilted to the side as if warming itself up for more vigorous movement. Rose wheeled her shopping trolly slower than usual to ensure she wasn't too far along the street when the commotion would inevitably begin.

'Ivan Winstanley, you promised—'

A frail lady opened the door, '—Sorry June, love. Our Ivan's not up yet. Perhaps come back in a couple of hours. He was on the whisky last night and you know how men are the morning after the whisky.'

'But we're going to Birmingham, Mrs Winstanley. He said we were going today.'

June spoke to the staircase, not the lady. She only pronounced her name to extend the reach of her voice.

'Aye, love, I'm sure he did. That's men for you.'

Mrs Winstanley sighed, but then lifted the energy, projecting hope. 'But I'm sure he'll still take you later; it'll just be in a few hours mind. So go on now, love. Have a cup of tea, and a bath. Then, pop back round.'

Rose's pace picked up, disappointed there would not be any drama.

'Mrs Winstanley, you tell Ivan I'll be back at 10 and that he'd better be ready. Otherwise—'

June spoke past Mrs Winstanley again, her voice sliming up the staircase toward the bedroom, but she couldn't think of an ultimatum. Her sentence lingered unfinished.

'Oh love, I don't think he'll be ready for 10. I think you—'

'—Tell her to fuck off Ma!' Ivan's older brother shouted from the kitchen. 'If she harps on like that, our Ivan will send her to the spinsters club, never mind Brum.'

'Fuck off, Waverley!' June shouted over Mrs Winstanley's shoulders. She felt like a tennis net.

'Ma, shut the door before crazy gets in the carpets. It's a bitch to get out.'

'Winston, you know I don't like the language.'

Mrs Winstanley pushed the door, edging it closed.

'Fuck off, Waverley!' June shouted again.

'You already said that cray-cray.'

Winston laughed at his reply.

'June love. Come back at 12; see whether he's up then, hey?'

Mrs Winstanley pushed the door further shut, but squeezed one last reassurance through the gap. 'I'm sure he'll be ready then, dear.'

Rose was near the end of the street. June sighed and twisted to see her disappear around the bend. She nodded at Mrs Winstanley, who nodded back before shutting the door. June returned home and began clock watching. The hours passed. Slowly.

'For fuck's sake. How is it only 11.30?' June said, muttering to herself as her body slumped further into Ma's armchair.

Make Your Own Furniture played on the small T.V., but none of the Finch sisters watched or even listened to it. Aunty Fran had her hands wedged under little Lilly's armpits and was pretending to walk her across the sofa. Ma was peeling potatoes for the Sunday dinner, and Evelyn was working her way through LP covers, imagining the songs playing in her mind as she admired details of the artwork.

June was reaching her limit. 'I can't wait until 12.00—I'm going in ten minutes. He's had long enough.'

'Aunty June is very impatient, isn't she Lilly? Yes, she is. She is too impatient, isn't she? Yes, she is.'

Fran cooed as she guided Lilly's pseudo-steps across the cushions.

Evelyn ignored June's nonsense. 'Fran, can I come to The Swan with you on Friday?' She asked while pulling an LP from its case: *Don't Stand So Close to Me* – The Police's new number one record.

'Okay. But you're not to go near any men, ok?'

Fran spoke in her normal voice, but she didn't stop playing or looking at Lilly. Evelyn placed the record onto the machine and the spindle brought Sting's high tubular voice into the living room.

June uncrossed her arms and sprang from the sofa. 'That's it I'm going now!'

She thumped his front door and bellowed before Mrs Winstanley hurried to open it. 'Ivan! It's time to go!'

Her words bounced off the wood and floated to the upstairs window.

'Sorry June, love, he still isn't ready. Perhaps, go next week instead, eh? You'll only have a few hours in the shops by the time you get there, so it's probably better to go next week, anyway.'

'Ma, shut the door. I'm trying to watch the tele,' Winston said, shouting from the leather armchair in his sweaty boxer shorts and vest, his toe-nails waiting on the coffee table for Iris to throw them away.

'I'm not going anywhere, Mrs Winstanley.' June replied, emphasising her name so Winston did not think she was speaking to him. 'He promised. And that's it. He needs to get up. Can you tell him?'

'Love, I don't think that's a good idea. You know how men are when—'

Ivan's bedroom window opened. The net and curtains shifted to one side and his head dangled out. '—For fuck's sake, June. Give it a rest, will ya?'

Rose reappeared at the end of the street, her shopping trolly full. She sped up so not to miss any commotion.

'Ivan, you promised we'd go this week. You promised.'

June switched to pleading reason.

'Why all the drama? I was going to get up and get ready in a minute. I never said a time. But now you come round giving me Ma hell and shouting on the street like some crazy bitch. Well, you can fuck off if you think I'm going to do anything for you now.'

Rose picked up her pace. She could hear raised voices, but no specifics. Needed to be closer.

'Ivan, that's not fair. Come on. You promised.'

Mrs Winstanley placed her foot onto the pavement and reached out to brush June's arm. 'Love, honestly, just give him twenty minutes to wake up and cool down. I'm sure he'll still take ye then.'

'No Ma. I've had enough.'

Ivan's voice passed down the staircase and out the window. 'I wasn't even bothered about going. Just thought I'd do something nice for her, given the shit time that's been happening with Evelyn and the babies. But what's the point? She's an ungrateful gobshite, and besides, I'm obviously sending the wrong signal.'

Mrs Winstanley clenched her fist and moved it to her heart. Her face crinkled in sympathy for the Finches and poor Evelyn in particular. A wisp of air leaked as she went to offer a kind word. But she caught herself; knew there wasn't nothing to say.

'I'm sorry, Ivan,' June said, her feistiness evaporating. Her eyes levelled with Iris'. 'I'm sorry, Mrs Winstanley. I didn't mean to be rude to you.'

'Love, you don't need to apologise.'

'Yes, she does, Ma!' Winston chimed in from the living room. 'She's disrespected us, and Ivan's right to tell her so.'

'Winston, shhh,' Iris said, stepping back into the house and twisting toward her son. 'The girl's been through an awful time. A little kindness.'

'Ma, she ain't the one that had the kid taken. You don't need to feel sorry for her. Now shut the fucking door. I'm trying to watch tele.'

'Ma, he's right,' Ivan said, shouting from the window. He directed his attention to June. 'It's over. Not that there was anything to begin with. I was taking you to Brum to be friendly, but it was wrong. You're not mine and I shouldn't have led you on. Anyway, we're not going, so fuck off. Go home and leave us alone.'

'I'm pregnant!' June shouted on impulse.

Ivan and Winston's laughter doubled up like hyenas, and Mrs Winstanley felt like that tennis net again. This time, as if Bjorn Borg had smashed a serve straight into her.

'She ain't fuckin pregnant, Mam,' Winston said, cock-sure. 'It's what the crazies say when they can't accept no for an answer.'

June flushed red and withdrew, making room on the pavement for Rose to pass with her shopping trolly. But Rose parked it and stilled herself. She faced June and asked, 'Dear, are you really pregnant?'

Rose patted her on the back. 'June dear?' She repeated, pressing for an answer.

'I could be.'

Winston's snicker drifted out the living room. 'Some twat would have to shag you for you to be pregnant, you moron!'

Rose's pat transitioned into a gentle rub. 'Dear, you either are, or aren't.'

'I'm not,' June confessed.

Rose brought the rub to a stop, gently placed both hands on June's shoulders, and manoeuvred her gently to the kerb. She re-clutched her trolly and shook her head softly as she wheeled on, passively condemning, and consoling. She patted one last time while passing by.

Mrs Winstanley, still hovering in the doorway, scrunched her face. 'Sorry love, just to be clear, you aren't pregnant?'

'No, I'm not.'

Ivan shut his window, and the curtains blocked the light.

'Why did you say you were, love?'

Iris Winstanley realised why before she'd finished the question. 'Oh, dear. I see. Look, have a cup of tea and a soak in the bath. Let him calm down and I'm sure he'll take you for a shandy later on.'

June accepted defeat. She nodded to convey her surrender, and Iris closed the door. 'That's a good girl.'

Evelyn re-placed the LP's spindle to the disk's edge when June returned to the living room, even though the song hadn't finished. The track played from the beginning. June sank into the armchair and avoided eye contact with her sisters. Not that they gave any.

' "Don't Stand!" ' Fran sang to Lilly, who was bouncing between a sitting and standing position on the floor with Fran's help. ' "Don't stand!" ' she sang again, shifting Lilly back and forth, making her chuckle.

'You know what this stupid song is actually about?' June said, snapping and crossing her arms.

'Who cares?' Evelyn replied. 'I like it, anyway.'

'Some pervert teacher having it off with his student. Men are complete dickheads.'

'June, you know I don't like the language,' Ma said, calling from the kitchen as she peeled the last spud.

'Fuck off.' June muttered under her breath such that Ma couldn't hear.

Evelyn examined the artwork on the LP's cover. A burnt orange and electric blue triangle encased Sting and his bandmates. She stared at its thick lines, wrapping around and around the men stood inside the shape, shoulder-to-shoulder, proud and together.

'I don't know how you can stare at that stupid case for so long,' June said, snapping at her little sister.

'Well, I thought you were going to Brum,' Evelyn replied, leaking sarcasm.

'Evelyn,' Fran said, warning Evelyn while keeping her eyes on Lilly. But it was too late.

'Sometimes, you can all be such bitches!' June said, tossing herself up and storming out of the living room. She slammed the door, thudded the staircase, and then slammed the bedroom door, too. She lay on the bed without removing her boots and stewed. 'I'm going to teach that bastard a lesson.'

Chapter 5 — Adult Lilly (1990s, Court)

The judge scrutinised Lilly. His eyes were like fireballs, his stare burning the ropey noose around her neck. 'Acquitted,' he said, the fire dampening and the noose loosening at his command.

Lilly looked at the fancy women in black robes and a white wig for direction. The barrister lady returned a smile as everybody else in the court shuffled papers and left. She strode to Lilly from the bench behind her pedestal. 'You're free to go,' she said.

'Now?'

'Yes. You can collect your things from the kiosk at the front of the building.'

Lilly didn't need telling twice. She unclipped the latch and left the wooden cage. A foreshadowing of the permanent incarceration had the prosecution been successful. She paced between rows of maple benches and pulpits; hurried through corridors of imperial architrave; and ran through the courtly hallways larger than the streets she grew up on. She snatched her bundled clothes, sealed in a translucent plastic bag on the kiosk, and after taking £40 from the clerk for travel expenses, left.

Black cabs jammed the road, but Lilly scuttled past. She wasn't going home. With the £40 and her bag of clothes, she trudged south. After crossing London Bridge in the rain, she disappeared into London's warren of backstreets and alleyways. Estates of concrete tower blocks rose into the grey sky.

Deep into Elephant and Castle, Lilly snaked up an outdoor staircase attached to a decrepit council block. She drifted along the corridor of the seventh floor, her hand icier than the rail separating her from the dark wet air. Nets and curtains blocked the windows and a couple of flats had iron bars across them. Lilly rapped on a dirty lilac door with flaky paint peeling off, flat 724.

A sickly voice asked who was there.

'The queen,' Lilly replied, her voice meek and brittle.

The bolt rustled and dropped, and then the door crept open. The man behind withdrew into plumes of smoke and the flat's dim lighting. Lilly followed. Wading through the filth, she inhaled the stale, almost solidifying air, the nearest thing she'd eaten since her last job: the bloke had a weird fetish. They often do. Three men lay spaced out on a brown flecked carpet, flea ridden had the smoke not exterminated them. Syringes, teaspoons, and armbands scattered between their bodies. The man stumbled past and then kneeled to fiddle with tinfoil on the floor. 'You know I can't give you anything without cash up front anymore,' he said.

Lilly pushed the two twenty-pound notes into his hands. The money disappeared before the rank air could smother it and Lilly fell to the carpet to shoot up just as fast. Heaviness weighed into her bramble-like legs, while a feeling of elevation swept her mind into euphoria. Fire flushed her cold, stiff body, making her feel warm for the first time in days. Her nose and eyes became wet and sticky, but her mind drifted and eased. She became too serene to care about anything. She fell into peace, but the timer had started. In four or five hours, nausea would bring her back to the seventh floor, and her spaced out body – stuck like lichen on rock – would peel away in agony.

She left the flat as soon as her heart-rate elevated enough for her to stand. The winter dark settled on London hours ago and though, only 7 o'clock, it felt like midnight walking along quiet backstreets. On the main-roads, young girls strutted past Lilly and her hunchback bin liner. They dressed in tiny skirts and bikini tops, ready for nights out despite the biting cold. Lilly needed to look like them: nobody would pay for her while she had rheumy eyes, phlegmy nostrils, and smelt like a stale ashtray.

She ducked the barriers at Bermondsey tube station and zipped along the Jubilee line. At Canary Wharf, a drunken lady stumbled into the carriage and Lilly helped herself to the women's purse. At the next stop, Lilly hurried off the carriage and ran along the platform to re-board much closer to the front of the train. In Stratford, Transport for London guards patrolled the barriers. One guard kissed his teeth as Lilly bleeped through with the women's tube pass and her own bag of clothes. Somehow, he knew she'd stolen the pass.

Outside the station, Lilly pocketed the ten-pound note and dumped the purse in the bin. She glanced back to see the guards denying the drunk women access despite her pleading that she'd had her purse stolen. Lilly played the sound of the guard's kissing teeth over the visual of the judge's fireball eyes while quickening her pace.

She whipped past closed shops and busy pubs before sliding down a dark alleyway that fed along the railway. A group of teenagers eyed her, assessing whether she was fair game for their boredom. A valid target for their cruelty. Her nasty smell and dilated pupils protected her. They thought better of messing with her. One kid spat beside her shoe as she stepped past, and another shouted an obscenity. But that was it. A passing train thundered by.

Lilly exited the alley onto a street of shoddy terraced houses. Paint peeled off most doors and weeds competed with wheely bins in the bits of concrete between the pavement and pseudo bay windows. Lilly snuck through the lane, cutting between two joined houses, letting herself into the unlocked back gate. The Alsatian in next door's garden barked as if it were ready to kill. Had Lilly cared much about her life, the dog would have scared her.

Lilly knocked on the back door after securing the gate. When the dog's bark eased, she could hear the whistling of the unmowed, waist-high grass stretching to the fence, separating the garden and railway. Light from the bathroom window illuminated a small patch, but London's light pollution left elsewhere dirtily dark. Lilly knocked again, causing the

Alsatian to bark once more. Still, nobody answered. Lilly slid down against the back door. On the floor, she wrapped her arms around her tiny kneecaps and leant her anorexic face on the drainpipe.

Her stomach ached as if somebody had punched her. She wanted to vomit and die. But Lilly swallowed hard and prevented bile from rising and spilling out on Madam's yard. Eventually, the door opened. An elegant woman with a Mancunian accent stood, cigarette in hand. 'Are you coming in or what?'

Chapter 6 — Baby Scarlet, 2 weeks old (1980s, Pub)

'That's too much, Lyn. Wait there,' Fran said, moving over to Evelyn, who sat in front of the dressing-table mirror. Fran rummaged through the make-up bag and found more appropriate tones. She wiped down Evelyn's existing eyeshadow and lipstick and then touched them both up with more subtle shades. Still garish.

'I think it looked good before,' June said, zipping up her boot and moving to stand behind Evelyn and Fran. She squared her shoulders to the mirror and glanced at herself. Her eyes then went to Evelyn. 'Men find a bold blue alluring. You've softened it too much,' she said, attempting to take the original eyeliner stick. Fran grabbed it before June ruined Evelyn's face.

'Don't encourage her!' Fran said, elbowing June away from the mirror. 'You look lovely, Evelyn. And you don't need any men.'

'Thanks,' she replied, 'but I'm not sure about the curl—' Evelyn examined the flick shooting outward from her straight hair. '—What do you think?'

June wedged herself back into the mirror and said, 'It looks great.' She had forced the same flick on her own hair.

'Time to go,' Fran said, less convinced of the flick and hurrying to avoid discussing it. 'Come on, Joanie is waiting.'

They took a final breath in the mirror before leaving the bedroom. June tore down the steps and Fran turned off the landing light. 'Are you sure I look alright?' Evelyn asked in the dark.

'You look lovely; besides, you're not to go with any men anyway, remember?' Fran squeezed her little sister's hand and led them downstairs.

'Remember your keys if you're coming back late,' Ma said, amplifying her voice from the living room.

'We will,' Fran replied, swinging her head into the living room and cooing at Lilly, asleep in Ma's arms. June and Evelyn had already left.

'She's asleep. I'll put her down when you've gone,' Ma said, almost whispering so as not to disturb the baby.

Fran air-kissed Ma and Lilly, then left. She closed the door gently, as if it would disguise her slipping out for the evening.

Music thumped the ground inside the Black Swan. Evelyn swigged a Bacardi and coke at the bar while her sisters chatted with friends. Men and women danced everywhere, most holding a cigarette, drinks, or both. More people clustered along the bar and at standing tables.

'What' ya drinking'?' A brummy accent said from behind Evelyn. He wore khaki trousers and a tight-fitting white T-shirt.

'Bacardi,' she said, drinking in his pseudo-military outfit.

'Can I get ya another?' He asked as Evelyn drank the remaining half of her drink. 'You can knock 'em back quicker than most blokes.' He handed a note to the barmaid, who poured Evelyn another Bacardi.

'Easy though, love. They hit you fast when you're not used to them,' she said, eyeballing Mr Pseudo-Military a warning to go easy on her. And then, she added in a quieter voice reserved for Evelyn's ears, 'and you don't want to end up like ye sister, do you?' Evelyn smiled. She knew the barmaid meant June, and that she didn't mean any proper offence. Everybody in town knew June was a tad unhinged. 'Besides, these barrack boys only want one thing from you, darling,' she said, resuming her usual volume. 'Trust me.'

'And what's that?' The Brummy asked, but the barmaid shifted to serve another customer. She was a veteran in dealing with flirtatious, entitled men.

'She means you just want sex,' Evelyn said. Her blue eyeshadow thickened in the pub's light. It was a good job June hadn't reapplied the heavier shade.

'Does she?' The man gulped his pint of fosters while maintaining a poker face.

'Women can be horny too?' Evelyn matched his gulp and her cheeky grin peacock'd in the glass.

'Aye, some kinds can,' he said.

'And what kind am I?'

Before he answered, Fran grabbed Evelyn's arm. 'Come for a dance, Lyn,' she said, pulling her away.

Evelyn pushed her empty Bacardi glass, and it slid on the counter. She gave a sultry glare to the man while drifting to the small circle of women dancing near the DJ's flashy lights. The music transitioned from Abba's Super Trouper to Madness's Baggy Trousers, and pissed men began hopping from one foot to the other, knocking and causing people not pissed to spill their drinks. The floor became sticky fast.

The group of women pounced into the empty alcove table, lit cigarettes, and laughed at the drunkards, who looked like they were having seizures. Evelyn slipped back into the bar crowd. Fran and her friend noticed straight away.

'How's she doing?' Jodie asked.

'Our Lyn's hard-faced,' Fran said before humouring Frank Boucher, gesturing at her to join his awful clown dancing. She shook her head and continued the conversation with Jodie. 'She hasn't mentioned giving her away. I know she's not the most maternal girl, but you would think—' Fran shook her head, but feeling herself getting angry, changed the conversation. '—If we don't keep an eye on her, there'll be another.'

'Never. You really think?' Jodie asked, prising gossip from Fran.

'Lyn's a madam. I love her, of course, but she's always been one to watch.'

Frank Boucher continued whooping at Fran while spilling more drink over himself and everybody dancing nearby.

'So Frank then?' Jodie asked, acknowledging the buffoon capturing Fran's attention.

'No — I'm not interested in any useless men.' It was true, but she indulged the flattery when tipsy. She hid her rare non-baby induced smile by sipping her gin.

Frank swept forward and stumbled into her. Fran slapped his forearm, resisting his insistence that she dance with him. He enjoyed the sting and responded with a vigorous pull on her arm. She resisted again.

'Oh, give him a dance. It'll make his evening,' Jodie said, squashing out her cigarette and shuffling off to the toilets. Frank took advantage of the situation and pulled more vigorously, yanking Fran to the dancefloor. Luckily, the track shifted to Blondie, which she found easier to dance to.

As the song ended, Frank leant in to kiss her, but Fran pulled back, resisting his fat, sweaty lips. He leant in harder, and Fran pulled back harder. 'No, Frank.' He spun her and tried again, scoring this time. He dragged his lips over her berry lipstick, smudging it. She tried but failed to push him away, and now his tongue had wormed its way into her like some alien predator. Her back crashed into the wall, and his hands pressed into hers. Fran bit his invading tongue, and he sprang back as if electrocuted.

'You bit me, you fucking bitch.'

'I said no, Frank.'

'Yeah, but you wanted it.' He spat blood onto the floor.

Fran grabbed her handbag from the table. 'Well, I definitely don't anymore.'

'You're all the same, you Finches: cock-teases!' Frank turned nastier. 'Except the little one, she puts out whenever.'

Fran's cheeks flared as red as the tampon she'd thrown in the toilet bin earlier. A small crowd gathered at the commotion. One of Fran's friends tossed a dreg of coke in Frank's face as they moved to another area of the pub.

'He's a twat, Fran, ignore him—'

'—Let's get another drink, duck—'

'—Don't listen to—'

But Fran interrupted them all. '—I'm just going to head back. I'm not really feeling it tonight, anyway. Jodie, will you watch out for our Lyn? There's a barrack-boy buzzing around; don't let him do anything with her, will you?'

'Of course, I'll keep an eye out,' Jodie replied, returning from the loo. She'd not witnessed what Frank had done, but didn't doubt he deserved the thick lip. She squeezed Fran's hand, feeling guilty she'd encouraged her to dance with him.

Fran waved goodbye to the women. 'Thanks, and if you see our June, tell her I've gone home too, not that she'll mind.'

'Will do, love,' Jodie replied. 'And don't dwell on that dickhead. Everyone knows he's an idiot.'

Fran slipped through the disco crowds and out of the pub's oak panelled door. After wading through more smokers outside, silence and darkness replaced the music and flashing lights. She paced home without incident, isolating her house key from the collection of work keys, to let herself in quietly, not wanting to disturb Ma or Lilly.

'Is that you, Fran?' Ma asked, hearing the front door open and close.

'Yes.'

Fran placed her coat on the rack and slipped off her shoes. She rubbed the mark on her shoulder where Frank had jabbed his dirty fingernails.

'Are Lyn and June still out?'

Fran nodded as she entered the living room. Lilly was asleep in her cot beside Ma's fabric armchair. Ma updated Fran on the smallest details of the baby's evening. 'She's been good as gold, drifted straight back off after feeding; as soon as her head touched the pillow, that was it. I thought she was almost going to wake up once, but no.'

Fran leant into the cot and kissed Lilly on the forehead, but wanting more, she lifted her out for a cuddle. She moved to the sofa and sank into the cushions, resting Lilly in her micro-bouncing arms. 'Hello precious, you are gorgeous, aren't you?' She whispered. 'Yes, you are. Little Lilly is the most gorgeous. Yes, she is.'

'I thought you'd be out longer. Was it not busy?' Ma asked, lifting herself from the armchair and continuing to speak before Fran could answer the question. 'I'm going to have a quick cup of tea before bed. Do you want one?'

'Yes, please.' Fran replied as Ma shuffled into the kitchen. She waited for her to return with the mugs of tea before elaborating on the evening. 'It was packed, but Frank Boucher was being an idiot.'

Ma already had a premonition that a bloke was involved. She blew her tea and changed the topic. 'How were Lyn and June?'

Fran blew on her tea. 'They're alright. Lyn got chatting to some squaddie almost straight away.'

'Oh, she didn't,' Ma said, the closest she came to judgment.

Fran sipped the hot tea. 'I asked Jodie to keep an eye out.'

'She's not like you or June,' Ma said. It was unlike her to comment on one child in front of the others. Her neutrality would impress Switzerland.

Fran brushed Lilly's sleeping cheeks. 'I know Ma.'

Chapter 7 — Adult Scarlet & Nick (2000s, Hakasan Restaurant)

The virgin train pulled into London Euston. Scarlet separated herself from her old life via a 58 minute journey of high-speed rail. She trudged past Upper Crust with two cases, crossed the foyer and entered the underground, where she bought an oyster card with a monthly pass. Unlimited journeys. One of the biggest commitments she had ever made. She thought of Lilly zipping around on tubes with her own bags and it gave her an unearned familiarity and mock confidence.

People grunted at the space she took up with luggage. They were trying to get to work. Why had this stupid woman chosen to move her possessions on public transport at this sacred hour dedicated to them? Crowds thinned once she passed south of the river and entered anti-commuter territory. At Clapham North, she clambered off the carriage. Only one case had wheels, so she intermittently exchanged the one she pulled and carried.

Outside, uninterrupted sun covered the Highstreet in a warm glow. People ate croissants and drank lattes in a never-ending stream of cafes. Scarlet rippled past, admiring the flamboyant outfits and edgy haircuts. Before a crossing, she stopped to catch her breath, wedging the cases against the shop window. She arched her back, one hand supporting the bend and the other palming across her pregnant stomach. The urge to pee came strong, but she would have to hold. With stiff legs, she pulled a scrap piece of paper from her back pocket and unfolded a hand-sketched map of the area. She could turn off the Highstreet for the flat. Her new home. Or continue and visit her little brother first.

'Get in touch when you're clean.'

Scarlet recalled Nick's last words to her. She pocketed the map and gripped the case. On she went, crossing the road. At Blockbuster-videos beside the next crossing, DVDs displays continued to glisten as Scarlet turned for the side street. 'He'll be at work anyway,' she lied to herself, knowing it was half-term. She then convinced herself she would only walk past and peek at the house; she would visit later.

Fancy terraced houses bordered both sides of the street, most three stories high. Halfway along, she stopped at a black door. Fresh paint. She flattened her palm on it and held there as if performing a ritual, but really the urge to pee overpowered her strength.

'Are you alright, love?' An elderly lady asked while wheeling her trolley. 'You look pregnant.' She sounded like she smoked forty cigarettes a day.

'I'm fine,' Scarlet said, sighing from the pain but nodding to confirm she was pregnant. 'It's just becoming more difficult to hold for the loo. Just taking a minute.'

'Need help getting in?' The lady could barely shift her own body, let alone help Scarlet lift hers into the house.

'No thanks. It's not my house.'

'Thought they looked too fancy for you, love. No offence.'

Scarlet gripped her cases, and the old lady watched her work against the pain. Once they started walking, the old lady explained herself. 'Just the wanker-banker types and their plastic girls take most of these places. You don't look like one of them is all I meant. Anyway, I haven't got all day to stand around chin-wagging; I'll be off if you're not in labour,' she said, more question than statement.

'I'm fine—although—' Scarlet withdrew the map and pushed it to the lady. '—I'm wondering if I can get to Benson Tower without going back to the High-street.'

'Follow me, darling.' The old lady began shunting along the street and Scarlet followed beside her. 'What's your business?'

Scarlet thought about saying she was a reformed prostitute, but didn't.

The old lady sensed her unease and clarified her question. 'I mean, with the building.'

'Oh, I'm moving in. Fresh start.'

'Well, welcome, love. I've been there most me life. It's alright really. Watch out for the little shits, prozies, and crack heads – they'll steal your knickers if you give 'em half a chance. But as long as you got your wits about you, it's not too bad. What floor you on?'

'Ninth. You?'

'Third. I began on the ninth but can't cope with that many stairs nowadays: the lifts are out most the pissin' time!' Affection warmed her voice and she continued speaking. 'You better be prepared to haul the pram up and down, love.' She grimaced, turning Scarlet's future misfortune into something to laugh at. Dark humour; compensation for the good who've seen too much bad. 'Apart from that, though, the ninth floor isn't too bad: few junkies, and like I said, they'll leave you alone as long as you don't make it easy for them to steal anything.'

The fancy town houses faded in the distance as Scarlet and the lady bent along an alleyway, feeding them onto the Benson Estate. Scarlet had visited her fair share of tower blocks and the supposed crime didn't much worry her. The thought of pushing a pram up nine flights of stairs did.

'I'm Sophia,' the old lady said.

'Scarlet.'

'Nice to meet you, Scarlet. Next time you won't have those bags and so you can give me a hand with my trolly.'

She winked at Scarlet while waving goodbye and entering the one working lift - Scarlet wouldn't fit with her cases. She reciprocated the wave and waited for the lift to return. People joined the queue, and they seemed to wait a lifetime. Scarlet refused to feel guilty for taking most of the space when it finally rocked up. She'd waited long enough. A bearded man - more hair than face - rode with her. He smelt of marijuana and Radox bubble bath: Scarlet's sense of smell had always been good, but in pregnancy it became ultra sharp. She tried to stop herself sniffing such that her nose wriggled. The man kept his eyes on the floor and ignored the pregnant women inhaling him. The lift juddered its way to the ninth floor of Benson Tower, her new home.

Nick shut and bolted the front door. He slotted his shiny black work shoes into the sideboard and hung his brown-green coat on its allocated hook. His brown satchel bag went upstairs with him.

Although it was half-term, he had popped into school that morning to teach a revision class for students about to take examinations. He pulled a bunch of their exercise books from his satchel and left them on his pristine dining table while he entered the immaculate kitchen. With a cup of tea, he'd get the books marked now and then enjoy the rest of half term.

Steam hissed from the kettle, disrupting his trance and prompting him to finish making the tea. He returned to the dining room, mug and a Kit-Kat in hand. After putting them down, he moved an onyx figurine from the centre of the table and began marking his students' work, dipping the Kit-Kat in the tea but carefully so not to drip liquid on his student's work. He stacked the marked books in the figurine's spot, and forty-five minutes later, when he had almost completed the pile, the doorbell rang, disrupting his self-imposed target. Completing the entire pile in 50minutes.

His white socks trod the beige carpet back to the front door downstairs. The bolt loosened, and he opened the door. His sister said hello, and he prevented his face from dropping. 'What are you doing here?' he asked.

'Hello, Scarlet,' she said, mocking his warm welcome and mustering an ecstatic smile.

'Scarlet, you know what I said.'

Nick moved outside the door; his white socks flattened on the pavement, and the door rested ajar on his back. Scarlet rubbed her stomach and increased her smile to include the sight of teeth.

'I'm clean, Nick.'

'You look pregnant.'

'I am.'

Scarlet's teeth clamped together, her eyebrows lifted, and her shoulders lowered.

'I'm glad you're clean, but I meant what I said. Three years. A couple of months isn't enough.' He said, avoiding eye contact. Scarlet's enthusiasm waned, but she went in with a reserve, so had plenty to spare.

'How many months has it been?

'Clean or pregnant?'

'Clean, but I guess both.'

'Eight months.'

'What are you doing here eight months pregnant?' Nick glanced toward the High-street.

'I'm not eight months pregnant, you idiot. I'll be bigger than this then. Eight months clean.'

'That's great. I'm proud, Scarlet,' Nick said, facing his white socks.

'—But,' Scarlet said, anticipating he had more to say and losing patience. Her nostrils flared, and Nick lifted his glance to look. Their eyes met and locked.

'—But I meant it. Eight months isn't three years.'

'Come on Nick. I'm done. When have you seen me clean for this long before? I'm done. For real.'

Nick broke their eye contact; his socks came back into view. 'Sorry. I know it sounds brutal, but it is what it is, so...'

'—So that's it?' Scarlet's palms opened and lifted like a music conductor telling the orchestra to raise the stakes.

'I'm sorry, eight months is brilliant—' Nick wasn't budging.

Scarlet swallowed hard and nodded. '—I get it,' she lied.

A long silence brewed, which Nick eventually broke.

'I've got a pile of work, so I—' He leant on the door behind him, causing it to open.

Scarlet took the hint. '—Yeah, ok, well, it was good to see you.'

'You too.'

Nick stepped backward into his house and lifted his palm to offer a meek wave goodbye. He closed the door, replaced the bolt and went upstairs without turning to see if his sister still stood outside.

But Scarlet had walked away, more angry than upset. She expected Nick to avoid inviting her in for a cup of tea, but she did not prepare for his coldness regarding the baby. She thought they would chat on the doorstep. For longer than they did.

Nick returned to his marking and finished behind schedule, pissing him off. He squeezed the marked books back into his satchel bag and positioned the figurine back to its central spot on the dining table. After showering, he put on an expensive jumper and travelled into the city to meet Matt for dinner, but he felt dirty. Infected. Scarlet had planted a seed of guilt somewhere inside; somewhere he couldn't scrub; somewhere fertile. It grew fast, spawning vine-like, parasitic tentacles leaching his organs, and sprouting toxic acids inducing head and especially heartache. He felt ashamed of how he had treated his sister, but more than that, he felt resentful that she had made him feel ashamed.

Matt, suited and booted, browsed fancy restaurants during his afternoon slump at work. The market was quiet. Graphs unremarkable. He booked a new upmarket Chinese restaurant, offering pricey dumplings and even pricier spring rolls. The photographs showed a luxurious room with elegant wait staff where everything - from the dark paint to the wall sized water features - looked chic and ultra expensive; it bore zero resemblance to the cheap, all-you-can-eat buffets of China-town.

At the restaurant, Nick used his chopsticks to dip a piece of salmon sashimi elegantly into a dish of soy sauce and then into his mouth. After swallowing, he began his confession.

'My sister called round earlier.'

'Oh, really? Did she want money?' Matt asked, dipping a dumpling into soy sauce, unfazed by his partner's revelation.

'No.'

Nick went to pincer another piece of sushi.

'It's good, right?' Matt said, pointing his chopsticks at the piece of tuna heading for Nick's mouth.

'Yeah, it's really good.'

They ate several more items from the shared plates clustered in the centre of the table. Neither could speak for a moment.

'Come on then,' Matt said after chewing and swallowing most of his food. 'What did she want?'

Nick poked his chopstick into the small bowl of rice and transported a couple of individual grains into the small dish of soy sauce. 'I don't know.'

'What do you mean?' Matt replied, laughing. 'Why are you being so cryptic? She must have said something.' He wedged a spring roll into his chopsticks and shifted it to his mouth quickly, not trusting the soft grease for longer than was necessary.

'I said I couldn't see her until she was three years clean.'

'Was she clean?'

'Yeah, but that's not the point.'

'I wasn't judging. I get it. Anybody can do a couple of weeks.'

Matt hovered his chop sticks above the last piece of tuna and gestured to Nick whether he minded. Nick shook his head. Matt could have it. He then sheepishly corrected Matt's assumption that it'd only been a few weeks.

'It's been eight months.'

'Oh, wow.'

Matt paused his chewing.

'That's impressive, right? She's never been clean that long before?'

The tuna rested on his tongue.

'I think it unnerved me,' Nick said, scratching the skin behind his ear. 'I wasn't expecting it, and while I'm obviously happy for her—' he looked away from Matt, '—it's sort of easier, you know, if she's not around.'

Matt placed his chopsticks on the empty, soy-sauce smeared plate, and folded his arms on the table, sensing Nick had more to say.

'And?' he pressed.

'And... she's pregnant.'

Matt's jaw dropped. 'No way!' he said with his mouth open.

Nick nodded while stirring wasabi paste and ginger into the soy sauce. Matt picked his chopsticks back up, even though the food was gone. He jabbed the edamame bowl, checking for a leftover bean. 'Who's the dad?' He asked, but didn't leave space for a response. 'Jesus, can you imagine having a baby at that age with no career or prospects? How far along is she? Is that why she's clean?'

Nick's cheeks flushed the colour of tuna sashimi as his partner fired question after question.

'I didn't ask.'

Matt waited for him to elaborate. He was an upper middle-class city boy, not attuned to the nuanced manifestations of embarrassment. He'd had little experience of it; couldn't grasp its deep-rooted, insidious nature. Matt didn't pick up the signs; couldn't pick up the signs. This part of Nick - this morality - he did not understand. He continued to wait for Nick to explain why he turned his sister away, not registering the inherent wretchedness the action (let alone the talk) caused. To Nick, the reason was neither here nor there. It didn't matter whether the reason was good. He felt a deep-rooted, terrible shame for abandoning his sister. His family. Facts or circumstance would never change that.

'I had work to do and didn't have the mental energy to deal with her,' he said, lying to himself and his partner.

'And how'd you feel about that?' Matt asked, still none the wiser to how raw a nerve the matter went.

'Shit.'

Chapter 8 — Adult Lilly (1990s, Brothel)

Madam Perez closed the door after Lilly traipsed inside; the Alsatian barked at the twisting of the lock. 'You got off then, you jammy cow,' she said.

Lilly scratched her anorexic elbow and moved her fringe away from her eyes.

'Get showered and cleaned up.'

'I need a little something to keep me going.'

'No chance, love. You know the crack.'

After lighting a cigarette, she placed a hand on her slender hip. She took a long toke and then gave the cigarette to Lilly.

'That'll have to do for now,' she said, patting Lilly on the back, and forcing her forward. 'The sooner you get yourself cleaned up and looking presentable, the sooner we'll get you a client.'

Lilly drifted through the kitchen, smoking the cigarette, like a small lost child. She wrapped around the banister in the dingy hallway and pulled herself upstairs. Grunting and pornographic squealing leaked from behind the bedroom doors. Lilly quickened her pace along the corridor. In the bathroom, she removed a black dress and leather boots from the trunk.

While hot water filled the bathtub, she stared at the overgrown grass stretching to the railway fence at the rear of the garden. An Eurostar train on its way to Paris blasted along the track. 100 miles per hour. It wasn't there the year before. People reading books, drinking coffees, and sipping champagne flickered past in little rectangles of yellow light, colouring the darkness.

Bubbles clustered on the surface of the bath water. Lilly's granny legs slid through them like thin poles. Heat submerged her body as she slunk into the tub. She felt like a fish taken from the freezer and placed in the oven. The change in temperature, drastic and cruel. Her face sank into the water, and she closed her eyes. Waves of hair stretched in every direction like tentacles, then unified as she rose for air. She breathed for the first proper time since shooting up. Pity it wouldn't last.

She wanted to lie in the warm tub forever, but Madam Perez knocked on the plastic door, letting herself in without waiting for an invitation - her keys opened every room. She dropped the toilet lid, sat down, and lit another cigarette. 'So, what's the deal?' she asked, peeing.

'Acquitted.'

The women shuck her head, smiling and blowing smoke over the sink. 'You have more lives than a witch's cat. I was sure I wouldn't see you again. Well, good for you, love.'

She gazed at Lilly like a mother and then snapped herself out of it.

'Now come on, Mr Spencer's on his way. Ten minutes.'

She shook, wiped herself, and stood; flushing the chain afterward. Her demeanour hardened.

'He's become handsy. Moreso than usual. It can happen when they get too comfortable. Stand your ground. Be firm. But not aggressive - it'll encourage him. Understand?'

Lilly nodded, despite not understanding; she no longer cared. She dipped her head underwater a final time. Madam Perez squeezed Lilly's shoulder on her way out.

'There's a little something on the side,' she said in the doorway. She'd left a greyish powder on the sink. 'I must be getting soft.' The door closed behind her.

Lilly climbed out of the bath, dried herself, and dressed in the skimpy black dress and leather boots. She applied makeup from the bits and pieces left in the mirror cupboard, including some deep blue eyeshadow, which reminded Lilly of her mother. Once ready, she waited on the toilet until the doorbell rang, staring into oblivion.

At that point, she snorted the greying powder, hoping it would last longer than Mr Spencer's needs. High, she left, closing the bathroom door behind her.

Chapter 9 — Baby Scarlet, 3 weeks old (1980s, Higham Lane)

'The tutor's here, Evelyn,' Ma said, calling from the kitchen after hearing the front door knock.

'I'm back at school next week; I don't need him,' Evelyn replied, calling from the living room.

'He's at the door. We need to say something.'

'Can't you just tell him the truth?'

Evelyn licked her finger and turned a page of Smash Hits magazine. Ma shuffled to the front door, huffing. 'I think Evelyn goes back to school next week, so we can probably leave it, don't you think?' she said to the old man. The tutor coughed into his fist and then removed his hanky to blot his elderly lips.

'I'll get on with the lesson since I'm already here. She could do with the help.'

The tutor scratched his elbow beneath the patch of his scraggy jacket and stepped his shoe onto the doorstep. Ma moved out of his way. He walked into the living room and sat in Ma's chair, panting like an exhausted dog. Evelyn shut her magazine and moved onto the far end of the sofa.

'Morning Evelyn. This is our last session, as I hear you're back at school next week. Shame really; you're making good progress,' he said, removing three archaic textbooks from his bag and placing them on the coffee table, still panting.

'Would you like a cup of tea?' Ma said, calling from the kitchen.

'Yes. Two sugars.'

The tutor opened the Maths book and quizzed Evelyn. 'Express 2/5s as a percentage.'

'40%,' she said, toeing her magazine beneath the coffee table, not wanting him to ask about it with his touchy fingers.

'If the Co-op has a sale on nappies - let's say, 2/5s of the usual price when buying two packs – how much will you save if the usual price for one pack is £6?'

Evelyn stared at the gas fire attached to the wall as she calculated the answer in her head: 10% of a single pack would be 60p; 20%, £1.20; 40%, £2.40; 40% of two packs, £4.80; £4.80 off £12.

'£7.20.'

'Smart girl.'

Mr Rogers scanned the small room, noting the ornament cabinets, crammed side tables, and stripy curtains. 'Make sure you don't get short-changed when you're shopping. You can't always trust the cashiers,' he said.

Ma entered the room and passed him a cup of tea.

'Thank you, Mrs Finch. I was telling Evelyn to be careful when paying for her things in the Co-op. You'll know more than anybody: you can't rely on cashiers counting accurately or being 100% honest, can you?'

Ma attempted to shuffle away without being pulled into Mr Rogers' observations and judgments, but he drew her back.

'Sorry Fae,' he said, switching to Ma's first name. 'I appear to have forgotten my cigarettes. You don't have a spare I could borrow?'

'Of course,' Ma said, turning back. She placed her packet and lighter on the coffee table within Mr Roger's reach.

'Thank you—' he said, observing the packet before taking one out and trying to identify whether it had come from a multi-packet. He couldn't tell. '—Where did you buy these from?'

'Work, why?'

'Hmmm—' he said, his glasses sliding down the bridge of his nose as he attempted to read the small print. '—I'm trying to see whether they contain a price.'

He fingered his glasses back to his eyes. 'How much is a single packet vs. a multi-packet?'

'97p for a single packet, or £9.70 for 200. They don't change the price for buying in bulk.'

Ma slipped into the kitchen before he asked her anything else. He re-focused on Evelyn. 'Well, let's pretend there is a discount for buying in bulk. There should be—' he said, injecting his commercial moralism into the arithmetic, '—Let's say, 200 cigarettes costs £8.73. How much discount will you receive for bulk buying 10 packets? As a percentage, naturally.'

'10%.'

Evelyn didn't think about the specific problem. She knew he'd remove 10% and didn't need to do the exact Maths. Mr Rogers loved a 10% discount.

'I don't understand Evelyn. You are a smart girl. Certainly not retarded. With your mathematical proficiency, your mother could have easily got you employment at the Co-op, despite having a baby. I mean, you wouldn't be the first girl to get pregnant at school. But twice? That, my dear, is not so common, and people won't understand; won't understand it at all. It'll make it very difficult for the managers to trust you. People make a mistake, but two?'

Mr Rogers' glasses slid down his nose again. 'Two dear is pushing it. Such a shame. Such a shame.'

He twisted his neck from side to side and Evelyn shifted her stare from the fire to the window, waiting for Mr Rogers to work through his musings. Every week, he said the same things. On he went. 'And it's such a shame, you know, because, like I say, your proficiency is above average. You answer problems with speed and only very, very rarely are you incorrect. You could have been a fine cashier. Fine.'

After an hour of monologues about lost potential, broken up by intermittent Maths problems, mostly involving 10% discounts on nappies, baby food, cigarettes, or washing powder, Mr Rogers left.

'God, I'm glad he never has to come round again,' Evelyn said, pulling out her magazine from beneath the coffee table while Ma lifted the cushion from the chair he'd sat at. She hit it mid-air. Flecks of dandruff and dry skin fell to the floor, which she then vacuumed. After cleaning up, she sank into her clean chair.

June stomped down the staircase. 'God, I'm glad that idiot doesn't have to come round ever again. He alone makes me never want a baby.'

'Don't be rude,' Ma said, turning on the television.

June passed by and sat beside Evelyn on the sofa. 'Nobody even cares about exams, Lyn. I wouldn't bother going back to school at all if I were you. I'll get you a job at the old people's home.'

'I want to go back.'

June snatched the magazine out of Evelyn's hands. 'Really?'

Evelyn lifted her feet onto the sofa and relaxed into the cushions. 'Yeah — I like school.'

June flicked through the pages of Evelyn's magazine. 'Why?'

'Dunno, I just do.'

June chucked the magazine onto the coffee table, bored. 'But aren't you worried about what everyone will say?'

'Not really.'

Evelyn leant forward and picked-up her magazine. 'They said nothing before. Why would they this time?'

Ma got up to use the toilet, and June eyeballed her leaving. 'She still not said anything?'

'No.'

Evelyn flicked through the pages of her magazine, and the conversation stopped. The noise from the television and Ma's flush of the toilet replaced the sound of their voices. As Ma re-entered, a re-run of Blankety Blank played out. An hour later, keys jangled in the front door as Fran let herself in. She removed her work shoes and entered the living room, asking where the baby was before saying hello to anybody. She jolted upstairs before they could answer and lifted Lilly from the cot where she slept.

'You shouldn't wake her if she's sleeping,' Ma said, turning down the volume of the television.

Fran tiptoed down the steps, baby in arm. 'She's still sleeping,' Fran whispered back on the staircase.

'Are you going to The Black Swan again this Friday?' Evelyn asked, as Fran entered the room with Lilly and sank into the empty armchair beside the T.V.

'I suppose so.'

'I'm assuming you've not heard from Frank Boucher?' June said, munching on a packet of prawn cocktail crisps.

'No. I shall ignore him if he's there.'

Fran rocked the baby, though not enough to wake her.

'He'll be there. You'll have to speak to him.' June said, leaning both elbows onto the arm of the sofa and staring at Fran.

'No, I don't. I'm not interested in the pig—'

June raised her voice and dug her elbows harder into the armrest. '— But how can you suddenly just stop being interested?'

'Not everybody gets obsessed,' Evelyn said, covering her face with the magazine to avoid June's wrath.

June speared her toe into Evelyn's waist. 'What do you mean by that?'

'Ouch! Don't do that, you cow!'

Evelyn whacked June's leg with her Smash Hits magazine, and Ma eyed them both, huffing and puffing.

Fran intercepted the fight. 'You can come Lyn, but you've got to stay away from those squaddies.' Lilly's eyes flickered open as Fran's rock transitioned into a bounce.

'I know what they're like. I'm not stupid.'

'I wasn't saying you are. I'm just saying be careful.'

June snaked her toe back toward Evelyn and hovered it by her waist.

'I'll hit you again,' Evelyn said, rolling the magazine into a tube as a warning. June ignored it and jabbed her toe into Evelyn, then sprang off the sofa, dashing past and knocking Lilly's head as she moved.

'You knocked her head, you idiot!' Fran said, pulling Lilly into her bosom and kissing her hair. Evelyn chased June with the tubular magazine around the coffee table and Ma kept telling them to stop running. Evelyn struck out, attempting to swipe June's exposed arms and legs. But she missed. She tried several times, but the magazine axed the air to no avail. Eventually, June crashed into the sofa and Ma stood up to prevent Evelyn following.

'Enough!' Ma said, physically cutting Evelyn away from June, and triggering Evelyn to resort to verbal combat.

'Go and stalk Ivan, you sociopath.'

'Fuck off.'

June rushed off the sofa, pushed past Ma's barricade and through Evelyn's folded arms. She slammed the living room door and stormed upstairs. Ma spewed about her swearing, but June was gone.

'You shouldn't wind her up. You know what's she's like,' Ma said, turning the television back up. Evelyn didn't argue back, and the commotion faded. Everybody went back to doing their own thing: Lyn read her magazine; Fran cooed the baby; and Ma watched another episode of Blankety Blank.

On Friday night, Evelyn applied her own lipstick and eye shadow, refusing Fran and June's help. She layered on more than the previous week.

'That's a bit much, don't you think?' Fran said, licking her finger and attempting to rub smudged lipstick from Evelyn's cheek.

'What're you doing?' Evelyn said, defending her face.

'You've smeared a bit of lipstick—hold still—there!'

The smear disappeared as Fran won the battle.

'You know she's going to cause him to flip,' Evelyn said, changing the conversation to June, and checking her lips in the mirror to ensure Fran hadn't wiped away too much colour.

'That's her business, so don't get involved.'

Fran examined her own lipstick and eye shadow in the shared mirror.

June returned from the bathroom smelling like a perfume shop. She waltzed back and forth like a hyper child. 'Come on! Let's go! Everybody will be there already!'

She urged them to hurry and then dashed downstairs, too impatient to wait any longer.

'She means Ivan will be there already,' Evelyn said, an enormous grin stretching across her face.

'Enough. I mean it, Lyn. Don't wind her up—' Fran air kissed her rouged lips before the mirror and fluffed her hair. '—Come on,' she said, squeezing Evelyn's shoulders.

Downstairs, she popped into the living room to kiss Lilly's forehead and say bye to Ma. Evelyn went to wait with a manic June bouncing up and down on the cobbled street.

'Remember your keys if you're back late,' Ma said, switching the T.V. to channel three, ready for Emmerdale.

'Will do. Love you, Ma.'

Fran waved and left. She slid the front door shut gently, minimising the volume, which was wasted effort, given June's screaming for them to hurry. 'Shh, besides, the band doesn't start till 8, so calm down.'

June ignored Fran and rushed ahead. Evelyn smirked, and Fran rolled her eyes. They linked arms and strolled arm-in-arm, ignoring the cold and June's irritating pleas to walk faster. She skipped ten feet ahead.

Inside the pub, they separated. June, wolf-like, tucked herself into a group of women hunting beside Ivan's pack; Fran, flamingo-like, chit-chatted rubbish with a flock of women from the sewing factory; and Evelyn, deer-like, ambled beside the bar alone, looking like Prey. A squaddie offered her a drink as she bought her own.

Mid-way through his come-on lines, Evelyn's attention hawked to another man. He stared at her, but with his pint hovering in front of his face, blocking all features save his penetrating hazel-green eyes. The squaddie looked over his shoulder to see what had caught her eye. 'What?' he asked, detecting no competition. 'Not the old dude?'

Evelyn lifted her glass and gulped her Bacardi and coke. She turned away from the older man staring at her. That was enough. For now. She indulged the squaddie.

'You're playing with me, ain't ya?' he said, grinning. He had a stronger brummy accent than the squaddies from last week. Evelyn smirked and then slipped away, brushing her body against his arm as left. He tracked the direction of her movement but didn't twist his body to lock in specifics; finding her was part of the fun.

She slid through gnarled limbs and bodies interlinked along the bar and found an empty slice of wall to lean against, closer to the man with hazel-green eyes. He would need to twist his body to see her. He didn't. But he knew she was there, watching him.

Evelyn shifted closer once the trio of women were served and moved away. She crept into their position and imagined the bristle of his stubble on her neck. He gulped his pint without adjusting his posture or gaze: his back remained hunched and his eyes fixed on the whiskies lined up along the bar.

'Remind you of school?—' Evelyn asked, facing the bar so they could speak without looking at one another. '—The bottles lined up like good little children, doing exactly as they're told.'

'What do you want, Evelyn?' He said, his voice flat and monotone.

'You've got a new jacket. It's nice. Did your wife buy it for Christmas?' She asked, leaning her elbow on the bar and planting her chin into a clenched fist.

'Scotch, please,' he said, getting the barmaid's attention, and pointing to the cheaper bottle of whisky before she could ask what he wanted.

'Ice, love?' The barmaid asked, tossing two cubes into his glass as he nodded back to her. He gave her a pound coin, and she returned him a twenty pence piece. He tossed-back the whisky in a single gulp and washed it down with a swig of his pint of bitter.

'You shouldn't be speaking to me. You shouldn't be in a pub.'

'You shouldn't be having sex with girls in pubs.'

Evelyn finished her Bacardi and then dug her other elbow into the bar. She interlaced her hands and her chin rested on the bridge. They continued looking at the bottles lined up against bronzed glass. A faint hint of their reflections formed. Both stared in silence. Evelyn broke the standoff by catching the barmaid's attention.

'You a regular now, Lynnie?—' The barmaid said, pouring a Bacardi and coke without Evelyn asking, and when Evelyn handed two twenty pence pieces to her, the woman placed three back in her hand, winking. '—Go easy, darling.'

She shunted along the bar and poured pints for paying customers while the man beside Evelyn drank. He blew nostril air into the glass, an expression of his anger, designed for only Evelyn to notice. 'This isn't right,' he said, his words plunking into the bitter and triggering ripples of spite to circle in the glass.

'Being left alone to have two babies isn't right.'

'I'm not responsible for both, and I didn't need to be responsible at all. You choose to have it.'

Evelyn drank the Bacardi like a shot, twisted her body, and leant back against the bar. 'Don't worry about it. Neither of us is responsible now. See you at school, sir.'

She walked away.

Meanwhile, June edged her way through a group of dancing women, positioning herself close to Ivan. As he danced, she inched nearer. Each brush of her body against his was electrifying. Emboldening. The smallest touch flooded her with confidence, thickening her esteem like water to flour. Drop by drop – or brush by brush – she gained substance; a solid mass, making her sturdy enough to embrace him head on. June spun to the music and crashed into him with an expectant euphoria. He could only respond joyfully to her forced collision.

Ivan pushed her away, hard, and everyone retreated several steps, the women gasping at June's undignified fall, and the men giggling at Ivan's blunt shove. June did not rise. Like sticky dough - flour with too much water - her limbs peeled to the floor. An awkward silence emanated from those close by, eerie amidst the pub's loud music and background hustle and bustle.

'For fuck's sake, June, get up, will ya?' Ivan said, breaking the deadlock.

June remained stuck to the floor, opting to be the subject of his hostility rather than inattention. Ivan grabbed her arm and yanked. She resisted. His anger intensified, and he imitated every short-tempered father figure he'd known. He yanked harder and spoke firmer, his voice deepening and darkening. 'June, I mean it. You're embarrassing yourself. Get up.'

Her counter yank almost pulled him to the floor rather than her off it. 'June, I fuckin mean it. Get up!'

Fran rushed over and pushed Ivan away. She scooped June up and shuffled her away from the crowd, which, by this point, lost interest. Dancers claimed the vacuumed space, and the pub returned to normal.

'What was that about?' Fran asked, lighting two cigarettes beneath the pub's outdoor lamps. She handed one to June.

'I love him,' June said, her body contorting like trippy shapes in a kaleidoscope. Fran gripped June's shoulders and coaxed her to sit down on the bench. It was snowing, too cold, for people to linger so they had space, privacy.

'You're just upset.'

'I love him,' she repeated, her heart hurting.

Fran took a long drag of her cigarette and blew smoke into the freezing air. 'Shall we go home?'

June shook her head: leaving would break her heart. If Ivan was here, she would stay. They sat on the bench together and smoked the rest of their cigarettes, watching the smoke drift into black air. Fran held her hand the entire time. After they finished, she stood. 'Come on. Let's get a drink, but promise you'll stay away from him.'

'I will,' she lied. Fran placed her hand flat on June's back and they pottered back into the pub.

Evelyn had returned to the squaddie from earlier. His thick forearm wrapped around her torso as she sat on a barstool and leant against the bar. Fran and June strode over. 'Come on Lyn, let's get a drink,' Fran said, huffing.

'She's got one,' the squaddie said, squaring his shoulders, puffing his chest, and smiling like a cheeky teenager.

'Lyn, come on, you know they're only after one thing,' Fran said, ignoring him and avoiding physical contact despite the crowds and their proximity.

Evelyn glanced down the bar for the teacher, but a young woman had taken his seat. He was gone, but his pint remained a quarter full. Maybe he hadn't gone, gone. Evelyn popped off the barstool, causing it to screech against the floor, but the music absorbed most of the noise. The squaddie released his hooked arm, granting an exit for Evelyn, but he pulled his torso closer so that her body slid against his as she moved away. He winked at her and smiled wider, believing the night was still young.

'You shouldn't lead them on,' Fran said, while claiming a booth for them to perch in.

'You talking to me or her?' Evelyn said, tipsy and with only half her attention present. She was searching the pub for the teacher. June was doing the same. For Ivan.

'You. I'm serious, Lyn. They're trouble. Stay away.'

She couldn't see the teacher anywhere, allowing her full, soured attention to coalesce. 'I know. I'm not stupid. It's only a bit of flirting, nothing serious.'

'No Lyn, you can't. Not even a little.'

'I'm going to the loo,' June said, having located Ivan and rushing to follow him toward the toilets. Fran shook her head, irritated. She was giving up on her sisters. Evelyn, though, watched June and as she did, she saw her slide past the teacher coming out of the toilets. He hadn't left. Yet.

Evelyn made an excuse so she could rush off to follow him, careful to ensure Fran wouldn't watch her. 'I need the loo, too.'

But before leaving, she waited for Fran to look at her. When she did, Evelyn mustered a sober, sincere voice. 'I'll stay away. Promise.' False earnestness.

Fran squeezed her hand, pleased and relieved with Evelyn's maturity. Maybe she was getting through to at least one sister. She smiled and relaxed into the booth's leather backrest.

Beside the exit, Evelyn checked over her shoulder and ensured Fran was not looking. She dipped out. Thin snowflakes settled on the ground and austere, orange light branched off the pub's lamps like lunar hanging-baskets in the thick of winter. Through the dimness, Evelyn watched the man fade in the distance. She followed, staying far enough away for him to not hear her light crunches on the snow, but close enough to track his movement.

The pub's glow dimmed to spartan blotches of streetlamp as Evelyn tracked faint footprints through darker streets. Rows of terraces turned to semi-detached houses, and after fifteen minutes, detached houses with pretty gardens filled the streets. The man turned into a driveway. Lights flickered on as he approached the porch. Evelyn watched him jumble through his coat pocket – and failing to find what he was looking for – bend down to retrieve a key from beneath a plant pot. But a woman answered and ushered him inside. The key returned under the pot, and the door closed. The porch light fizzled out, leaving Evelyn with the meagre streetlight. She knew she should leave, but the desire to see his wife, his children? overwhelmed her rationality.

She checked the windows and driveways along the street: curtains were closed. Gates shut. Nobody around to see her. She scuttled along his driveway, past the fancy Ford Sierra he drove to school in and leant against the house, her heart thumping. Light poured from the upstairs window, illuminating a square patch of bush in front of her. It must be the bathroom. He must be in there washing away the smell of whisky on his stubble, clean for his wife's bedsheets.

Evelyn continued shuffling along the house until she reached the fence to the back garden. She waited for the bathroom light to disappear before opening and slipping through. Dim moonlight coloured the slither of snow settled on the lawn. No other light. She edged to the backdoor and pressed her face on the glass. Unlike her own, it led into a long hallway rather than the kitchen. Light from the upstairs landing cast a subtle internal glow, allowing her to see straight through to the front door. Pictures hung on the wall, but she couldn't make out the subjects. Then the light went off altogether. They must have gone to bed. She pondered the key under the pot, but couldn't bring herself to use it. Instead, she stared through the glass, trying to notice anything significant, but it was too dark. She turned and sank against the door; her bum perching on the step.

She sat, wondering whether they were having sex; whether there were any children inside; whether they were boys or girls; if he was nice to them; if she was nice to him. But suddenly, the door opened, and a hand fired out to clamp her mouth. She tasted his fingers. He had been smoking. His breath slid over and under the tiny hairs on the back of her neck and then his whispered words poured into her arteries like a hit of opium. 'What the fuck are you doing at my house?'

He slid the tip of his finger into her lips, allowing her to suck, and engulfed her body from behind. 'We cannot do this here.'

He unzipped his jeans and then pulled at her underwear.

'Marc?—' His wife said, calling from the top of the staircase. '— Everything alright?'

His hand clamped harder as he spoke to his wife. 'Yes, sweetheart. Just getting some water. I'll be up in a minute.'

His voice returned to a pornographic whisper as he focused on Evelyn. 'I knew you were following me—' he said, sliding his finger into her. '— But you are out of your fucking mind coming here.'

He pulled his fingers out and forced her body to twist. His stubble levelled with hers eyes and his hand still clamped her mouth. 'Come to my house again, and I'll kill you.'

His hazel-green eyes bored into her soul, and they did not blink. Slowly, he peeled his hand from her mouth. Stunned, she didn't move or say anything. He pushed her gently backward so they no longer touched. 'Now get the fuck out of my garden—' his voice unintentionally raised. '—Now.'

He closed the door, and Evelyn heard the key turn. Her legs had turned to jelly, but she willed them to transport her even if it was in tiny infant-like steps. After passing through the gate, she lowered the latch as quietly as possible, and tip-toed across the drive, taking care not to be noticed as she snuck away. On the street, she stopped caring about his wife seeing. She ran hard and fast, unconcerned with how it looked or whether her heels made a racket. She ran hard. Hard and fast.

Back at the pub, Fran and June separated into their own groups. Evelyn slipped back into the crowds, her absence un-noted, apart from the squaddie, who'd circled the place several times, looking for her. Upon seeing her, his smile bloomed. He crept behind and, with his thick forearms, lifted her into the air. 'I thought I'd lost ya!'

Placing her down, he wrapped his face around her neck and pecked her cheek, then he twisted her body. Their eyes levelled. He wrapped his arms and interlaced his hands around her body. Evelyn gripped his hair and yanked his head back. But, as quickly, she jerked it forward. Their faces squared, and she dived into his lips, kissing him hard and fast.

'Come on then,' Evelyn said, taking the lead. She grabbed his hand and strode toward the exit. The squaddie reached for his jacket just in time. He didn't want to slow or interrupt her stride. Outside, the snow thickened. Evelyn and the squaddie kissed repetitively beneath the orange lamp, mounting with flakes. Evelyn pulled away from the kiss to propose their next steps. 'Let's go to yours.'

'Look, I'm not actually that kind of guy—' the squaddie said, holding Evelyn tight to his chest, a vulnerable and hitherto genteelness replacing his boyish bravado and banter. '—I like ya, babs, and I don't go to bed with women that I like. Not just like that.'

Evelyn squirmed in his arms. She wanted to push him away and punch him.

The squaddie exerted greater force to restrain Evelyn; to stop her exploding within his arms. 'Hey, hey. What's up?'

'Get off me! Get off!' Evelyn said, kicking him in the shin and triggering him to let go.

'Fuck—' he said, sighing at the sting. '—I was only trying to be nice. What's wrong?' He flattened his palms into the air, showing he wasn't angry or a threat, and then, while stepping forward, slowly lowered one arm. He stretched it out and opened his hand toward Evelyn, inviting her to take hold.

She twisted away. 'Just forget it.'

The squaddie continued approaching her, slow and steady, the way he would approach a traumatised soldier on the battlefield. He went to place his hands on her waist. To hug her softly from behind. She pelted him in the stomach, and despite being a tough military man, it winded him.

'Fucking hell—' he said, bending over and clutching his stomach. Evelyn stepped onto the road. '—I don't even get an apology?' He asked after regaining composure, lifting his back straight, and keeping one hand on his stomach.

'I know this ain't about me, bab? Look, I'm not saying I don't want ya; cause I do: you're beautiful. I'm just sayin' that I'm a bit more old-fashioned than people presume. I like to know me women afore we get intimate, you know, like?' He said, his white, well-formed teeth appearing as his mouth opened into a joyous cheeky smile.

Evelyn sat on the kerb and gave the tiniest of smiles back. It was enough. The squaddie joined her on the step. 'I don't know anythin' about ya, babs. Let's spend a bit of time together, eh?'

Evelyn went to push her hair behind her ear, but the outward flick she'd styled prevented it from moving as it would normally.

'What are ya doing tomorrow? How about I take ya to Brum?—' He said, offering his hand again; Evelyn taking it. '—I can call for ya at 10 and we can get the train together? How about it?'

She nodded.

'And how about a little kiss—for the road?' He wrapped his arm around her shoulders, and as they leant in, Fran and June stormed outside.

'Get off her!—' Fran said, pulling Evelyn up. '—You squaddies are all the same. Just piss off and leave us be!'

Evelyn and the squaddie smirked. Neither took much notice of Fran's hostility. 'Where d'ya live?—' The squaddie said, standing tall as Fran and June carried Evelyn away in their linked arms. '—I'll call for ya tomorrow.'

'Piss off!' Fran and June said together.

'Gadsby Street. Three doors up from the Palace,' Evelyn said back, smiling over her shoulder between her sisters' heads.

Fran laughed, disbelieving a squaddie would honour his promise. She saw no threat to Evelyn telling him their address. He wouldn't call. June, though, twisted, intrigued and surprised by his eagerness despite their abrasiveness. She offered a sultry stare at him, wondering whether he'd be interested in her.

'See you tomorrow. I'll be there!' he said to Evelyn, his beefy arm waving her goodbye.

Chapter 10 — Adult Scarlet (2000s, Lambeth College)

The lifts were out, yellow tape roping them off, so Scarlet took the stairs. Again. Her hand slid along the red plastic rail encircling the grey concrete staircase. At least she was going down. Every few steps, she stopped to rub her stomach, which had grown large during her stint in London.

Reaching the ground, she exited the building and approached the bus stop. The 137 rumbled away. She'd missed it by seconds, but it didn't matter. Unlike home, buses came every ten minutes, and she'd allowed plenty of time to get to class. On the bus, a dishevelled man with messy wire-like facial hair and a scrawny dog, gave up his seat. She took it, wanting to show gratitude, but feeling uneasy about the potential for residue fleas.

Scarlet was 8 months pregnant, and the struggle to stand upright had kicked in. She perched on the edge of the seat and avoided leaning back. On the approach to Lambeth College, she grabbed the pole to lift herself up and pressed the little red button for the bus to stop. She stumbled off, one foot at a time.

Inside the college foyer, the security guard opened the gate beside the turnstiles. She waddled through, hurrying to catch the fancy lift ready to close. It was rarely out of action, which irritated her. She could climb three stories: it was mounting nine that exhausted her.

'Good to see you, Scarlet—' a short woman said, holding a whiteboard pen. Splashes of leather peppered her outfit and gave an edge to her dyed grey hair. '—How are you?'

Scarlet stumbled to a seat before she panted an answer. 'Good. Good. I enjoyed the stories.'

The woman smiled. She had a capacity to make people feel fully seen when they spoke. 'I'm so glad you enjoyed them. Quite the scandal.'

'I'm assuming it's where Freud got the name?' Scarlet said, removing her notepad and a copy of The Three Theban Plays.

' "Most men are blatant thieves, blinded by ambition for self-gratifying greatness—" ' she said, chuckling at the quote. '—We'll talk more about Freud later. Though, it's quite convincing that Sophocles' Oedipus must have energised his thinking. Hello Rochelle—'

She paused the conversation with Scarlet to greet more adult women coming into the classroom. '—How are the children? How's work? Is your mother getting on alright?'

Scarlet observed the way she related to each of her students with genuine interest. It wasn't just a job to her.

'Ok. I think that's everybody, as Sonia won't be joining us this evening.'

She picked up her board pen and removed the lid. 'Antigone—' she said, spelling the name on the board in big letters. '—Conscientious warrior or reckless fool? Brave or idiotic? Inspiration or spoilt brat? In the tradition of Greek drama, the text opens up the range of possibilities. It makes room for the audience – them, us – to decide.'

Despite her age, she wore a short leather skirt and perched on the edge of the desk like a slender twenty-year-old. The board settled into the background. She paused for dramatic emphasis, giving the class ten seconds to gather their thoughts.

Latisha broke the silence; Latisha always broke the silence. 'Spoilt brat if ya axe me. Wid so many actual problems, the girl choosin' to die for the honour of a dead white man! Yes, she standing up for what she believe in, but damn, she needs a better cause. Is that all the girl really care about? She got nothing bigger?'

Emilia, a bookish girl, rebuked Latisha. 'I mostly agree, but we have to be careful about judging beliefs from a universalist perspective.'

Scarlet nodded, agreeing with the bookish woman sat at the front. She had been swatting up, reading recommended articles during the long days alone in the flat, and she recalled lots of writers warning about being too universalist in perspective. Not that she understood what that exactly meant. It was over her head. She enjoyed reading, especially as a girl, but the scholarly material for the course was a bit much. Yet the gear was out of her system, and she was enjoying the challenge. Her clarity of thought and sophistication was returning, and she had faith she'd get there. She was enjoying her mind again.

'I suppose it's dangerous to presuppose what makes a person tick; to assume that what will tip one person into despair or cause them to lash out, will be the same for somebody else.' Scarlet said, her pulse quickening as she spoke aloud in front of the class.

Scarlet's contribution buoyed Fatimah to share her thoughts. 'What might seem stupid to one person could give somebody else a reason to live.'

They smiled at one another. They had spoken once or twice and knew they would be friends. The teacher moved her hands further back on the desk and drew her shoulders apart as if she were doing a yoga stretch: her chest puffing out; her head bobbing up and down; her eyes focused on an imagined drishti point.

'Yeah. I get that—' Latisha said, waving her hands as she spoke. '—But equally, we must admit that some tings affect everybody, no matter dis or dat. Not everything subjective. Some tings simply right and wrong.'

'I'm not so sure. Herodotus, the Greek Historian, argued morality is a product of social customs. And he thought people are prone to hold their own customs as superior. I think he might be right,' Emilia said, drawing a smile from the teacher for additional reading.

'So, there's no right or wrong? That doesn't seem right to me,' a woman, sat at the back beside the window, said, keeping her gaze on the desk and her big hair covering her face. Although her voice was quiet, her words fell heavy, like suitcases packed with buried emotions. Despite her hesitancy, something stubborn, within, made her speak. 'I just think some things are absolutely wrong.'

Out of compassion, Latisha and Emila paused the argument. They sensed the lady had suffered some sort of injustice or abuse; sensed her comment was personal, about more than academic tit-for-tat.

A silence brewed, and the teacher assumed the responsibility of steering it away. 'There are things we feel with complete conviction. Things certain. Certainly right and certainly wrong, no matter to whom or when they happen. People believe they are true regardless of philosophic or scientific proof; regardless of whether we can know for sure whether the thing really is true for all people, at all times, in all places. The question is, does it matter? Does or should philosophy and science interfere or lessen the strength of such convictions? Should faith ever guide our actions and decisions, individually and collectively, in the here and now?'

'Are you asking whether people and societies should still have convictions and commitments even if we accept some things are unprovable?' Scarlet asked, resting her pen on her lower lip. The teacher resumed her previous yoga posture, her chest puffing out and her shoulders relaxed. She left the question for the class to ponder.

'I think so—' Fatimah said, filling the void. '—We can believe in things; we can have faith, trust and standards despite lacking absolute proof. But perhaps that's why it's so important to not be blind about the decisions we make.'

The others looked at Fatimah expectantly. She stumbled to express her point of view several times, but found the words eventually. 'I mean, perhaps it's important to acknowledge that convictions come from us, and so we must be humble and tolerant; I mean, we shouldn't hide the reality that much of what we are — laws, customs, worship — are acts of faith, attempts to govern fairly and intelligently. Attempts to serve

God, while humbly accepting we can never be 100% sure it's what he'd want. That really it's all our effort.'

Scarlet thought of her mum, and Nick, and the father of her unborn child. She rubbed her belly and added to the conversation. 'I think you're right, Fatimah. There's so much we can't prove; we can't prove a higher power exists or whether it'll punish us for doing wrong, yet we should still try to make the world a better place. For each other.'

'This is what I said to begin wid—' Latisha said, her hands animated. '—there is simply a consensus on tings we want and don't want to allow. Me don't care whether bastard rapists are going to be punished by the Lord; me going to also rip his balls off and ensure he feels the pain in the here and now, and damn the man dat try to get in me way.'

The room filled with smiles and chuckling as the women sympathised with Latisha. Amid the joy, the teacher slid off the desk and picked-up the board-pen. She wrote 'logical positivism' and then explained the term. 'The text invites us to think about Athenian Democracy; the idea that humans can set direction and frame the conditions of their future co-existence through enactment and enforcement of law.'

'Fuck me!' Scarlet shouted, dropping her pen and crunching her body in response to the cramp.

'Is it the baby?' Fatimah said, leaping from her chair.

'Do you need us to call an ambulance?' The teacher said, shuttling over to Scarlet too. She and Fatimah placed their hands on Scarlet's shoulders.

'Shit, I'm so sorry. I'm not due for another month.'

'Don't apologise. Breathe. In—And—Out. In—And—Out,' the teacher said, her shoulders rolling backwards and her chest raising as she inhaled; then rolling forward and decompressing as she exhaled. Scarlet imitated the movements, and Latisha called an ambulance.

'It's too early,' Scarlet said, shaking, but the teacher cradled her cheeks and stilled her head. She locked eye contact and continued modelling the animated breathing. The rest of the women flocked around, forming a semi-circle.

The ambulance arrived within ten minutes. Fatimah allowed Scarlet to clutch her hand the entire time. As the paramedics escorted them through the building, the teacher darted to her office to look up and call Scarlet's next of kin. 'Hello, is that Nick Finch? This is Dr Bronwyn. I'm a teacher at Lambeth College. Scarlet Finch is one of my students and she listed you as her emergency contact. She is going into labour—'

Dr Bronwyn paused, but Nick didn't know what to say. Short of time, she continued. '—I wanted to let you know the ambulance will take her to St. Thomas' Hospital. Are you still there, Mr Finch?'

'—Yes, I'm here. I'm just not sure why she put me down as her contact.'

'She says that you're her brother—'

'—Yes. No. I mean, yes, I am her brother, but we're not really in touch, so not a brother, brother.'

'Does she have anybody else?—' Dr Bronwyn asked. Another long, awkward silence lingered. '—Look, she's going into the hospital a month early, and she's afraid. She'll need somebody she knows. Are you going to go?'

'Doesn't she have anybody at the college that she's friends with?' Nick said, hearing his own callousness. Dr Bronwyn hung up. She grabbed her leather jacket, handbag and keys, and dashed outside to join Scarlet and the paramedics. The ambulance door was ready to close.

'—Wait! Please,' Dr Bronwin said, calling to the paramedics, not seeing Fatimah was inside. They helped her climb into the ambulance before shutting the doors. Dr Bronwin and Fatimah clutched Scarlet's hands. 'Everything is going to be ok,' they said together.

Chapter 11 — Baby Scarlet, 4 weeks old (1980s, Gadsby Street)

Evelyn stepped out of the bath. Water trickled to the floor as she stretched for a blue towel. She doubted the squaddie would show, but got ready just in case. After securing her body, she wrapped another towel around her hair, tucking the end beneath the mounting bun on her head. She left the bathroom.

Fran laid Lilly flat in the cot and twisted away. 'Evelyn, hurry-up! I need to get ready. Some of us have work,' she said, leaving the bedroom.

They passed one another in the hallway, Fran huffing and Evelyn avoiding her chastising stare by rushing past. In the bedroom, she sat at the dressing table and fingered Fran's make-up set, wondering which eyeliner would look best. Lilly winced as the bathroom door closed. She wanted fussing, and Evelyn, finding herself alone with her, realised she would have to do it.

She fetched her from the cot, and placed her on her lap, facing the dressing-table mirror. They glanced at each other's reflections, and then Lilly quietened down, becoming fascinated with her mother's examination of the different colour eye shadows. Thumps on the staircase announced June was back. She dashed into the bedroom. 'That squaddie is down the road!' She said, jumping on the bed without removing her boots.

'It's only a quarter to ten. I'm not ready.'

June yanked an apple from her jacket pocket. 'I can't believe he's turned up—' she said, biting a good chunk and causing juice to squirt on her upturned wrist. '—I thought it was him as I walked along the main road, so I ran, to check if it really was, and as I got—'

'—You didn't talk to him, did you?' Evelyn said, unimpressed with June's rambling.

June rolled onto her back, licked the juice from her wrist, and took another chunk out of the apple. Her head lolloped off the edge of the bed. Upside down, she glared at Evelyn and smirked.

Evelyn pressed for details. 'What did he say?'

June gnashed the pulp and force-swallowed. 'I didn't say anything.'

Evelyn stood and hung Lilly over June's body.

'—Ew, no way!' June said, pushing Lilly's plump legs away from her face.

'Come-on, I need to get ready if he's really coming.'

June twisted onto her belly. 'I could go if you're not ready.'

'—Don't be a cow.'

Laughing, she rolled back onto her back. Evelyn dangled Lilly's legs over her face, irritated that she still had not taken her. Lilly's feet landed on June's stomach. 'Come-on—' Evelyn said, desperate to release Lilly and get ready for her date. But still smirking, June spread her arms wide across the bed. '—You're such a cow.'

Lilly's legs shot into the air as Evelyn pulled away. 'Never ask me to—'

'—For God's sake, just give her to me,' June said, but before she moved into a more appropriate position to take Lilly, Fran re-entered the bedroom, and Evelyn plonked Lilly into her arms.

'Who's a good girl?—' Fran said, blowing raspberries into Lilly's cheeks and cooing, but also moving her toward the cot. '—Sorry, I've got to go to work. I'm covering Gina's shift. You'll have to get Ma to fetch her.'

'The squaddie's here.' June said, rotating the apple and biting into more of its green skin.

Fran huffed as she reached for her handbag and dashed to the mirror to apply a little more lipstick. 'I haven't got time for your nonsense June;

and Evelyn, I've told you already, they're bad news, but you'll learn the hard way.'

Lilly cried as Fran retreated in shunting backward steps. 'I know, Lilly, I know, baby, but Aunty Fran has to go to work.' She said, blowing a last kiss and pulling the bedroom door closed behind her. Evelyn pulled up a lime green skirt she'd borrowed from Fran's wardrobe and raced to get ready over the crying.

June, after finishing her apple and exhausting her patience, lifted Lilly out of the cot and took her down to Ma. On the staircase, she called to tell Evelyn that somebody was at the door.

'—Tell him I'll meet him outside the Crystal Palace in five minutes.'

With Lilly still in her arm, June headed to the front door, passing Ma in the corridor. 'Don't worry Ma, I'll see to it. It'll be Evelyn's man,' she said, still smirking. Ma went to take Lilly, but with a mischievous smile, June tightened her grip. 'Don't worry, I'll hold her.'

Ma tutted but shuffled along the narrow corridor, not getting involved.

'Alright?' the squaddie said, raising his brows. 'I didn't realise you had a bab.'

He let Lilly hook her tiny hand around his pinky finger. 'Ya've got a little beauty there, ya've; hello bab, y'll'right ain't ya?'

'Oh, she's not mine,' June replied, straightening her back and pushing her thigh forward, causing her skirt to lift and reveal more leg-flesh.

'Right, well, I was callin' for Evelyn. She about?' The squaddie rubbed his hands together. The weather was crisp. He glanced along the street, wanting to evade June's flirting. She swapped Lilly from one arm to the other, emphasising her bosom. The squaddie took no notice. His tongue pushed against the roof of his mouth as he allowed the silence to linger rather than ask another question and prolong the conversation.

'Whatever.' June said, snapping at him. She hadn't provoked or received the attention she was hoping for. Lilly clung to her chest as June turned away. 'She'll meet you outside the Crystal Palace in five minutes.'

She slammed the door.

Outside, Rose, the next-door neighbour, pulled her door shut. 'Oh, don't mind her love. She's like that with everyone.' She said, pulling her shopping trolly toward Brummy John. 'Fran's a lovely girl, though. Nothing like June.'

'Well actually, I'm here for Evelyn,' Brummy John said, stepping onto the road to allow Rose to pass by with her trolly.

'Oh, I see.'

Rose struggled to conceal her judgment. She quickened her pace, wanting to hide her facial expression from the man. 'Well, Evelyn's lovely too, I suppose. Nice to meet you. Goodbye.' She said, not looking back. Brummy John didn't think much of it. He stood on the road to look at the upstairs window. He thought he'd seen the net twitching, but it lay flat like the rest of the nets on the street. Stepping back on the pavement, he strolled along to the Palace, three doors down.

He leant on the frosted window and lit a cigarette; the smoke drifted to the pub's placard before dissipating into the blue sky. Evelyn emerged before he'd finished smoking. Her red eye-shadow emphasised the penetrative glow of her blue eyes as she met his gaze. John stamped the cigarette butt and embraced her. He took her hands and leant in for a kiss, not a proper, mouth to mouth kiss, but equally, not a prissy, dad-like, full cheek kiss either. He planted his lips to the side of her mouth, clipping the corner of her lip, keeping control and ensuring she didn't need to respond by opening, moving or refusing to open her lips to his, heightening the erotica without seeming un-decent. 'Told ya I'd call.'

He released one hand and swung the other, still clutched to hers. They strolled along the street toward the train-station. 'So ya sister's a bit of one, eh?'

Evelyn rubbed her earlobe. 'Just ignore her. She says stupid stuff to provoke a reaction.'

'Yeah, I got that. I was pretty sure she was hitting on me.'

'She was definitely hitting on you. She's like that with men. Comes on way too strong and scares them away.'

'Oh yeah? You a good expert on men, then?'

His tongue poked out the side of his mouth and his face tilted across to Evelyn so that he could examine her reaction. She ignored him, gave off no reaction. Deadpan, they continued walking, but his face illuminated at her evasion. Her perceived coyness only strengthened his enthusiasm, cheekiness, and dash of passive-aggressive insecurity. 'Yas a proper fine gal, ya know. I've got a good eye; know when I spot a good one.'

'So you're the "good expert" on women, then?' Evelyn said, releasing the smallest of smiles and Brummy John capitalised on it. He pulled her into his body, squeezed her tight, and planted another kiss.

'See, yas got a good humour. I knew it. Total keeper.'

At the train-station John bought return tickets to Birmingham, where they continued to flirt and get to know one another. Meanwhile, Fran was at the warehouse depot, picking items for the old biddies. It wouldn't be long before she reached Mrs Elliot's house where she would bump into Sally and Joe McGuinness, meet little Anabelle, re-name her Scarlet, and bring her home.

Part 2 — Summer

Chapter 12 — Uncle Nick (2000s, Maternity Ward)

'She's beautiful,' Nick said, perched on the hospital armchair as he held Summer. He stood, kissed her forehead, and passed her back to mum. Scarlet rocked her newborn in her exhausted yet protective arms. Dr Bronwyn blew a kiss beside the door; she was leaving.

'Thank you so much,' Scarlet said, her fingertips twinkling as she mustered a goodbye to the teacher who had stayed with her throughout.

'Not at all. Get plenty of rest. Your brother has my number,' Dr Bronwyn said, patting Nick's back. 'Call me if you need anything.'

She blew another kiss and left the hospital room, her leather jacket in hand. Nick followed her out.

'I wanted to say thank you,' he said, calling and walking over to her. 'It's a long story. She was—'

'—An addict. A lot of the women in my classes are,' she said, shifting her leather jacket into the other hand. Nick looked at the floor. Black-and-white tiles. 'You came. That's what matters,' she said.

Her fingers brushed his arm as he opened up. 'I hadn't written her off,' he said, still looking at the tiles. 'I'd just said she needed to prove herself. Three years clean.' He looked up, expecting to see condemnation in her eyes. Seeing none, he asked what she would have done.

'She isn't my sister,' she replied, her face deadpan. His gaze returned to the floor, and he studied the chequered tiles as if they contained his judgment.

'You would have done more?' he asked.

She patted his shoulder, resumed her exit, and said one last thing before leaving the corridor, 'Only you can answer that, but sometimes, answers aren't as important as you think. Give yourself a break. You're here now, aren't you?'

The door closed behind her and Nick felt dissatisfied. The fortune-cooky platitude she dished out would stick with him for weeks. For now, though, he accepted Dr Bronwyn's sentiment and returned to the delivery room.

'Thank you for coming. It means a lot,' Scarlet said, her eyes earnest. She stroked away wisps of Summer's hair. Nick sank into the armchair beside the bed.

'What are you going to call her?'

'Summer. I hadn't decided for sure. Thought I still had a few weeks, but I'm certain now she's here.'

Nick's bum scooted to the edge of the chair. He leant over. 'Princess Summer,' he said, positioning his hand close. Her crinkled fingers clutched his thumb.

'Less of the princess: she's my little warrior,' Scarlet said, mustering a smile to cover the pain creeping in as the drugs softened.

'Who's the father? I meant to ask when you came round to the house,' Nick said. A knot of guilt tightened as he mentioned their last meeting. 'I'm sorry for the way—'

Scarlet placed her hand on his and shook her head. '—Don't. Please? I'm sorry too.' Shame rouged her fatigued cheeks. 'Can we just start fresh?'

Despite his feeling wretched and apologetic for his ruthless exile. Despite the sincere plea in his sister's voice. And despite the inducing vulnerability and softness Summer brought about, he couldn't pretend; couldn't start fresh. 'I can't,' he said.

She felt like he'd shut the door on her again.

'But I'm here,' he said, wanting to take her hand, but interlacing his own to stop himself. 'I can't forget the past. I just don't work that way. God, I've tried and I wish I could. A baby won't change that.' He moved his hands into a prayer-like position, his knuckles mounting upward. '—But that doesn't mean we can't be a bigger part of each other's life. If you want that?'

'—Of course, I do.'

She felt the door open.

Nick asked about the father after a few minutes of comfortable silence.

'I don't want him involved,' Scarlet said.

'Who is he?'

'He's married. Has grown-up kids.'

'How old?'

'Late forties. It began as a casual thing, but then, he started talking about leaving his wife, his job. It's not what I wanted.'

'You don't want to be with him?'

'Not like that. I don't want to break-up his marriage. His family, and I definitely don't want Summer feeling that sort of responsibility.'

Scarlet kissed Summer on the forehead.

'That's not on you or Summer. It's his marriage.'

'That's not how everybody else would see it. She'd be—' Scarlet said, pulling Summer closer to her breast, and re-thinking what she was about to say. '—Besides, I'm not even sure I want it.'

'You wouldn't want to be with him even if he wasn't married?'

'I don't know; it's too hypothetical. He wouldn't be who he is if he weren't married.'

Nick looked unimpressed, and she felt obliged to elaborate.

'It was exciting, a bit of a fantasy. But in reality, we hardly know each other. Plus, if he's the kind of man to wander, it'd only be a matter of time before I'd become—'

'—The other woman,' Nick said, relaxing into the chair, grateful for her honesty. 'Does he know about the baby?'

Scarlet shrugged. 'He suspected. I never told him outright, but he could see I was bigger and that I didn't want to be naked around him anymore. He's not an idiot,' she said, knowing deep down he knew.

'Has he been in contact?'

'He's sent messages, but I haven't responded.'

'Are you going to?' Nick said, placing one leg over the other. 'Do you want me to con—'

'—No,' Scarlet said, closing him down. 'I need some time to think; to think about how I tell him; how to play it out.'

'It would be good to have some help... raising a kid alone is going to be hard.'

Scarlet smiled at Summer. 'I'll be fine,' she said, believing in herself, believing that she would be a good mum.

'You say that now, but it's going to be hard. Kids are—' Nick's thoughts drifted to the naughty children playing up in class. After the bell went, they were no longer his problem. The parents they went home to though, they were stuck for entire evenings, weekends, years. Decades.

'I'm going to be fine. You don't have to worry. I'm going to love her so much,' Scarlet said, squeezing Summer and planting gentle kisses on her forehead.

Nick thought about the stressed mums arguing with teachers on parents' evening, their refusal to hear that their little warriors were behaving like complete brutes. He never bothered with the confrontation; knew it would only cause arguments and deplete the rest of their spartan parental energy. Knew the kids would end up with even less attention at home as a despair that dares not speak its name, crept beneath the skin: the dark, guttural knowledge that their own child's soul was rotting. Instead, Nick told the parents mistruths; that Jimmy or Megan was a tad cheeky or a little over-enthusiastic, but that deep-down, they were good and likeable; wanted to do well, even though he had zero evidence to support the assertion. Nick feared Scarlet would become one of these parents that he needed to lie to; that she would become a mum, so knackered and unintentionally neglectful of a kid morphing into a living nightmare.

'I know you will,' he said, not willing to argue.

'I'm not stupid, Nick. I know you don't believe I can do it,' Scarlet said, remaining calm and loving as she spoke. '—But just watch.'

'I don't believe you won't do your best. I'm just saying that it's going to be really hard, and that if there is a dad that wants to help, then why not let him? You don't have to be together.'

Summer squirmed and cried a little. 'Hey baby? You're ok. You're ok. I'm your Ma. Yes, I am. And I love you. Yes, I do.'

Scarlet released her boob, and Summer's lips locked onto her Ma's nipple. 'I hear what you're saying, and I understand,' she said, her shoulders dropping away from her neck, and her upper back relaxing more sincerely into the pillow, propping her up. 'I'll tell him; think I was always going to. I just need a bit of time so that I can do it properly.'

She closed her eyes and breathed deeply, satisfied at the milk transferring from her body to Summer's. 'I need to feel strong enough to ensure it's on the right terms,' she said. Her eyes re-opened, and her neck leant onto her shoulder, enabling good eye contact with Nick. 'You understand what I'm saying?'

Nick broke the gaze. 'I get it, but I think you're more likely to settle for something you don't want, the longer you leave it.'

'Jesus Nick!' Scarlet said, causing Summer to pull away at the sudden jolt of emotion; but she was very hungry, and so plunged back onto the nipple almost immediately. 'I've literally just given birth. Can you let up, just a little?'

'I want the best for you.'

'I know you do. And you're right,' she said, eliciting a smug smile from her little brother as she pierced him with an intense stare. 'You're always bloody right. I'll call him as soon as I'm home.'

Nick eased, appeased by her surrender. 'What's this job he's willing to leave, anyway? Is he rich?'

'Hardly. He's a teacher.'

'—Not from George Eliot?' Nick said as mental profiles of male teachers rolled through his mind as if he were reading an attendance register.

'You cannot tell anybody, Nick. I mean it.'

'—Who is it?'

The gossip drew out an enthusiasm he'd lost over the years. He was genuinely enjoying being with his big sister for the first time since he could remember.

'He's been there for like twenty-five years or something.'

'—Mr Andrews?'

'Ew, no! He must be over 60,' she said, a sobriety sweeping over her as the name of Summer's father settled in her mouth. 'Mr Cliff; Marc.'

Nick scrunched. It took him a moment to conjure a face. 'Really? He seems so—'

'—Normal?'

'Yeah. And he doesn't seem that old, but I guess he must be. God!' he said as his mind wandered further. 'You didn't get together while we were still at school?' Nick was apprehensive of the answer but prepared himself to react stiffly.

'Of course not. He's not a paedophile. We met at the pub last Christmas. I wasn't in a great place; neither was he. Anyway, we met in the pub. Let's leave it there.'

'I'm a bit stumped. Mr Cliff? He's quite—'

'—fit?' Scarlet said, chuckling at her brother's prudishness as Summer released her lips and burped. 'You can talk about men in front of me; your gayness is hardly a secret. You loved Nan's dresses too much.'

Nick stuck up his middle finger but smiled whilst doing so: he still felt uncomfortable in revealing his sexuality around family.

'How about Ma? When you going to tell her?'

Scarlet wriggled back into the pillow. 'I hoped you might—'

Nick's lips expanded into a giant protest. '—Come on! I think you need to ring her, Scarlet.'

She closed her eyes and asked Nick when he last spoke to her. He closed his eyes, too. 'I dunno,' he said, trying to remember. '—Couple of months ago, I guess. She knew you were pregnant, didn't she?'

Scarlet kept her eyes shut. 'No,' she said.

'Who have you told?'

'From home? Nobody.'

'Why?'

Summer removed her lips and rolled her cheek to rest on Scarlet's boob. 'I want to do it on my own,' Scarlet said.

'But they'll help. They'll be glad, especially aunt Fran. She loves kids.'

'You don't get it.'

Scarlet reopened her eyes.

'I don't,' Nick said, strident. 'Why refuse help if it's there?'

'Would you want them to help if you and Matt had one?'

'That's different,' he said, stiffening.

'Because you're gay?'

'No. Because there are two of us.'

'What about if he died?' Scarlet said, rubbing the small mark on her earlobe.

Nick's fingers stroked the top of his own hand. 'I've never thought about it. I've barely thought about children, let alone raising one alone.'

'Well, think about it. Would you want them around all the time?'

'Probably not,' he said, feeling humbled. He wasn't arrogant, but could be a little snobbish.

'I want to raise her my way. I want her life to be different.'

Scarlet tilted Summer onto her back so she could see her face. She brushed her cheek. 'I don't blame or resent any of them,' Scarlet said, smiling at Summer as she spoke to Nick. 'There were plenty worse off than us.'

Nick didn't feel as generous regarding his upbringing, even though he displayed more surface gratitude and compassion for his family. 'I think I get it,' he said.

'I want her to know that I'm her Ma. Just me, nobody else, and that I'll always be there for her.'

Nick stood to withdraw the mobile phone from his pocket. Apart from playing a game called Snake, he barely used it. 'Matt's calling,' he said, standing and walking over to the door. 'I'll be back in a minute.'

He pulled the door shut gently behind him, making sure he didn't make any noise. 'Hey, I'm at the hospital—'

'—Sorry, babe. This is urgent. I need you to go home ASAP, go into my office and get my little black book from the bottom drawer of my desk,' Matt said.

'What? Where are you? I'm at the hospital. Scarlet has—'

'—Nick, I'm sorry. I need you to do this for me. It's really important. I can explain when you get here.'

'Ok,' Nick said, slowing down as he began to entertain something serious had happened. A nurse pointed to the mobile phone and waved her finger in a censorial manner. Nick ducked his head to thwart her gaze.

'I'm at the City of London Police station. It's near Spitalfields Market. I took you there a few months ago, remember?' Matt said.

'What? Why are you at the Police station?'

The nurse tutted from the other side of the glass and moved from her desk.

'Matt—'

'—Nick, it's urgent. I will explain later. Get my black book from the bottom drawer of my desk and bring it to the station straightaway.'

The nurse emerged from the door, but Matt had ended the call. The phone was back in Nick's jean pocket. 'You cannot use those in here,' the nurse said, wearing the severest matron outfit.

'I'm sorry, it was urgent.'

The nurse tutted, went back into her office and closed the door, dismissive of Nick's excuses. He returned to tell Scarlet about the phone-call, then kissed her and Summer on the forehead. 'I'm sorry I can't stay longer,' he said, feeling sincere. He wanted to spend more time with them. He slipped his arm through his jacket sleeve. 'How many weeks do you think you'll be here for?'

' "Weeks?" ' Scarlet said, chuckling. 'Men haven't got a clue, have they? I'll be home tomorrow. If she wasn't early, it would be today.'

'I just thought—'

'—She's healthy, and so am I. There's no need for us to be here more than a day. Two most. They'll need the bed.'

Puzzlement swept Nick's face. Going home alone with a baby was ludicrous, but he didn't have time to ponder with his husband in a cell for reasons unbeknown.

'Go,' Scarlet said, shooing him with her free hand. As he stepped to the door, she thanked him one last time. 'Thanks Nick. For coming,' she said, mustering strength and courage from a deep well of memory. 'I'm glad you exist.'

He stopped to face her, and with a sincere stillness he hadn't felt in years, he repeated the cheesy tagline from their childhood. 'I'm glad you exist, too.'

Chapter 13 — Aunty Lilly (1990s, Turbine Crescent)

Mr Spenser put one foot into his pin-stripe trousers, and then the other. His flabby legs disappeared from view. Lilly lay on the bed, almost naked. She had a skirt rolled up to her chest and a hairband. She was bleeding, but the drugs in her system numbed the pain and allayed her panic. Mr Spenser didn't worry. He wafted his sky-blue shirt beside the bed, attempting to banish the creases. One overweight arm slid into the sleeve, then the other. His barrel of a stomach disappeared from view. Twenty years of bacon sandwiches and secretaries fetching him fatty lunches. He looked at Lilly while putting on his jacket. She remained spaced out.

'Hey,' he said, prodding her loose ankles and avoiding the saliva he'd left on it. 'Oi, come-on. Get yourself cleaned-up.'

Lilly didn't move. She was aware of his presence, his intention for her to act and move under his will, but she had lost control of her own body. The awareness meant nothing. It prompted no reaction. Lilly continued to bleed on the bed, her mind continued to withdraw from the suffering of her body, and her soul continued to flee the materiality of her mind. She was dying.

Mr Spenser's chubby hands now gripped her thin, brittle ankle. 'Oi, you fucking bitch, you need to get-up.' He said, almost spitting the words.

He yanked her ankle, sending a tremor through her leg, pelvis, chest and neck, but Lilly didn't move. She had given up; her body submitted to violation. He applied greater force, yanking the ankle harder. Nothing except more tremors, riding her body like waves to the shore. Her mind was an inanimate flotsam. 'Fine. I understand, you fucking whore,' he said, pulling his wallet from the pin-stripe trousers now buttoned into his stomach. He scrunched three twenty-pound notes and threw them onto the bed. 'That's all you're getting out of me, so you can stop the charade.'

He walked out of the room without waiting to witness her miraculous resurrection.

'Can we book you another appointment, Mr Spenser?' Madam Perez asked, appearing beside the banister with her diary as he stepped into the downstairs corridor.

'Next Tuesday, 3pm. But I don't want that scammy cow. Get me someone more experienced. I don't like feeling taken advantage of. Pay up front. Get that side out of the way. Professional. You understand? Or perhaps a younger girl, less willing to take advantage.'

'Of course, Mr Spenser,' Madam Perez replied. The customer was always right. Her stern brow and severe poker face seemed to appease his feeling of being slighted. He felt reassured she would administer justice and rectify the lack of professionalism once he was on his way.

'Pleasure doing business. It's good to know there are respectable establishments left.'

Madam Perez smiled with an earnestness that eased Mr Spenser's smug exit from the property. She shut the front door behind him, slowly, but once he waddled away, she fired the latch across and bolted upstairs to evaluate the damage. Seeing the bloody bedsheet, she rushed straight to the bathroom, grabbed towels and pegs, and then ran back to Lilly. She wrapped the linen firmly around and between her legs, applying pressure on the blood, and pulled a little powder from a tin hidden beneath her shawl. She rubbed the white stuff along Lilly's gums. A little cocaine to keep her ticking.

'Hang on, love.' Madam Perez said, darting away. She hurried back down the staircase and then along a corridor hidden behind a disguised door, blending into the staircase's panelling. It led directly through to the neighbouring house. 'Ahmed!' she said, calling to the property's elaborate staircase, carpeted with thick red fabric. 'One of the girls has a bad bleed.'

A Turkish man with a soft beard shunted to the top of the staircase; he gripped a medical bag in his slightly hairy hands. 'Berat, bring the sling,' he said, calling to someone behind him before rushing down the staircase to follow Madam Perez.

She returned to the original house. Ahmed followed. 'How much blood has she lost?' He asked, his voice quiet and confidential.

'At least a pint, maybe more.'

Light-footed, they climbed the staircase and entered the bedroom. Ahmed glanced at Lilly and the bed. He didn't need to think. He knew. 'We need to get her next-door straightaway. With her heart beating that fast, she must have shed at least two pints of blood.'

Berat entered, carrying the sling.

Madam Perez cupped one hand around Lilly's cheek and ran fingers through her hair with her other. 'You'll be alright, love. Hang-in-there.'

Ahmed and Berat moved her body into the sling as delicately as possible. As a British girl, she was an expensive commodity, and so they handled her well. They took small, controlled steps to limit the movement of the sling. Madam Perez hurried ahead and unlocked the airing-cupboard door. It didn't open to a boiler. It opened to an empty passageway, a secret route into another neighbouring property, the house with the Alsatian in the garden. Lilly was unconscious; unaware of how many of these houses connected.

Ahmed and Barat angled the sling to slot through the passageway without putting Lilly down. It was tight, but they'd done it before. They entered a room which originally had been a bathroom. Now shelves lined every bit of wall. It looked more like a pantry. Medical equipment, boxes of drugs, and random paraphernalia filled the space, and a dirty blanket covered the window, making it appear squatter-like if passengers looked at the property from the railway.

Madam Perez locked the airing cupboard door from the pantry side and slid an empty rail to fill the void. She also locked the interconnecting door in the pantry itself. Security.

Ahmed and Baret didn't waste time. They passed through the room into the corridor, Ahmed now stepping backward, one-foot at a time, as he carried his end of the sling. They twisted in unison and got Lilly into the master bedroom, which was set up as a small, makeshift ward with several hospital beds wedged close together. Madam Perez helped them move Lilly into a spare bed and within seconds, Ahmed needled a vein in Lilly's upper arm. He attached a thin flexible tube, an intravenous line, to it, ready for blood to pump into her ghostly body. Beret returned with sachets of various blood types and Madam Perez flicked through her diary before telling him which bag to use. 'O+. How long will it take?' she asked as Ahmed and Baret fiddled with medical instruments.

'A couple of days, perhaps a week,' Ahmed replied, removing the towels Madam Perez had wrapped around Lilly. He washed his hands in preparation to stitch Lilly's injury. 'Baret will keep you informed.'

Chapter 14 — Uncle Nick (2000s, City Police Station)

Nick had used his mobile phone more in one day than the last few weeks combined.

'I know you've never taken time off, and I feel terrible for asking, but we really need you in,' Nick's Head of Department said through the phone. Ofsted had called the school, informing they would arrive tomorrow for an inspection.

'I'm really sorry. I can't. There's something else now too. Can you—' Nick said before allowing his boss to interrupt. He wanted to check the problem didn't involve his sister's baby. '—No, no. Nothing like that. The baby's fine. Healthy. It's unrelated. There's an issue with Matt.'

'This is a career defining moment for us, Nick. Surely you can get here for just a few hours? I covered your top set year 11s earlier. They were great, but they said you had their books and mock papers. We really need them. Can you bring them in later so that I can at least cherry-pick ten-to-fifteen as examples of the challenging material we've covered? Also, the data won't have any credibility unless we can back it up with hard evidence, which reminds me, I absolutely need you to get their scores into the system ASAP. That's a non-negotiable. We have to show decent progress. I know it's a pain in the ass, but they will hawk our bright disadvantaged kids. Your lot. You know it. It was the weak spot in our last review, and it'd be criminal to get slammed for it again when you've done such a brilliant job,' he said, barely stopping for air.

Nick sighed, hating that he was letting the team down, especially when he had worked so hard. His class of bright, poor kids were doing much better than national averages, and he wanted Ofsted to see that, but it didn't change things. 'I have no idea how long this will take,' he said, unwilling to mention the truth. Besides, he didn't have details; didn't know why Matt was in the police station. And sure as hell, he wouldn't volunteer that information. For now, he said what his boss wanted to hear. '—I'll bring the books and papers in later. It might be pretty late though as I don't—'

'—We'll be here until at least ten.'

That we irritated and induced Nick's guilt. It separated him from the team and reinforced that he was coming across as the weak link because of circumstances beyond his control.

'Hopefully, I'll be there way before that. I'm sorry, Neil. You know that I'd—'

'—I know it must be important. You're never like this.'

Nick felt stung. Neil's remark acknowledged Nick's excellent record, his reliability. But it also emphasised he was messing up when it mattered most for him not to. 'See you later,' Nick said, all he could muster.

The tube remained busy and sweaty even though commuter traffic eased hours ago. Beside armpits, Nick dwelled on what Matt could have done, and specifically on why he needed that little black book from his office. What was in it? Thoughts of his school inspection drifted into mind, but it just didn't seem to matter against the absurdity of Matt going to prison. Nick thought his fiancee was as straight and clean as they came: a grammar schoolboy from a quaint English hamlet where people owned bookshelves, read Shakespeare for fun, and got tutored into red-brick universities, which guaranteed them high-powered, satisfying (non-criminal) jobs for life. This had been the entire attraction. Matt had a history that Nick idolised. What is he doing at the police station?

Back at the flat, Nick filled a glass of water from the tap and drank it in one. He continued contemplating what could have happened, trying to push away the anxiety that he'd ignored things about Matt. Red, inconvenient flags. The glass clinked as it landed on the countertop. Nick wiped his hands on the tea-towel and then tossed it beside the empty glass. It was time to look in the black book.

Matt's office was exceptionally clean and unexceptionally beige. The walls, the carpet, and the furniture were all beige. The bookshelves were beige, and they contained no books. Matt had spaced small modern ornaments out on them. Why doesn't he have any books? Nick thought, allowing a suppressed line of enquiry to surface. He's educated. Grew up in a bookish house unlike Nick, who didn't enjoy reading, and put it down to not coming from a middle-class, cultured family. Although as he thought about it, he remembered his aunts and sisters, his gran, having library books lying around. They read even if they didn't own many books. They didn't seem to talk about what they read, but they definitely read. A lot. The more he thought about it, the more he pictured them with a book and himself without one. The odd revelation that his family might not be as simple and unrefined as he had become accustomed to think, disturbed and disrupted his sense of order. A flicker of doubt burned the back of his eyes. Perhaps he had not quite understood the world as accurately as he believed.

He opened the metallic drawers beneath Matt's pristine desk, letting loose pent-up feelings of insecurity and paranoia. He had never allowed himself to look through Matt's things. Not something loving or trusting people do, he told himself. And though he never thought of love or truth as genuine; not real natural forces like gravity or magnetic poles. He did believe people could produce it, a sort of manufactured product. It was his sophistic way of getting around the fact he was an unbeliever, without wrecking the sub-conscious mysticism at the core of his own romantic relationship. Nick and Matt told each other they loved one another. They spoke of being each other's 'one'. Monogamous. Fated together. Though neither would use that language. But it was a lie. A contradiction at the centre of their life.

Nick didn't believe in love. His class conditioned him to believe in subjection and his own snobbish self-delusion prevented him from joining the resistance against it. Unlike the acerbic women of his family, he allowed the mystical concept of 'the-one' to go unchallenged. He granted it a safe home. He allowed it to feed the moralism of devotion.

His devotion to Matt. His devotion to untruth. Nick stared at the bookless shelves and felt the betrayal of his simple wondering about Matt not reading. He knew he wasn't just making a silly observation. He knew he was upending the foundations of their relationship by changing the terms. Embracing the truth even if inconvenient.

They were not a team. Nick was not his spunky, witty partner. He had signed up to become a Victorian spouse, the kind that knew their place. Gilded privilege. Doubting the concept of 'the-one' was an act of rebellion. It would heighten and complicate expectations. Being 'the-one' would no longer be enough. Their relationship would require sturdier foundations. He would want more intimate knowledge of who Matt really is. He would want to exam and analyse his experiences; would want a properly shared life.

Nick didn't love and trust Matt with his heart, but deep-down, he wanted to. He wanted to re-negotiate what they were about. The terms of their commitment. To no longer perpetuate the myth that genuine couples are only about the head. That relationships are not only about suspending short term self-interest for longer term self-interest. Rather, they hinge on the sharing of happiness; of seeing a beloved thrive.

He remembered Matt telling him that the black book was in the bottom drawer. And although he stilled his interior monologues and rebellion, he worked through each drawer. Top to bottom. Just in case there was something revealing. Stapler. Hole punch. Empty pads. Tat. Nothing shocking or exposing. With each disappointing revelation, Nick grew more frustrated. He had opened the floodgate of mistrust, and failing to find evidence for his changed disposition only exacerbated the feeling and knowledge of a deeper and darker betrayal. 'Something is being hid. Something isn't right. Matt is not committing in the way I am,' he thought.

Nick nudged the computer mouse, and the monitor automatically awoke. The screen displayed a beach-like image with a neat box in the centre requesting a password. He keyed words into the box, but each activated a pop-up box: 'Incorrect password. Try again'.

'I'm never going to discover it,' he said, while thinking, 'I'm not even sure I want to.' He came away from the keyboard and returned to the drawers. The bottom drawer. He opened it and a small A5 black book sat alone. His knees dug into the carpet as he flicked through the pages, trying to make sense of the swirls of numbers, names, doodle-like calculations, and scribbled nonsense inside. Nothing. It shone no light on the situation. It felt nothing more than an insignificant scrapbook. All the drama for this. He picked himself up and slammed the drawer shut.

Before leaving the flat, he removed his students' books and exam papers: they weighed his satchel too much. He'd have to return and collect them after visiting the police station. For now, he slipped the black book into the bag, locked-up the house, and made his way back into the city.

The tube remained as busy, sweaty, and armpit heavy as earlier. He considered removing the book to read through the scribbles again, but decided against doing so, judging he had gone too far. It was only right Matt had a chance to explain the situation. Nick thought himself having no evidence to think wrong of him yet. He felt wretched at how much he'd doubted the relationship; at the extent of his own mistrust. He was letting the relationship down and dishonouring his end of the bargain. If there was something awry, he'd wait and hear it directly.

At the police station, a surly officer told him to wait in the tiny reception. She didn't say it would be a two-hour wait. The place looked like a militarised holding cell. The occasional officer drifted behind steel and glass counters, but on the whole, it was eerily quiet. Nick lost count of the times he checked his watch. He thought about the classes he should be teaching, and ahead to the classes the inspectors would observe, picturing the few empty seats in the classroom where they would sit. Eventually, a weaponised, padded lady with plaits and no smile buzzed him through to a meeting room.

'Nick,' Matt said, relief washing his face as he hawked Nick's satchel bag. 'I promise I'll explain everything; is the book in there?'

Nick shifted the bag to his pelvis and removed the book before sitting down on the burgundy plastic chair opposite Matt. He laid the book flat on the table. 'What's going on?'

Matt stretched his hands across the table and fingered through upside-down pages without drawing the book away from Nick.

'Matt—' Nick said, sitting upright with his shoulders squared and his face levelled at his incarcerated boyfriend, who did not mirror his body language at all. Matt's shoulders hunched together and slunk toward the table; his face focussed entirely on the book. Nick wasn't even sure Matt had properly looked at him.

'Please trust me.' Matt said, his hands flattening the spine of the book, ensuring the opened page did not fling shut. He forced the edges and let go. The pages didn't flop. He took Nick's hand and quickly gripped his index finger as if it were a pencil.

'What're you doing—why aren't you looking at me?' Nick said.

'Look. They're doing me a favour by letting us see each other—there's no actual right. So we need to be quick. That book has a number. I need you to call it,' Matt said, pulling Nick's finger beside the number in the book. 'Promise me you won't look at the name. I mean it, Nick. I don't want you involved, so the fewer details you know, the better.'

'What? What're you talking about? Is this even legal?'

'Of course. I'm complying with the police. That's why they're letting us talk. You're doing nothing wrong, but promise me you will not look at the name. Promise?' Matt said, pushing three fingertips down on Nick's index finger, which he had positioned on a specific part of the pad.

'What should I say?'

'Tell them the police have arrested me for Turnpike.'

'What?'

Matt closed the book with Nick's hand and finger pinned to the spot inside. 'Call from a random payphone and then burn the book.'

Matt pulled his hands back to his side of the table and interlaced them. He lifted his shoulders and face for the first time to look Nick squarely head on. 'I've done something mightily stupid, and it's time to pay. I'm sorry,' he said, his words confessional but unemotional. He needed to be clear the first time around, lacking confidence he'd have the strength to say what he needed more than once. 'I'm not coming home for a while, Nick... the crime is work related, so they won't drag you into everything. You don't need to worry about ramifications. It wasn't about us. It was separate from our relationship. Remember that, ok?'

Nick stared in shock and disbelief, only semi-accepting what was going on. He had nothing to say.

'I've been helping some pretty bad men legitimise businesses that aren't and shouldn't be legitimate.'

A vacant expression swept Nick's face as he turned ghostly white. He was grateful Matt had tasked his hand and finger with gripping the page. He channelled his focus there. 'How long?' He asked Matt. They both avoided looking at one another.

'Perhaps five years. Three, if I'm lucky; give the police what they need.'

Nick lost the spot in the book as his hand shot to cover his mouth. He was asking how long he thought the police would keep him detained, not the length of an expected prison sentence, which had yet to enter his thoughts. It made sense, though. ' "It's time for me to pay," ' Nick said, recalling Matt's words. Things had gone from zero to a hundred too quickly. Prison. Five years. 'Prison? You're certain. What have you done?'

Matt broke his posture. He immediately flicked through the book to re-find the page and re-secure Nick's connection with the important number. 'You must keep hold and call this number. Nick!' Matt said, demanding his attention. He waited until Nick acknowledged the seriousness. Until he looked at him. 'Do not look at the name. Call the number. Tell them I've been arrested. For Turnpike. Hang-up. Don't wait for a response, Nick. Hang-up. Do not engage in a conversation. Hang-up. Do you understand?'

Nick nodded, staring at Matt for traces of information.

'These are nasty fuckers. People trafficking sick son-of-a-bitches. It was one thing for me to be involved, but I don't want you or anybody—'

'—What do I tell your parents?' Nick knew Matt was thinking about them.

'That I've got into trouble at work. That it's my own fault and that although it'll be alright in the end, I'm going to have to suffer the consequences of my own making,' he said. He had rehearsed the speech. 'Make sure they know it's deserved.'

He had not rehearsed this part. 'I don't want them thinking it's some miscarriage of justice. I want them to know what's about to happen needs to happen; that it's right, and not to fight it. I don't want them thinking they need to do anything. This is my fault. I did it. They need to know that. I don't want them to think I'm somewhere I shouldn't be,' he said, unusually earnest and emotional. Nick understood. He looked at Matt in a way he had never looked at him before, saw a nobility and truthfulness he'd not known was missing, a vulnerability that exposed him to the suffering of others despite the very real trajectory of his own shrinking future. At that moment, ironically, Nick loved Matt with his heart.

'Times up,' the padded, unsmiling police lady said, entering the room.

'Call the number. Speak. Hang-up.'

Both Nick and Matt stood, pushing the burgundy chairs behind them.

'I love you, Nick, and I really am sorry.'

Chapter 15 — Aunty June (1980s, Ivan's Bedroom)

'Ma, this isn't right,' June said, following her and Fran into the living room with Lilly and Scarlet gripped in their arms. Evelyn gone.

'Don't talk nonsense,' Fran said, snapping at June on behalf of Ma, whose eyeshadow smeared with tears. She was too upset to talk about Evelyn leaving. 'It's her choice. And that's the end of it.' Fran put a bounce in her voice. She wouldn't allow the situation to affect them any further. Her mind moved to calming the babies.

The conversation was closed. Scarlet was staying, and Evelyn could come to terms with it, or not. If she wanted to live on the streets or sofa-surf with squaddie John, it was her prerogative. Any homelessness would be entirely her doing. She had a home; could re-join whenever. But she would have to share. She could not deny Scarlet her place. That is wrong, she thought, giving June a final dagger'd stare.

Ma lowered herself into the armchair and folded Scarlet into her crotchet cardigan. She wiped away her own tear and flooded Scarlet with a joyous smile. 'Evelyn will come around, you'll see,' she said to the baby.

To June, the situation stank like soured milk, but what good was pointing? Besides, this really wasn't her thing. She disregarded what happened. Threw it out of her mind and moved on. Went upstairs, away from the babies. The fussing. The disfunction of it all. She lay on the bed and fantasised about Ivan. About getting into his bedroom. His socks. Pants. Tissues... Dirty magazines. Smelly t-shirts. Unwashed sheets. Euphoric smiles smothered her face as she touched herself.

After cleaning up in the bathroom, she focused on logistics. She jumped on the bed and scratched thoughts into her tatty diary. 'Iris = Bingo, Monday, 7-9pm?' she wrote, her pen tracing the M on Monday repeatedly until the letter was thicker than the others combined. As the space eclipsed, she moved her pen onto the 7. It was going to work. She could feel it with the expanding ink.

'Aren't you going to come and play with little Scarlet?' Ma said, her head poking into the room and taking June by surprise.

'Does Iris play Bingo every week?' June asked, ignoring Ma's stupid question.

'I don't know. Why are you asking me that?'

Ma circled the bedroom, looking to remove things and make space for another crib. 'You don't need this?' she said, her voice lifting, making the statement sound like a question.

'Does she?' June said, stressing her original question while attempting to balance the diary on her domed kneecaps.

'I suppose so.'

Ma continued shuttling around the room, picking things up and putting them back down. Keep or bin? she thought to herself repeatedly, tallying up the bins and ignoring June's interest in Iris. After twenty years, she took little notice of June's nonsense.

'Don't you know for sure?'

Ma huffed as she threw two empty bottles of hairspray into the bin. 'She does. Jean from work goes with her, but why you want to know about Iris playing Bingo is beyond me,' she said, wobbling the mirror that rested on the dressing table to see whether she could displace it easily. She could. She heaved it up and moved it onto the bed beside June, whose diary tumbled from her knees as the bed springs caused her legs to sway.

'What're you doing?'

'Help me move this dressing table up a bit,' Ma said. She had already positioned herself at the side of the dresser, ready to lift. 'Come on.'

June shifted to the dresser, her thoughts too preoccupied with Iris to challenge Ma's moving of the furniture. They lifted the dresser together, shuffling it one mini-step at a time, a meter along the wall. 'That'll do. Now bring the mirror back and we'll put it on.'

Ma anchored it so that the glass angled safely between the dresser and the wall. 'Perfect,' Ma said, approving the relocation while avoiding her reflection in the mirror. 'Sharon's got an old crib that we can borrow. You've got time to pop down and fetch it before you start work, haven't you?'

'Are you 100% sure she goes every Monday?' June asked, refusing to let the conversation drop.

'What is it with you and this bloody bingo?' Ma said, walking away. 'I'm obviously at home, so can't know for sure, but as I already said, Jean says they usually go together.'

Ma swung her head back as she reached the door, chastising June with a serious face. 'Don't be getting involved with Ivan or Winston. I don't like to speak bad about anybody — God knows we've our problems — but those two are no good, June. Stay clear if you've any sense,' she said, before adding. '—And remember to pop down to get the crib from Sharon's. I've phoned to say you'll be coming.'

The door shut without June confirming. The lack of protest implied consent.

With part of the crib wedged beneath her armpit, June stumbled along the pavement, stopping periodically to catch her breath and adjust the awkward thing. As she approached the pub, she rested the crib against its wall. She could continue carrying it alone, but she'd spotted Ivan walking toward the pub with Winston.

'That shit show almost made you look like the normal one, eh?' Winston said to June, laughing and elbowing his brother for reinforcement.

June stuck her middle finger up and told him to fuck-off. However, there was an unusual lack of fire in her response. She smirked at Ivan, thinking about getting to his stuff. Winston and Ivan shrugged off her mild wetness and disappeared inside. They scented there wasn't anything further to gain from hurling hostilities when she was in one of her weird, non-combative moods.

June lifted to her tiptoes, and through the translucent glass above the frosting, she watched the tips of their heads bob along to the bar: Ivan's luscious black hair and Winston's prematurely balding bird nest. With their pints, they drifted to a corner table and joined a group of men playing dominoes. June flattened her feet and checked her watch. 6.45 pm. She wondered what time they went for a drink in the week. Monday. They must go at this time. They have to. What else do men do after work? She thought, desperate to know for sure. She contemplated sitting in the pub for a few consecutive Mondays to check. However, women didn't really go into the Crystal Palace. They could. Technically. They just didn't. It was one of those things. Besides, she also knew that she lacked the patience to wait weeks.

Bending down to lift the crib, she committed to having one drink. She'd get there for 6.30, and leave as soon as they arrived—if they arrived. People would stare and frown, but fuck them. It would be worth it. Delight flushed her cheeks as she heaved, crib-in-hand, back home, hopeful. All they needed to do was turn up. They will.

Fran helped transport the crib upstairs and into the bedroom. Evelyn didn't return. Not that evening or any of the following. June and Fran slept in the room with her two babies. Her bed empty.

Come Monday, June was manic. At work, she irritated the residents with her erratic restlessness. The old people liked quiet in the mornings. A good graveyard atmosphere; staff difficult to spot. No fussing. No bothering. A place they could wake glacially.

'Piss off!' Gladys said, slapping June's hand as it pulled at her arm. Gladys was a sharp old woman who liked to do things on her own terms; naturally, she didn't take kindly to June forcing her to move into the lounge and play cards.

'Leave my shitting slippers alone, you pilfering cow!' Bernard said, stamping away from June's hands as they attempted to slot slippers onto his feet after he had told her several times that he didn't want to leave the snug. 'I don't want my bloody shoes on. I'm happy here. And I'm not an invalid; I know you can hear me.' Bernard actually wanted his slippers on, and ordinarily he would have graciously accepted support, but June's condescension rubbed him up the wrong way. He chose inconvenience over comfort. It wasn't so much her smug happiness that bothered him, it was her evangelical expectation that he must feel happy because she was in a crazy mood.

'Yeh piss off and leave us be!' Eugenia said, joining the chorus of complaints. She grabbed the remote and turned the T.V. back on. June had switched it off to promote the card game, the one nobody wanted to play. The resistance had no effect on June's mood. She irritated the residents until the last minute of her shift, losing no momentum. Nothing could ruin this day.

After work, she dolled herself up with heavy blue eyeshadow and far too much red lipstick. She looked like a little girl who had broken into her Ma's makeup bag, and afraid she'd never get another chance, applied as much of everything as possible. She slipped out without Ma or Fran noticing her union Jack, clown face, or to ask where she was going.

In the Crystal Palace, Big Kev over-frothed her half-pint of lager shandy, entrapped somewhere between the fact he had a young woman drinking alone in his pub and the extreme colouring of June's makeup. '25p change, love,' Big Kev said, placing the silver coins onto the counter where June had left her 50 pence piece. She scooped the twenty and five pence pieces and headed for the table built into the window beside the entrance.

After each sip of her lager shandy, she checked her watch. Fifteen minutes elapsed and not a single person came in. Three blokes old enough to be her father played dominoes and a handful of blokes old enough to be her grandfather sat alone, chain-smoking cigarettes and sipping large sips of ale. An unnatural silence circulated over the clacks of dominoes, the occasional spluttered cough, and the more occasional ring of the till. How do people spend so much time here? She thought, deeming the place drearier than anything she'd experienced, including christenings. No wonder the women went to Bingo. Her enthusiasm drained as the drab reality of the pub invaded her hopes of getting into Ivan's bedroom. As she thought he wasn't coming, Winston walked through the door.

'What the fuck do you look like?' he said, offended at the state of her face and her presence in the pub.

Her heart struck, but like a stroke victim. Too hard. Too vigorous. Too singularly. Desperately hopeful that Ivan was behind; that he, too, was about to enter the pub. The beat paused. Her blood stopped pumping. She held her breath. Each second passed like a day. No, Ivan. Still no, Ivan. A week passed. He wasn't coming.

'Hello?' Winston said, pressing her for a response. But she couldn't focus on anything but her disappointment, oxygen starved muscles, and the door that Ivan was not walking through. He shook his head, snorted to himself, and walked to the bar. 'Two pints of Gold Label please, Kev? How long has she been in here?'

As Kev pulled two pints, Ivan entered the pub. June's pseudo heart-attack ended. Air rushed to her organs as she gulped air, electrifying her insides and jolting everything alive. She jumped up, adding to Ivan's weariness. 'Enjoy your evening,' she said, brushing her body against his arm as she slid out. Her half-pint of lager shandy remained on the table, half-finished.

The smokeless, non-stale air hit her flushed cheeks like serpentine ice-water, and her adrenaline spiked. Game on. She rushed home, let herself in quietly, and snuck straight upstairs while Ma and Fran played with the babies in the front room. June positioned the chair from Ma's bedroom beneath the attic hatch and pulled herself up, biting down on the Maglite torch to keep it gripped between her front teeth. She resealed the hatch in the loft and only then switched the torch on as if it had secret powers beyond illumination. Bin bags of forgotten stuff glowed like treasure in a pirate's cave. Shin-by shin, June traversed the plank to the boundary wall, climbed over it, careful not to hit her head on the beam, then back on her shins completed the journey to Ivan's hatch.

Dust layered on every bag. Nobody had been up in years. June listened hard for signs of life below and breathed heavily, attempting to balance the fear of being caught with the overexcitement of touching Ivan's things. Socks. Pants. Tissues. Fuck it. Her fingers locked into the hatch's groove, allowing her to lift it off.

Brown carpet stretched along the dark and musty hallway. June dangled her legs onto the banister, unintuitively bordering a staircase on the wrong side of the house. The layout back-to-front. The simple difference thrilled her. She pressed against the ceiling for balance; then slowly, palm-by-palm, took herself away from it, guiding herself down the wall until she could carefully jump from the banister without making too much noise. Although, if anybody was downstairs, they'd definitely have heard the thud. Her body froze in its lowered position like a bat waiting for sonar information. Her upper body squashed between her bent legs, and her face hovering close to the floor. Nothing. She was safe. Yet she remained still for another 20 seconds, just to be sure. She listened for any movement. Clear. Iris was definitely out. She unbent her legs and launched her torso upright, grinning like a Cheshire-cat that had caught the cream. She was in.

The stale smell of cigarettes reminded her of the pub. At home, Ma made them smoke outside. Now she realised why. The place reeked.

She endured the stench and ventured into the front bedroom, shared by Ivan and Winston. It was disorientating. Ma had the front room, whereas Iris had the back; how upside down the world order was. Simple laws of nature. Not natural. Not law.

Both beds remained unmade. Duvets scrunched in heaped piles atop crusty bedsheets that hazed in the lingering smoke, which seemed to ripple around the entire house like some sort of afternoon dust storm. Ivan's double denim trademark outfit signalled his side of the room. Acid-washed jeans and a knock-off Levi jacket slung on the bottom of the mattress. June climbed onto the bed, skipping to the end of the Goldilocks fairy-tale by getting straight to the one that was just right.

She wrapped the duvet around her body, pressed her nose against his pillow, and inhaled aggressively, extracting the smell of his sweat. Dosed-up, she twisted to lay her cheek flat, and watched herself finger the stain on the bedsheet, perhaps drool from the night. She shifted her mouth onto it, kissing the fabric. Licked it. Not so much to leave her own saliva. This was about him. She felt cocooned and though she had never taken drugs, assumed it made people feel this. No wonder they became addicts.

The promise of more eventually motivated her to get out. She slid his drawers open one at a time, her hands swimming through the items as if they were marvellous fish in the Great barrier reef. His underwear stingrays. Thrilling. Electric water. She pulled out a pair of black boxer shorts and covered her face with them, again inhaling aggressively. These had once wrapped his upper thighs and framed his pelvis. She removed them from her face and exchanged them for a worn pair beside the wardrobe, although this time she merely scrunched the fabric and pressed it into her nose. A rotten fustiness sent her into dizzy euphoria. Like an addict, she dosed-up to breaking point, breathing harder and heavier until her system overloaded.

She examined everything. Saw value and richness in ordinary crap. A clump of dirty tissue rested beneath his bed. She reached under and pocketed it, convincing herself he wouldn't notice, telling herself it was the one and only thing she could take without jeopardising her illicit visit. Visits. Much better to play it safe. Avoid getting greedy and being found out. Not to take too much now. Later. She would return. Again. Again and again.

The bedside clock flashed 7.50 pm. Time to get back. Bingo wouldn't finish for another hour, but better to play it safe. There was no guarantee beyond Ivan and Winston would stay in the pub for much longer, beyond the general principle of male gluttony. Before leaving, she skirted Winston's side of the room, quickly browsing through his things. There was no way she'd touch his underwear or smell his duvet. Dirty pig. However, she noticed a grotty glass on the bedside table. He clearly used the same cup without washing it: a gunky rim of grime encircled the inside. June smirked, simultaneously staring at the glass, and hearing memories of Winston taking the piss out of her. Revenge. A little taste of his own medicine, she thought, taking the glass to the kitchen and searching for something nasty; something to slip in and make him choke. She didn't want to kill him. Just give the fat bastard an unpleasant experience. A sour taste as his dehydrated, hungover ass leant in for a gulp of water in the early morning.

Though the desire to inflict pain surpassed the commitment to play it safe. He deserved to suffer. Besides, he couldn't possibly know or even think she would be responsible. He should clean his glass more often.

She searched through the kitchen cupboards, looking for something nasty, but not too nasty. Beneath the sink, she noticed a bottle of Thallium. Rat poison. Scary image of skull and bones on the bottle. She realised why no rats had been scurrying around the garden for a while. While unscrewing the lid, she stretched her arms far away, assuming that the stuff would stink. She controlled the bottle, ensuring that only a couple of drops fell into the glass, not wanting him to actually die; despite her intense hatred. Also, too much, and the smell would be obvious: he'd change the water. The whole point was for him to notice. She wanted him to spray the stuff all over himself and his bed sheets while hungover and hazy; wanted him to drag himself out of bed and suffer; wanted him to wash his mouth out when he was most desperate; when he most wanted to bury his head beneath the duvet and sleep. Fat Bastard. She stirred the glass with her finger and then smelled it. Nothing, really. Good.

She bent to replace the bottle under the sink, but then an intense reservation kicked-in. Perhaps it was too weak for him to tell. Perhaps the stupid idiot would drink it without noticing. Ignorant dickhead. June decided it was safer to put more in, enough that he would definitely taste it; definitely know to spit it out. She couldn't risk poisoning him. Not seriously. She didn't want to get into actual trouble. She poured a little more into the glass, making it obvious. Better to play it safe. Then, she worried more, and so poured more, intent on making it idiot-proof.

She placed the bottle back on the shelf beneath the sink and shut the cupboard door. Carrying the glass, she headed back to the landing. But as she reached the front door, she froze. This is a bad idea, she thought. Too dangerous. The thick bastard might be stupid enough to drink it. She would throw the water away and abandon the plan. She turned, about to retrace her steps to the kitchen, but as her first foot landed on the red living room carpet, Iris and her Ma's voice sounded on the street outside.

'Not at Bingo tonight?' Ma asked Iris as she put the bin outside ready for the morning collection and as Iris searched through her handbag for keys.

Inside, June darted back to the kitchen, tossed the glass onto the counter, almost spilling it, and then sprinted upstairs to get into the attic before Iris let herself in. She struggled to climb onto the banister without a chair to stand on. Hadn't thought about that part. Her heart thumped as her thighs pounded into the bar, almost breaking the entire banister and bruising herself. Iris must have heard something, surely? June didn't wait to find out. Inelegantly, she pulled herself up, palms treading the wall; body swaying and narrowly avoiding falling back down. She slid the hatch open with her fingertips and lifted herself up.

Outside, Iris found her keys and replied to Ma while moving them toward the lock. 'I left early. I've got a terrible sore throat and my tastes awry. Can't shake this metallic, tarry texture. Horrid. Think I might be coming down with the flu,' she said, twisting the key. She paused, let go of the keys to cover her mouth, and coughed.

Ma wished her well, speaking as if there had been a death. Iris thanked her and returned to twisting the key. The lock unfastened and just before opening the door, she said, 'I couldn't take the smoke in the Bingo Hall either. Think it might be time to finally quit—' she referred to her cigarettes. '—if this flu doesn't take me first,' a self-deprecating touch of exaggeration to accompany her bidding farewell to Ma as the door opened, and Iris hobbled inside.

'Take care, love,' Ma said, waving to Iris's back, and then fastening the flap on the bin-bag, and going inside herself. Both doors shut as the hatch slotted back into the ceiling. Operatic timing. June scurried back through the conjoined attic, praying Iris couldn't hear anything.

She couldn't. Iris could barely hear her own thoughts: her ears rang and her head split over and over. She couldn't focus at all. In the kitchen, she placed her handbag on the counter and took the glass. She shut her eyes and braced herself to endure the pain of swallowing something as simple as water. One of the worst sore throats she'd had in a long time. She gulped the entire thing stoically, dismissing the vile taste as a derivative of her flu, and nothing to do with the water itself. She was dead before Winston and Ivan returned home.

Chapter 16 — Nanny Evelyn (1980s, School)

Squaddie John had been good to Evelyn. His intuition told him to run. His own preservation told him to run. Paedophile, that's what they'll call me. Yet he stuck by her. After the door closed, ending the short-lived reunification with Scarlet, John took Evelyn into his arms and then into his home. Her hardened body accepted his hug and her homeless soul accepted his offer of accommodation. He slept on the sofa, and she took the bed. The barrack officers weren't happy, but they agreed to a grace period. One week to put things right. She needed to go by the following weekend, even if it meant the streets. Charity had limits.

She ignored school on Monday and went to the council house instead. But she couldn't bring herself to go in, worried that they'd make her go home. She tried again the next day and forced herself inside.

'We understand the situation, but the problem is that we can't provide accommodation until you're 16. Technically, you need to be with a foster carer, but I'll level with you love. That's won't happen at this stage,' the well-built lady at the counter said. Her voice was warm and soothing; exuded confidence and experience, earnt through dealing with these sorts of cases every day. 'Can't you go home just for the week, love? Put up with it and come back after your birthday? It'd make everything much simpler. There are a couple of decent places on Marston Lane coming up—I reckon we might squeeze you up the list if you can hold a week.'

The lady dangled a carrot to gage her situation. Many girls would hold out months for a Marston Lane property.

'Lovely street, you know, love. Half the tenants down that end of town have already pounced on Mrs T's right to buy. Shedding properties by the week, we are. You'd have some lovely neighbours. So what do you think? Come back next week and get the process started then?'

'I can't,' Evelyn said, her words slipping out before she'd meant to speak. The offer was beyond good. She never expected the council would actually give her a house. She spoke out of instinct. Fran's betrayal was fresh. Sore. It was too raw and painful to imagine seeing Scarlet. No house, regardless of size, could persuade her to go home. Returning wasn't an option.

Her cheeks flushed in embarrassment as her mind caught up with her instincts, and as she regretted declining the offer. Making do for a few weeks wouldn't be impossible: she could sneak into Gran's shed? Even rough it in the park? Options flittered. For her own place, the worse would be worth it. A home on Marston Lane. She fiddled with her hands, mounting strength to tell the lady she'd changed her mind.

The well-built lady sighed compassionately. She saw Evelyn's inner thoughts and intervened to disrupt the anguish. She was used to dealing with savvy and shrewd clients—could smell a negotiator before they approached and said a word. Evelyn was not a negotiator; she had too little self-interest; too little game. Not too much. Many girls that came knocking on her door internally somersaulted at this sort of deal even if they tactically withheld their reaction. Evelyn's guttural and earnest rejection communicated a deeper vulnerability (and strength), a more embedded willingness to put herself in danger; she had a capacity to detonate and die rather than compromise and concede. Evelyn was a warrior in an idealistic, patriarchal world, deeply uncomfortable with tolerating the reality of knightly women. The lady saw that and immediately liked her; she wanted to help Evelyn.

The lady prioritised the case; deemed it worthy of special consideration—beyond the default special consideration inherent in their work. 'Look darling, you are clearly in a bit of trouble, aren't you?—' she said, placing her hands on top of one another on the counter and while leaning her body back. '—Let's see what we can do.'

Evelyn frowned. Had the woman retracted the initial offer? What did she want? Why couldn't she just accept it and get out? If only she had reigned in her instinct. Been rational from the start. A few seconds of restraint, and she would have agreed to the original terms. Instead, Evelyn mistook the lady's affection for a smirk, and worried she'd blew her chance. She swallowed; the lump in her throat rolled down her neck. She nodded to the lady with grateful eyes.

'Oh, love—' the lady said, reading her apprehension. She had really taken to her. It happened now and again. '—Leave it with me. I'll see if I can rush something through. We can sometimes get you in early by delaying the paperwork, so the tenancy doesn't officially start until after you move in.' She winked while placing her index finger on her lips, implying secrecy. The lady looked like she'd blown out the candles on her own birthday cake and was ready to share out its large slices. She was a kind and trusting woman, capable of sensing and easing honest pain.

They moved into a small room where the lady filled out paperwork. Mostly simple administration. The lady didn't ask where she was staying, and Evelyn wouldn't have told her, anyway. She didn't want to mention the barracks to the council; they'd done her a favour. It wasn't right to get them into trouble, especially John. Better not to mention any of it. She gave Ma's information: name, address and landline number, and also the name of her school.

The lady told Evelyn to return the next afternoon and hoped, though stressing she couldn't promise, they might have sorted somewhere, even if it was a temporary. It was enough for Evelyn. It was more than enough. She had expected no serious resolution, yet they had offered near salvation. Things might work out. She left the building hopeful, but as she dismounted the steps, the thought of Scarlet in Fran's arms rushed into her mind. It crippled her. She crunched into a ball, wrapping one arm around her stomach as if struck by a cramp. With the other arm, she shielded her eyes, pre-emptively hiding tears building in the sockets.

Devastation was a typical sight outside the council house, and so nobody paid Evelyn much attention. After a moment, she peeled herself upright, mortified that somebody may have seen, and sternly told herself to pull it together. She wasn't that person; wouldn't be that person. With enforced pride, she made herself walk; made herself get to school.

Although she wasn't in uniform, reception signed her in and told her she could go to class. They lent her a pen and jotted down her timetable. Evelyn knew her timetable after a week at school, but the receptionist insisted on writing it down. They thought of her as the student with the babies; the one that hasn't got a clue and needed fussing over. She took the piece of paper and thanked them. No point challenging the stupid women. She glanced at the paper as if it helped. Home Economics had already finished, so she headed straight for the Science labs. Biology.

The other kids were good with her. Nobody mentioned babies, and they didn't seem to think, or at least show they thought any less of her. In honesty, most of the girls believed they'd be following in her footsteps in a year or two anyway, so Evelyn's getting to motherhood early provided a strange sort of celebrity status, not that they revealed they thought that either. School wasn't a place for sharing personal thoughts or showing how you felt. It was just a place people went in the daytime, a strange sort of pseudo-job or alternate reality where kids bided time; waited for real life. Not necessarily unpleasant, just unfamiliar and strange; a place filled with weird adults that differed from the rest of society. School was like a boring holiday with enough foreign things to keep students mildly attentive, but not so exotic they expatriated or became homesick. A fishing village in northern France.

Evelyn had English before lunch with Paedo-Stiffy, Mr Cliffy. He taught the sublime nature of poetry while getting erections for the girls with larger breasts, and scaring them witless with his severe manner. He lived in the posh part of town with his wife and kids, who knew nothing of his infidelities. A total hypocrite and not somebody who should preach love. The man had seen to girl-lovers at his backdoor while his un-scrutinising wife lay upstairs in bed. A scumbag. A dirty bastard who got away with murder.

Fifteen-year-old girls and boys in white shirts and loose ties drifted against tatty wall displays and faded paint as they entered Mr Cliff's classroom, hungry and ready for lunch. Mr Cliff sat at his desk finishing the rest of his pear, his gaze absorbed on life beyond the large windowpanes, rather than the students entering his room. The gentle hum of noise eased naturally as people sat at informally reserved desks; seating plans self-imposed by students themselves. Evelyn sat at the empty desk two rows back from the door. Mr Cliff didn't notice her until everybody was in, and the second bell rang to show the lesson had started. But when he noticed, he noticed hard. He speared the core of his pear into the bin, whereas he normally would have merely lobbed it. He bit his tongue consciously as he faced the class in front of the blackboard and then released a rush of air from his nostrils. The class knew he was pissed-off already. Several girls braced themselves in anticipation of a creepy question being directed at them. They hated having to speak in front of the class, but knew he'd zoom in on them.

'Miss Clarke, what is love?' he said to one of the nervous girls.

'I dunno, sir,' she said, muttering into her fists and hoping it would encourage him to move onto somebody else.

'But we've spoken about it before. Unless you are retarded, and you're not retarded, are you, Miss Clarke, then you will know something. Tell us,' he said, turning his back to the class and picking up chalk, demonstrating a readiness to write Joanne Clarke's response on the blackboard.

As she stumbled in search of anything to say, the chalk dragged along the board, leaving a long white line representing her non-response. 'Miss Mayol, care to enlighten the class as Joanne Clarke, evidently, has nothing to offer.' He stopped dragging the chalk, and the line ended.

Joanne looked relieved he'd moved on. 'Sex sir,' Deborah Mayol said, deadpan and unapologetic. She was one of the few girls in the class that saw herself as a woman, and who didn't allow Mr Cliff to intimidate her. He leant back against the board, holding the chalk in his hands, which came together and rested near his crotch. A standoffish silence rumbled between him and Deborah, as if radio waves streamed back and forth in magnetic collisions throughout the room. She held her own, and did not speak until he explicitly directed her to do so. She could handle the authoritarian, believing they were easier to play than people thought.

'Elaborate,' he said. She had forced his command, and in the process, undermined him.

'Love's a device to woo women into bed, "treasure in un-ploughed-up ground," ' she said, referencing a quote from the poem they'd studied last lesson. Mr Cliff smiled, a sleazy grin of a smile.

' "I must all other Beauties wrong / And rob thee of a new embrace".' He quoted back at her. The boys of the class looked gormless, and the girls remained nervous. 'What does the poet mean in these lines, Miss Finch?' He said, directing attention away from the confident Deborah Mayol and onto Evelyn. His question cruel. Though Evelyn didn't care, and neither did the class. They assumed Mr Cliff was merely being his usual dickish self. Evelyn shrugged, even though she knew exactly what the speaker meant in those lines. 'Come on, you must be able to work it out?' He said, not letting it go.

'I'm not sure, sir. What do you think it means?'

His face switched from the integrator to the interrogated, and his body turned stiff. Rather than leaning, he pressed against the blackboard, and his muscles tensed. He was no longer relaxed, but he would not shift his position and acknowledge the reversal of their master-servant dynamic; recognise her ability to upturn the natural order. Him, questioner. Her, questioned. She had really bothered him. He slowly unpeeled himself from the board as if she wouldn't notice; as if it he had done it in his own time.

'This isn't about me, Evelyn Finch. What I "think" is by-the-by. I asked you what the lines *mean*, objectively speaking, of course. I don't think your insolence is brilliant, given how much school you've missed. Do you—?' but before he could finish, the secretary knocked on the classroom door. The gormless boys awoke from their passivity and the anxious girls crept out of their caverns. Nobody ever came to lessons. Something interesting must have happened. Mr Cliff's uncomfortable and pissed-off tension at Evelyn's minor provocation now bubbled into full paranoia and fury.

'Apologies, Mr Cliff, Sir—' the secretary said, as if she herself were a pupil. Two ladies stood behind her. '—But we need Evelyn Finch to come with us. It's rather serious. I'm very sorry for—'

'—It had better be extremely serious. The girl's missed months of lessons and now you want to pull her out.'

He covered his terror with aggression; the damming notion she'd told somebody he was the father bleached his insides and forced him to fight back.

'No. It won't do. It's not appropriate to remove her right now.'

'I'm really sorry, Mr Cliff, Sir—'

The secretary felt like a minor clerk laboured with giving an unwanted message to a terrible king on order of a powerful but distant emperor.

'—but there're two ladies from the council and they need to talk to Evelyn urgently. I wouldn't ask if it—'

'—Yes, I can see the stooges hovering behind you,' he said, drawing his sword. He had an entitled fight (rather than flight) instinct; couldn't back down, even when he knew he was wrong. The sword was real. He kept it beside his desk, said it was a prop to bring Shakespearean fight scenes to life. Really, it just made him feel like a big man. If the bitch has fucked me over, she's got another thing coming if she doesn't think I'll defend myself, he thought, giving Evelyn a dirty dagger'd proprietary glance, and then addressing the women from the council. '—She's in class. You'll have to come back later, assuming council workers don't clock off at lunch.'

He waved his hand dismissively and directed another question to Deborah, who he knew would answer correctly.

'What do the lines mean, Miss Mayol?'

But the lady holding the clipboard manoeuvred herself from behind the door, cupping the poor secretary's shoulder as she moved past, as if saying, through touch alone, that she'd take it from here. Mardy, stubborn men with self-important arrogance didn't faze her. As she entered the classroom, Evelyn noticed it was the lady from the council house, whom she'd seen early that morning. 'I'm sorry, Mr Cliff, my love. I don't mean to disrupt your important lesson, but we weren't really asking dear; we're telling. Miss Finch is to come with us right away. I'm sure you understand, me duck.'

The lady twisted, her bodyweight shifting with her eyes, as she scanned the room for Evelyn and quickly caught sight.

'You don't have authority in my classroom, "duck". Evelyn isn't going anywhere. She's a student of mine and her education is too important.'

Mr Cliff strode toward the lady and stood uncomfortably close to her with a wide-legged, intimidating stance. It didn't bother the lady, or at least she didn't let on if it did. She ignored him completely and called over to Evelyn. 'Evelyn dear, come on now. Bring your stuff too, duck.' The lady's warm, buttery smile glowed as she spoke, suggesting she had good news.

The woman's lack of deference and simple command sparked a bomb of rage in Mr Cliff.

'Sit down!' He said, snapping at Evelyn, who had already tucked her chair beneath the table. She froze, awaiting further instruction from the lady.

She didn't give it straight away. Instead, she turned, looking at Marc Cliff in slow disgust. Head to toe.

'—I said sit down!' he repeated. But despite the increased volume and bile in his voice, Evelyn didn't pull the chair back out. Though she kept her hands gripped onto the blue plastic edge in case she might have to in a minute.

'Love, raising your voice will not work with me. This is a matter of child protection, and we have full rights to remove Miss Finch from her lesson. I apologise for—' she said, turning to look at the white line drawn across the board, derisively mocking whatever he had been professing to teach; clearly, nothing if he behaved like this. '—for disrupting this very important lesson, but needs must. Besides, resilience is everything in this world. Wouldn't you agree, Mr Cliff?' She said, leaving the question as a piece of rhetoric; not in need of answering. She turned away, stretched out her hand to Evelyn, and contracted her fingers in a come-this-way-dear. Evelyn nodded, and waded through the pew-like aisle bordered by rows of desks, her classmates staring as if she were an actress in a movie.

'Foolish bureaucrats. Never happy unless you're poking your nose into ordinary people's business and ruining lives.'

He walked back toward his desk, attempting to regain dignity through his moralistic condemnation, disdain and derision for an authority he refused to recognise. He leant against his desk in mock relaxation.

'I feel sorry for the poor girl. But take her. It's probably too late for her, anyway.'

His performance was remarkable. Marc Cliff quashed his own sweaty palms and convinced himself he had nothing to do with whatever was happening; no reason to be afraid that her child protection business concerned their sexual history. It would just be another delusional schoolgirl fabricating nonsense and any accusation would come to nothing... let somebody else deal with the shit, he thought. '—Just get out already so that we can continue, and this does not affect the rest of the class.'

He rolled his hand again dismissively, mocking and uninterested. Bored.

Evelyn left with the women. The secretary scuttled out last, leaking apologies through the narrowing gap between the door and its frame.

Outside, the lady from the council placed her hands on either side of Evelyn's shoulders. '—Dear, you didn't tell me you had two children now, did you?'

Evelyn's heart felt like a pile of boulders had fallen on it. The house wasn't happening. Marston Lane wasn't happening. They were going to force her home. The weight of the lady's hands became much heavier as the strength departed her withering shoulders; as her bones thinned like lifeless leaves, destined for the crunch. Sadness pulled heavily from within.

The lady removed her right hand from Evelyn's shoulder and used it to cup Evelyn's chin, applying a soft force to encourage Evelyn to tilt her head upward and make eye contact. '—Oh love, you should have told us. We can't have you waiting weeks with two babies to look after,' she said, her grin widening and her eye winking, theatrical and affectionate. 'Mind you, we'll still have to put the paperwork through afterward like we talked about.'

Sickness weighed Evelyn's stomach; it sludged through her pelvis, into her legs. She couldn't infer what was being implied. Refused to. The lady needed to say it explicitly before she would allow herself to believe. The other lady pulled a key from her handbag. She was much skinnier and her back had a bad curve to it. Though her face was as equally kind. The first lady, still staring at Evelyn, square-on, broke the news.

'We've got you a two-bed on Marston Lane. I won't lie, it needs work, which we could have done had we a few weeks, but given your situation, well—' she said, her teeth glistening, and her open hands adding gravitas to her message. '—well, it's better to have somewhere with potential than nowhere. Let's leave it at that.'

The second lady handed the key to Evelyn. 'An early birthday present, dear.' They both then reached in and gave Evelyn a hug.

Mr Cliff had set the class a task. He shifted to stand beside the door, listening for accusations, but failing. He couldn't hear what the women said. After five minutes, he opened the door, but Evelyn and the ladies had gone. The school corridor was silent, nobody scuttling along the grotty wall-displays updated ten years ago. He stood there, opposite the open door to the boy's toilet, with his paranoia and a class pretending to write about a cynical love poet, presented as a sublime God, when all they really wanted was to eat lunch, play football, and talk about Top of the Pops.

Chapter 17 — Aunty Lilly (1990s, Turnpike Crescent)

Lilly regained consciousness. She had been out of it for five days and Ahmed thought she was a goner. The policy was to not let them go past four. If they hadn't come around, put them out of their misery. But Ahmed hated doing it and bent the rules whenever there was hope. One more day if it might make the difference. Two at the most, but no more. And even then, it caused problems. Thankfully, Lilly only needed one. She was going to pull through.

'Drink up,' he said, tilting the glass of water, loaded with a pharmacy of powders and salts. She complied, looking at the unconscious Indian girl in the bed opposite. Lilly, herself, was docile. She hadn't fully come around, and Ahmed kept it that way. He administered another liberal dose of methadone, a heroin substitution; a larger dose than any clinic dished out, but not so large to satisfy the addiction. He kept pushing the tranquilliser until the drug numbed most of the pain, and until it warded off the effects of cold-turkey, that aggressive self-scorching rampage, the body inflicts on itself as the heroin leaves.

'Fetch Pam,' Ahmed said, injecting another thin needle into Lilly's arm. Baret obeyed his instruction; as he left the room, Ahmed removed the needle and dropped it into an empty dish where it rattled. He then removed his plastic gloves and plonked them beside. 'You are a lucky girl.'

He didn't expect her to answer, but he felt compelled to speak to patients when they made it against the odds; he had become accustomed to one-way conversations.

'Where am I?' she said, surprising him. Her words were weak but not hollow. Beneath the drugs and suffering, she was there.

'You are safe.'

She wanted an answer, but lacked the strength to command her throat muscles. She took in the sight of hospital sheets, machines, and a doctor, and her heart-beat fastened, believing police officers and prison-guards would be close by. Hospitals were part of the establishment. Not to be trusted.

'You are not in a hospital. Relax,' he said, placing his gloveless, hairy hand onto her bony arm. His voice was authoritative, conveyed a street intelligence that assured Lilly he was as much a part of the underworld as her.

She tried to recall her sense of self, the interconnecting experiences that made her who she was; the bits of her not lost in unrecorded, unmemoried history. But the darkness was too alluring. Her body craved emptiness. Simplicity. Her mind shut itself to warrens of memory; to history. She could barely process the reality of the room she was in now, let alone allow fragments of sense from the past to complicate things. Remembering was too difficult. Impossible. She couldn't summon, command, nor convince her mind to show her anything other than where she was right now. Out of self-preservation, her mind and body locked away her own history, her identity, behind picket-lined neurons, on strike against the past.

'Tell me where I am. I can't remember anything,' she said, panting and almost out of breath.

'It's normal. Don't worry for now. You're safe. That's all that's important,' he said; his eyelids remaining eerily wide and open as he stared at her from above; from her perspective angel like. 'Unfortunately, you will remember soon, and then you will want to forget. So enjoy the moment while you can.'

He wrapped his hand around her arm and pressed his fingertips into her skin, slowly, as if he were conducting a religious ritual where the action - his gentle touch - was as important in convincing her to do as he had said. It worked. Lilly relaxed. She stopped trying to remember, stopped trying to make sense. She drifted into a peaceful present and accepted the limitations of her knowledge. The incompleteness of her senses. She smiled at the world like a joyous, ignorant baby, and wise old philosopher, accepting the kaleidoscope of impressions and forces rushing through her mind and body without resisting or subjecting them to her own intelligence. She let them be.

'Oh darling,' Madam Perez said, entering the room. She was taller than most women and had a queen-like presence. Her movements were deliberate and full of content. They always meant something. Always conveyed something. Sexual energy. Regal grace. Indifference. Baret followed behind her, the short Turkish man, his movements meaning nothing at all.

'She's doing better than expected. Even speaking a little, which is unexpected given the potential brain damage,' Ahmed said, removing his hand from Lilly's arm and standing up from the stool beside the bed. 'He left a small bleed on her head, which swelled, but it's too early to tell if it's caused any permanent damage.'

'How long?' Madam Perez asked, placing her hand on Lilly's face and using her fingertips to stroke the cheek.

'Two days.'

She winced. It wasn't what she wanted to hear. 'She deserves at least that. How much will it cost?' she asked.

Ahmed moved equipment from a counter onto a tray: sachets of liquid, drip tubes and bandages. 'Baret will cost it up.'

'Ball Park?'

'He'll itemise everything so that you can see, but it was a bad tear, Pam. We used a lot of blood.'

Madam Perez held herself with complete grace, never appearing to stoop into the filth of negotiation. Her eyebrows raised, but the rest of her facial features remained poised as she waited for him to answer.

Ahmed continued moving the equipment. Only when he had finished entirely did he answer. 'Five thousand.'

His dark hazel eyes made his soul seem far away, burrowed deep, detectable only via a warren of refracted light bending through the networks of his biology.

Pam gave a single nod and did the mental arithmetic quicker than a calculator. She twisted to Lilly lying in the bed, placed both hands on her arm and thought about the amount of clients she had serviced, and the quantity she'd have to continue servicing to repay the debt. Ahmed knew exactly what she was thinking.

'We're both going to hell,' he said, dropping his chin to his chest and internally asking God for forgiveness in heavily accented Arabic. He lifted another tray of instruments and equipment and walked away. Baret's eyebrows curled as he frowned at his boss's conscientious brooding. Baret did not approve. To him, the girls were sub-human, and helping them was an act of merciful charity. They should be grateful for receiving his and Ahmed's help. End of story.

Madam Perez withheld her reaction. She shared Ahmed's sentiment, but knew he thought about the situation with the wrong tense. They weren't going to hell; they were in it. She leant forward and kissed Lilly on her forehead, praying she'd make it.

Chapter 18 — Uncle Nick (2000s, Benson Tower)

It had been a terrible week for Nick. The police had cordoned off his house by the time he returned from the police station, so he couldn't get back in to collect his students' mock papers and books, let alone any clothes, toiletries, or belongings. Ofsted hammered the school, removing its 'good' status, and although Nick was hardly responsible for the broader failings printed in the report like some BBC News Headline, he certainly hadn't helped. His boss was frosty, and the leadership lacked sympathy for the week leave he had proactively taken. The call Matt instructed him to make was deeply dissatisfying: he didn't have to withhold conversation; whoever was at the other end asked him no questions. He was none the wiser about what was really going on.

Scarlet was his saviour. Despite telling her she needed three years clean before popping inside for a coffee, she offered the spare bedroom in the flat without a second thought. Plus, after spending weeks without adult company, she appreciated him being around. Nick told himself she benefited from him being in the flat: he could help look after Summer. But he was useless, and besides, Scarlet was doing fine. She expected nothing from Nick; was just glad to see him; glad at the reconciliation of their relationship.

He visited the station every day, but the officers didn't allow him through to see or speak to Matt. He couldn't get past the generality of him aiding terrible men with their illegitimate businesses. What did that mean? The phrase looped his mind, especially when lying flat in bed. He needed details. Real information.

After four days, Nick demanded to see Matt. He became heated in the station, ranting about rights and civil liberties. The officer with the ponytail took pity, pulling him aside and revealing he couldn't see Matt because Matt didn't want it. He blocked the visits, not the police. Nick wanted to explode as fury sent shivers along his arms, but he kept it together. The officer acknowledged the underlying hurt and frustration he must feel as she guided him to the exit.

He had no idea what to do or why Matt was acting cruel. How could he continue living a normal life with everything as it was? It wasn't fair for Matt to cut off so severely. So Cold Turkey. Yet he had, and life had to go on. The last thing Nick needed was to lose his job. Without Matt's income, he'd need to think about money much more explicitly. Nick wasn't overly materialistic, but he had become accustomed to casual luxury; life that cost more than a teacher's salary. He would be fine whilst staying rent free at Scarlet's ninth-storey council flat, but a nice, little apartment of Clapham High-Street would absorb his income like a sponge taking water. The math was a no-brainer.

'Sorry,' Scarlet said, apologising for Summer's crying. 'She just won't settle this evening, won't you, sweetheart? You just don't want to settle this evening. No, you don't. But uncle Nick needs to get some sleep for work. Yes, he does.'

She bobbed and soothingly rocked Summer to no avail. She continued crying.

'Don't worry, honestly. I can't sleep, anyway,' Nick said, walking to the kitchen cupboard in his bed shorts and T-shirt. He removed a bottle of Jack Daniels still in the Tesco carrier bag and poured himself a glass against the lamplight, illuminating the open walkway on the other side of the kitchen window.

'That won't help,' Scarlet said, speaking over Summer's crying.

Nick moved to the sofa, sipped the bourbon whisky, and then placed the glass on the coffee table. 'I know,' he said, conjuring several excuses in his head. But hearing how each sounded, refrained from articulating any, and instead took another sip. After which, he repeated himself. 'I know. I won't buy another bottle.'

He meant it. They hadn't really been a drinking family, except for Nick's father, and even he didn't really drink in the house. Alcohol was a social thing; men drank in the pub. Everybody else, at the occasional party, but even then, it wasn't as prevalent as it appeared. Dancing was far more important.

Despite Summer's crying, Scarlet smiled as she sat down on the chair opposite the sofa. Nick leant back and as he breathed, Summer randomly settled down. A welcome miracle. She hooked onto her Ma's nipple, which was half-covered by the open blouse she'd never have worn before having a child. The non-crying silence made the air feel like a warm bath. Nick and Scarlet instinctively relaxed, their muscles letting go of the tension, and their shoulder blades unfolding from neck-hunched wedges.

'So, what are you going to do?' Scarlet said, closing her eyes in a satisfying peace as she asked her brother the question she'd held back for days.

'What can I do? Go to work. Find somewhere to live—'

'—You can stay as long as you want. I enjoy having you here.'

'I know, but I can't stay forever. I'll need my own space, eventually.'

Nick took a larger sip of the bourbon.

'I meant, what are you going to do about Matt? Do you love him?'

Nick sipped again. Talking about love directly was uncomfortable for him. Scarlet didn't fill the silence, though. She left it to fertilise their relationship. 'Yes,' he said, eventually. Scarlet continued to respect the space for him to think through his answer. 'It could be five years,' he added. He hadn't told her about Matt telling him that.

Scarlet remained calm: she assumed a prison sentence and expected it wouldn't be small. The police had cordoned off the house. Whatever he'd done was obviously serious. 'It's understandable if you don't want to wait,' she said, resting the back of her head in the armchair while Summer fed.

'It's not the waiting itself. It's the not knowing what he's done. The secrecy and lies. The uncertainty of whether it's something I should wait for.'

'Does what he did matter?'

'I don't know.'

Nick sipped again. Then spoke truthfully, 'Yes.'

Scarlet nodded. 'I think so too.'

'It feels like I'm supposed to say it doesn't matter; that I'll stand by him no matter what, but I need to know what he's done.'

'Have you got suspicions?' she'd asked when it first happened and he'd said no. But a week had since passed, and buried thoughts may have bubbled to the surface.

He shook his head and drank again. 'I honestly didn't have a clue. We were normal. Went to work. Dinner. Occasional night out.'

'Did he do drugs?' Scarlet said, rouging a little at her question. It was the last thing she wanted to ask, given her own history. 'More people do them than you think.'

Nick's hand wrapped around the glass, and he stared into the brown bourbon. He hated what he was about to say; it was something he ignored, pretended not to notice; refused to see in his partner. 'He took a bit of coke, I think. Not much though—he wasn't an addict.'

Now, Nick rouged. He had used the term judgementally. But Scarlet took no offence: this conversation wasn't about her. She maturely endured the sub-text with gutsy openness, as if the applicability of his words to her was little more than an uncomfortable, irritating aside; it would disappear if starved of attention. She refused to fight the blushing red of her face. The waves swept up and over and fizzled like an ocean in the sand, ending itself. No need for control. Focus returned to Matt. The uncomfortable presence of analogy gone. Nick appreciated her grace, the way she did not shut herself off, and close-down the conversation out of a destructive self-preservation. He continued.

'On a night out—I'm not talking about dinner and a couple of drinks with just the two of us. I mean, a proper night out with friends. He'd slip off to the toilets and then come back buzzing. He'd make out that he was just drunk, but we both knew he wasn't. We played along with the charade.'

Nick paused for another drink. He didn't want to say it, but did. 'He knew I hated any sort of drugs because of you and Lilly. So I suppose it was easier to pretend it was just alcohol.'

'Do you think of her often?'

'Try not to. You?' he asked, looking up and meeting Scarlet's eyes. They rarely spoke about Lilly since her passing.

'Lot, even more since Summer,' she said, breaking eye with Nick to smile down at her baby still feeding off her breast. 'It makes me feel sad they'll never meet, but—it sounds stupid—I'm glad I at least have the sadness. The idea of forgetting haunts me much more than remembering—' Scarlet looked back up at Nick, and spoke with an added, hearty strength to her voice, making her sound musical, as if a violin or guitar string accompanied her words. 'The feeling that one day I'll leave her behind terrifies me. She can't become history, Nick. The sadness keeps her alive.'

'But she is history. She has to be,' Nick said, bristling at Scarlet's point of view, which irritated him.

'It doesn't feel that way to me, and I don't want it to.'

'But you have to move on. For you.'

They both spoke with certainty. Their point of view absolute.

'I don't want to move on, Nick,' she said, fight in her voice for the first time.

Summer broke from feeding and scrunched her nose. She was clearly full and so Scarlet scooted her upward a tad and pulled her blouse across. She rested peacefully in Scarlet's steady arms. 'I don't need to move on by forgetting her; by forgetting anything. It's a lie, Nick. We don't need to forget. We need to remember.'

Nick placed the glass back on the coffee table, disgruntled. He didn't share Scarlet's philosophy, believing that people had to forget the past in order to move on. But he believed even more in not arguing about it. Doing so only indulged those hanging on. It was sentimental and prevented actual progress. Successful people knew this. Unsuccessful people did not. And it was a complete waste of time convincing unsuccessful people. Scarlet.

'I know you disagree, so you don't need to nod,' she said, still relaxed. Not combative or argumentative at all. But equally unwilling to permit untruth to re-settle into their relationship. 'We can have different outlooks and still be close. It's being honest that's important. Please don't pretend to believe in things I believe in and then drift away again because you feel you can't be yourself around us. Disagree. It's fine.'

Nick scrunched his hand and propped up his chin on it. His knuckles curled toward his lips, and he nodded again. This time, honestly, like a chastised little boy, soothed by the repentance.

'We love you, and it's not fair that you end up resenting us on the back of false nods that we never wanted or needed. We're different. And that's ok. You're wrong and we're right, of course,' she said, grinning and then winking, an emphasis of her friendly intention and a lightening of the serious conversation. 'Don't drink anymore of that stuff. You'll regret it in the morning.'

Nick poured the alcohol down the sink. He didn't really like whisky, anyway; didn't much like alcohol, if he was honest. He enjoyed the looseness, the effects of being a little drunk; the feeling of freedom he felt too rarely in real life. But the actual taste he could live without. He walked back over to Scarlet and kissed her and Summer on their foreheads. 'I'm off to bed.'

'I'll go in a minute too,' Scarlet said. Summer had fallen asleep on her lap, and she didn't want to risk waking her for the moment.

As Nick went to leave the room, his mobile phone rang. Luckily Summer didn't stir; her full little belly must have settled her into a deep sleep. The caller had withheld the number.

'Hello?'

There was no initial response, but Nick knew it was Matt; could sense a tearful, choked voice was about to speak. 'It's Matt—' he said, holding back tears. '—It's done. The police have what they need, and they'll have leaked information to the papers, so it'll be out in the open soon.'

Nick's stomach churned like an adult riding a crazy rollercoaster, for which he was far too old. He wanted to vomit the small dregs of whisky before even hearing the details.

'The papers will find you, but they'll leave you alone once they realise you had nothing to do with it—'

'—For fuck's sake Matt; you're scaring me.'

'—I'm so sorry, Nick. Please remember how sorry I am. I've been a selfish prick.'

Matt covered his mouth as if it would control his tears. Beside him, the policewoman pointed to her wristwatch, encouraging him to hurry-up. He pulled himself together and pressed ahead. He owed Nick enough for him to hear directly. 'I've helped this Belorussian guy move his dirty money into UK bank accounts. He runs a sort of brothel come drug house out of a row of shitty terrace houses in some backwater cul-de-sac. East London, Stratford, I think—' he said, knowing for certain that it was Stratford, but unable to speak as clearly and honestly as intended. '—he was using a lot of human-traffic—'

Nick felt the sick shoot up his throat like the little dials on a fairground machine. Matt was using language disingenuously, obscurity reality, rather than owning up to what he'd contributed to. '—What do you mean "he was using a lot of human-traffic"? You make it sound like he's a mechanic or some fucking car dealer.'

Matt clarified his language, eager to be straight with Nick. 'You know what I mean. He was transporting men and women, some underage, from abroad, exploiting them without proper pay; promising visas after stints of working as prostitutes and drug pushers; after putting them firmly in his pocket.'

Nick was stunned. He had no idea what to say.

Matt continued. 'I've helped the guy to put his profits legitimately into business accounts. I'm not talking a couple of thousand, but hundreds of thousands; millions. Over the years. But Nick, I've had no direct contact with the operational side of the business; I want you to know that. I've never touched the girls or boys; met the men or women. I've never even been to the street or seen the properties—' he said, lying. He had visited once. '—I'm guilty of fraud. That's what I'll go down for. The police won't pursue abetting or money laundering because I've been upfront and cooperative.'

The policewoman became more irritable. After huffing, she poked at her watch again, urging Matt to wrap up the call. She didn't like being privy to these types of conversations.

'I'm really sorry, Nick. Please forgive me.'

Tears streamed down his cheeks, and Nick could hear the suffocated sobs.

'—Please forgive me.'

But Nick turned cold and hard. Silent as steel. He had nothing to say. Perhaps ever again. This situation was too repulsive, and his only response was to switch himself off. He ended the call, placed the phone on the shelf built into the corridor wall, and returned to the living room.

Scarlet looked at his pale face and mirrored his apprehension. He sat down on the sofa, the same spot as before, but his soul had left the room. His body vacuous. Scarlet became afraid. She had never seen her brother like this; and as a family, she thought they'd been through it all.

'He's been helping some Eastern European with human-trafficking—' he said, his voice eerily deadpan. Cold, even racist. Robotic and devoid of emotion. '—He's been the money man. Making the business appear legitimate, transporting the profits into legitimate UK bank accounts. He's a piece of shit. A disgusting, scummy piece of shit. The whole time. Our entire relationship. He's been doing it. They can hang, draw and quarter him for all I care.'

Nick's voice remained monotonous, each syllable undifferentiated, unemphasized.

'I never want to see him again. Let him rot in prison. Let the inmates kick the fuck out of him. Leave him for dead.'

Scarlet had nothing to say either. Prostitution was an industry that had devastated both their lives; had taken their flesh and blood, never mind their dignity. How could he have been facilitating, profiteering from it the whole time? The fancy meals. The drinks. All of it paid for with dirty money. The sick resurfaced.

'I have to go to bed.'

Nick stood without waiting for Scarlet to respond. He said goodnight mechanically and left. Scarlet gave him space. There was nothing she could say. She remained in the chair with Summer asleep on her lap, almost as stunned as Nick. She'd not much warmed to Matt, but never did she expect him capable of something like this. He was the entitled rich boy from Grammar school; a holier-than-thou, condescending prig who thought without actively thinking, he was better than people like her because his job involved spreadsheets, shouting on the phone, and attending expensive, company-paid-for lunches where he drank too much. How was he connected to such a vile, sinister underworld? It chilled and surprised her as she lay back in the armchair. She gripped Summer tighter and prayed that she'd never grow up to fall for somebody like that.

After ten minutes of staring into space and mulling it over in her head, her mobile phone bleeped. Another message from Summer's dad appeared on screen: 'Message from Marc Cliff'. She clicked to open it.

Chapter 19 — Aunty Fran (1980s, Marston Lane)

Nets twitched as police cars drove up and down Gadsby street. Iris' body, zipped in a black bag and flat on a trolly, wheeled off with the Coroner the previous evening, and gossip about her death flared overnight. Although the autopsy showed poison killed her, the more dramatic rumours took hold: a burglar shot her; a druggy stabbed her; a psychopath smashed a brick over her head. Nobody yet suspected June.

The well-built lady from the housing department arrived amid the commotion and knocked on Ma's door. Evelyn had been to see her a few hours ago. 'Hello me duck. I'm Racheal Evans from the council. Do you mind if I pop in for a little chat?'

'If it's about Iris, I've already told the police everything,' Ma said, looking over the lady's shoulders. She saw official looking people hanging around. They held clipboards and whispered to one another. Must be discussing the details of how he did it, Ma thought. She also saw half-lifted nets in the houses across the street. The neighbours still snooping. Though she couldn't talk, she'd been looking out the windows all morning herself.

'No, love. It's nothing to do with that. It's about Evelyn, but I think it's better if we chat inside,' Rachel Evans said, flattening her palm in the corridor's direction behind Ma, inviting herself in. 'Shall we?'

Ma squashed herself against the door, making space for Rachel to pass into the house. After she'd squeezed past, Ma shut the door, taking another peek at the clipboard people.

Rachel strode into the living room as if she'd been in the house a thousand times before. 'Hello me duck. I'm Racheal Evans from the council,' she said to Fran, who perched on the edge of the sofa with Scarlet clutched in arm. Rachel settled in Ma's armchair before Fran said hello or invited her to sit down.

'Make yourself at home,' Fran said, deadpan. She looked like an interviewer for a job she would never give.

Ma scuttled around the coffee table and sat beside Fran and Scarlet. 'What is this about?' Ma asked, pulling her green cardigan across her chest and then breathing in.

'I had a visit this morning from Evelyn Finch. I'm assuming she's your daughter?'

Ma nodded above her now crossed arms. She and Fran both suspected the woman's motives. Their guards went up.

'We get plenty of young girls coming to ask for help, but there was something about your Evelyn that I couldn't put my finger on. She wouldn't tell me why she couldn't go home, but she was determined. Resolved—' Rachel said, deliberately pausing to see whether Fran or Ma would volunteer information. They didn't. And so she continued. '—The thing is, she had no expectations. Came in defeated as if nothing could be done and that's difficult to fake. I've got a good nose for it. They're unique smells, desperate and hopeless. We get lots of desperate girls, not so many hopeless ones. So whenever they come in, they get my attention.'

Rachel enjoyed her job and didn't seem to mind speaking frankly. This only deepened Ma and Fran's apprehension. 'What I'm saying is that your Evelyn came across hopeless, but when I made a few calls, things didn't add up. I thought there might be domestic abuse. It's common with the hopeless women... sick bastards grind them down until they don't care anymore. They're not desperate; they're—'

'—Evelyn isn't being abused,' Fran said, snapping at Rachel Evans for her offensive suggestion. She tightened her grip on Scarlet too, as if Rachel were about to snatch her at any moment. Take her back into care.

'I don't think any of you are abusing her, and duck, give that baby some space. I'm not from the social; not here to take her anywhere.'

'You know she's Evelyn's child?' Fran said, not loosening her grip on Scarlet, not believing a word Rachel Evans had to say. All state authorities deserved distrust. She wouldn't be fooled.

'Yes duck. Though Evelyn didn't say. I made calls, and it didn't take many for it to come to light that she had two children. What I don't understand is why she didn't tell me. It would have helped her application.'

Rachel looked at her pad to check a few details. Fran and Ma steeled their reactions. They would not ask about the application. Rachel brought it up. She should tell them without their having to ask. 'According to the social, there'd been a reunion between Evelyn and the second child after a—' Rachel said, glancing back at the pad for the duration of Scarlet's sojourn from the family. '—four-week separation?'

Ma's chin dipped into her cardigan. She didn't want to discuss their dirty laundry in public, and though they sat in her living room, Rachel was most definitely public. Whereas Fran's back straightened. She would fight, not cower. 'If you're not from the social, what're you here for? Why are you poking your nose into our private affairs? Stop with the games, and spit out whatever you have to say.'

'Easy, love. I'm here to help.'

Fran snorted. 'Nobody asked for your pissin' help.'

'Look—' Rachel said, reaching into her brown handbag, dumped on the floor beside the armchair. She rummaged through the contents, feeling for a set of keys. '—I'm here because we sorted a property.'

She held the key in the air. Ma's chin decompressed from her cardigan, her face lifting in surprise.

'Where?' Fran said, her shoulders relaxed, but her face remained scrunched.

'Marston Lane.'

Fran and Ma's ears pricked. Had they heard right? Or was it merely beguiling?

'But before we rush ahead, I need to determine whether the need is genuine,' Rachel said.

Ma and Fran's ears unpricked. Neither believed Evelyn was needy. Marston Lane was a false carrot to get them talking.

'Is Evelyn welcome here?' Rachel asked.

'—Of course she is!' Ma said, finding her voice. Her response was instant. No delay. No room for ambiguity. The idea of the council thinking she was a neglectful mother shamed her beyond embarrassment.

'—It's Scarlet that isn't welcome,' Fran said, still bitter at Evelyn's unforgivable behaviour.

Rachel sighed as the pieces slotted together. '—I see. Evelyn hasn't bonded with the baby, and it wasn't her choice for Scarlet to return, which is why she wants to leave,' she said, summarising the situation for her own benefit. She turned to her pad, and scratched inked sentences onto the pages. It sent Fran into a frenzy. She pivoted upward from the sofa, preparing to spit wasps if it came to it.

'It changes nothing! Scarlet is staying! The social already said. If Evelyn doesn't want to step up and raise the baby herself, we can, and will! We are her family, and you have no right—no right!—to take her away.'

'—Sit down, love. I told you, I'm not here in that capacity. I've no direct business with the children.'

' "No direct business",' Fran said, mimicking her language, and suggesting foul play. 'Aye, you've no business period. Now we think it's time for you to bugger off and leave us alone.'

Rachel leant back in the armchair and rested the pen and pad on her lap. 'Duck, I only meant that I've no business beyond the child having satisfactory accommodation. I don't know how many times I need to say it, but I'm not from the social.'

'But you'll say that our accommodation isn't "satisfactory," and tell the social she can't stay. I know how it works. Don't take us for fools.'

Fran rocked Scarlet in her arms — side-to-side in gentle sways — as she continued her challenge of Rachel Evans. 'I know how people like you work. You come in here, friendly-friendly, and then stitch us up. Don't take us for pissin' fools. Now piss off.'

Rachel grinned warmly. She liked Fran a lot. 'You're a pistol, if you don't mind me saying. We could do with more women like you at the office.'

Fran ignored the compliment. Another tactic. Another misleading, fake carrot, to get her talking.

'You're right, of course,' Rachel said. Fran looked vindicated, smiling not because she was happy, but because the woman had confessed her true colours. She was right; deserved to be righteous in calling it out.

'See Ma.'

Ma looked heartbroken. 'You're going to take her away from us, aren't you?'

Rachel saw the same trace of hopeless deference in Ma as Evelyn. Takes after her, she thought, her grin widening as her focus returned to the now pacing and nuclear Fran. 'You're right that I'll say your accommodation isn't satisfactory. There'll be six souls from three generations living in this tiny two-bed. It's not big enough—'

Fran went to explode, but Rachael stood, pushed out her palm, and delayed her. She had more to say. '—But you're also wrong to suggest I'll say, let alone recommend, that Scarlet, or Lilly, shouldn't live with you. For one, I'm not a liar. I said I'm not from the social, including as a deceptive indirect information gatherer. I don't decide where or with whom children should or shouldn't live. And even if I did, it would mean diddly squat. I work for the housing department and judge whether children have "satisfactory accommodation", solely so that I can justify allocating bigger or additional properties for the families to live in. I am here to ensure the children, and Evelyn, have a good sized home.'

Fran capitulated, at least a little. Rachael Evans was winning her trust. Mind, it was another thing to show it. 'How can we trust you?' She asked, poker-face still on. Rachael Evans picked up the key she'd placed on the table.

'The property is ready. I fast-tracked the case because of the children, and Evelyn being a minor. I'm reaching out to fill in details; make sure things add up. Now I obviously appreciate the situation is more complicated; that she doesn't intend on the children living with her—'

Fran scrunched her face, feeling slightly self-congratulatory for not fully abandoning her scepticism. Rachael Evans was still up to something; still had a card up her sleeve. '—Are you expecting us to beg?' she said, speaking over Rachel, who leant forward, placed the key onto the coffee table, and slid it forward.

'Please sit down, love. I'm not here to cheat you. I'm not here to negotiate either. Take the key if you don't believe me.'

'What use is a key? You can kick us out even if we took it,' Fran said, moving back to the sofa and sitting back down beside Ma. Rachael ignored the rat-hole of a question, sensing she had won Fran over to move the conversation forward. She really had taken a liking to her.

'It's more a question of whether the Marston Lane property is right. I'm catching-up with the family dynamics. Clearly, you are a tight unit, and it might not be the right thing to offer another two-bed—'

Ma realised that Marston Lane wasn't for all of them. It wasn't one of the obvious three-bedroom houses on the street, but a sneaky two-bed hidden somewhere out of view. It was a home for just Evelyn and the babies, an exit strategy. How hadn't she realised straight away? She felt such a fool and incredibly sad, believing deep down that Evelyn was coming home at some point; that things would resolve on their own; that everything would figure itself out, and they'd live happily ever after. Even if space was tight.

Fran thawed, realising that Rachael Evans wasn't there to screw them over, but to give them real options. She was really there to help. She laid down her weapons, unguarded herself. '—But can Evelyn really have her own home, at her age, just like that?' she asked, a rare vulnerability and openness to her tone.

'At 15, officially, no. But I'm willing to delay the paperwork a few weeks until she's sixteen, which is when it becomes possible. It's not common, but it happens when there's need.'

'But she can't live alone!' Ma said.

Rachael Evans smelt Ma's desperation. Not her hopelessness. She didn't believe what she had just said; she wanted it to be true; desperately wanted Evelyn to not live alone; desperately wanted her to stay at home forever. But knew she could; knew it was possible; knew it was not unlikely, unrealistic, or even unreasonable.

The conversation was over. 'Look, you need time to figure out how things are going to work, and the short of it is that I don't need to know the ins and the outs. There is a two-bed property available now, and between the six of you, you're entitled to it. Maybe Evelyn will want to be there with the kids. Maybe not? Perhaps you—' Rachael glanced her attention to Fran, '—might want your own place? Maybe your sister?' Rachel checked her pad again for her name. '—June might want her own space, freeing up space for the children here? Whatever you choose, it would be stupid to not take it when it's there. These things don't come around as often as you think.'

Fran and Ma both nodded, grateful for Rachael's consideration and extreme pragmatism.

Rachel lifted herself from the armchair, pulling her handbag up too. 'It won't be there next week if you decide against it,' she said, moving for the door. 'I'm going to visit Evelyn at school and update her on what's happened. I'll give her the second key and tell her you've got one too, and that you'll all have to get together and decide how to move forward.' Rachel twisted to look back at Ma and Fran. 'In your own time, of course.' She twisted back and continued walking along the corridor. 'I'll come back next week with the paperwork, and we can decide how best to fill it in.'

At the front door, she twisted a last time and winked, a reassuring gesture to assure them she'd make good the official side of things, whatever decision they came to.

Ma thanked her for coming.

'Don't worry about seeing me out. You've got plenty to discuss,' she said, gripping the handle of the front door. Ma and Fran followed, anyway.

'Rachael?—' Fran said.

Rachel removed her hand from the door handle and turned to her.

'—Thank you.'

'Duck, it's my job, and like I said, we really need more spunky women at the office, so if you fancy a job, get in touch.'

Rachel stretched out her hand, and Fran reciprocated. Their two palms met in a firm handshake beneath affectionate smiles. 'I mean it,' Rachel said.

She let herself out, squeezed between the boot of her ford fiesta and the bonnet of the police car parked behind. Ma and Fran waved as the engine roared to life and the car rolled away. Rachel was gone.

But just as they were about to go back inside, the police officer stepped out of the car and approached. 'Fae Finch?'

'Yes, but if it's about Iris, I've already told the officers everything I—'

'—Fae Finch, I'm arresting you on suspicion of murdering Iris Winstanley. You do not have to say anything, but it may harm your defence if you do not mention when questioned something which you later rely on in court. Anything you do say may be given in evidence.'

Chapter 20 — Pam (1990s, Quaglino's Restaurant)

Madam Perez wore two-inch black heels, adding height and gravitas she didn't need. At the brothel, she wore boots, professional trousers, and her hair up. It looked effortless. Sexy and authoritative. She was one of those women who didn't have to try. Even without revealing flesh, she commandeered men. She didn't need large heels. She kept the place running smoothly with limited accessories, gliding clients in and out with flats and charm, suggesting sex rather than giving it. Never putting herself on a plate. Keeping herself mystical.

Outside the establishment, for meetings with the big boys, she didn't have that luxury. She pulled her hair down where it draped her open back, and wore the skimpiest, glossiest dress, just about covering her thighs. Professional. She had clients to satisfy and expectations to meet. Dmitry, the biggest of the boys, liked the working girl look, and what he liked mattered. Pam adhered, with a bit of class thrown in.

She wore a diamond necklace and a gold watch to offset the cheapness of the dress. She hated these meetings. Hated having to wear the dress and the jewellery. She'd trade open legs and shoulders of the restaurant world for the burlesque shawl any day of the week. Madam Perez, like most long-serving, dutiful employees, had become institutionalised. She liked what she'd become accustomed to; defended what she had grown to feel was homely.

Her heels clacked against the cobbled west-end streets leading out of SoHo as her useless tiny handbag glimmered and bobbed against her glamorous bottom. She knew she looked the part, but felt resentful for having to play it at her age. She'd done the hard work: exploited, cared and repaired girls; schmoozed the dirty old bastards and bled their wallets. Yet little of it truly belonged to her. Serious profit and ownership rested higher.

'Pamela! Gorgeous woman,' Belarusian Dmitry said, taking her hand and kissing it with his bulbous lips as she strode toward his car beside the entrance of Quaglino's restaurant, their meeting point. The driver shut the car door. Dmitry had left it open, as he always did.

The driver returned to his seat and drove away. Dmitry was a man silently obeyed; his needs serviced without explicit instruction, like royalty born with servants, who attended to needs as if they were extra body parts rather than entities in their own right. No thanks. No acknowledgement. They were extensions of him.

'Excellent choice,' Madam Perez said, referring to the restaurant. She hated it. She preferred dark, private, un-glitzy establishments. Some pokey hole off a SoHo back alley. Quaglino's was the opposite. It didn't welcome customers. It peacock'd them. Sucked them into its imperial staircase, which pulled them down its spiral curve to a lower floor, where a string quartet played against a banquet of noisy customers, tossing oysters down their throats and forever clinking champaign flutes. Jewels twinkled in the black marble steps and screamed wealth. The place stank of money and entitled class; vain-glorious inheritors self-congratulating one another, waffling on about their entrepreneurial prowess and ingenuity when they were little more than carbon copies of their financier parents, whom they depended on entirely. Pam couldn't stand it. At least Dmitry wasn't one of those. He was a sick bastard in a whole other way.

'Cut, shit. You hate place, but I like cigarette girls and vodka,' he said, kissing both of Pam's cheeks and then wrapping his arm over her shoulders. His meaty fingers slid down her back and clutched her slim, but maturing hips. He appreciated an older lady when they looked like Pam, but still preferred them young. 'Come. Let's get to business.'

Arm-in-arm, they descended the staircase and emerged into the subterranean kingdom of Quaglino's. The ceiling height doubled that of the upstairs entrance. The open-plan sea of tables, napkins, waitresses, and rich balding men the size of three or four ordinary people gave rise to an ocean of sound rolling and crashing into the expansive walls at either end of the restaurant. Dmitry, carrying Pam's hand high, cut through the centre of the room and found his way to a good table at the back. The attractive waitress pulled out their chairs, and they sat.

Dmitry ordered an expensive bottle of vodka for the table and two glasses of wine for the occasional rinsing of the vodka. He ordered the taster menu to eliminate the need to choose specific things to eat and to maximise the quantity of food. Pam took a salad.

'I have investors to purchase last properties. Move junkies to number 5. Then I get more scumbag to incentivise further selling of house; "move along", as you say,' he said, waving a cigarette girl over. He continued talking as she headed to the table. 'You have opened to idea of apprentice?'

Dmitry had never mastered the grammar for formulating questions.

'Have you?' Pam timed her jibe well. The cigarette girl landed with packets of Marlborough Reds while another waitress arrived with the bottle of vodka.

Dmitry tried the vodka and lit a cigarette, blowing out a barrel of smoke, satisfied with both. He laid his hand on the table with the lit cigarette squeezed between two fingers, dangerously close to the tablecloth. 'I have many peoples. You are fool if think business not need many layer of peoples. We must have help. Too much proud. No. Must think.' He tapped his head with the cigarette in hand.

'I will,' Pam said. She wouldn't.

'No. You not change thinking,' he said, laughing and taking another drag. 'But for me is good, anyway. Keep cost down.'

His teeth closed on each other, and smoke vented through the gaps over a purposeful 'shh' sound he made by pressing his tongue to the roof of his mouth and blowing. He unclenched his jaws and a reservoir of smoke released in a single plume. 'Very true. We achieve a very good profit. Maybe too many profits.'

Pam raised her eyebrow. There was no such thing as making too much money. At least he was getting to the point.

'Cash is become big problem.'

'Clients aren't exactly going to hand over their credit cards,' she said. It was a non-starter, and he knew it. What did he want?

Dmitry grinned. 'Clients can use. No problem.'

He knocked back a shot of vodka, refilled his glass, knocked that back, refilled, and knocked back another. 'Problem is us. We not put big cash into bank account. Every bastard in UK now obsessed with how say? "Verification." People not want only money; they want know every fucking cunt touch every fucking note before; where money is from. We must new ways of moving big cash into banking accounts with verification.'

Pam thought of the bundles of cash sitting in her safe at home, her life savings; her ticket to retirement in the south of France where she'd see out her days once she became too old for it all. She liked cash. Cash was simple. Cash was honest. Cash was good as long as you weren't greedy.

'Cash, not like was. Must change big business, "diversify operations," he said, grinning. Chins layering on one another. He poured and shot another vodka, pleased with his advanced vocabulary. 'There new young "chaps" work in city. We "groom" these peoples after they finish big money schools. "Graduate schemes".'

He pronounced words he considered overly English like quotations, as if they didn't belong to him. They landed like alien words. An unknown language. Neither English, Belarusian or Russian. 'Too hungry and "entitled", these peoples. Filled with too much in self-believing. They big Gods. Think they bring enlightenment to London. "Toss-pots". Clever "tossing pots".'

He grinned again, squeezing the several layers of his chin tighter. 'Yes, much clever "tosser-pots" help us with big cash problem,' he said, sounding like a toddler, figuring out the boundaries of a new word as he bent it into unused forms.

Pam censured her thoughts, steeling a poker face, which prevented her facial gestures and body language leaking any signs of opinion. It wasn't her place to think.

'Can only put small cash on banking accounts for nail bars and kebab shop profits without tax office—How to phrase bullshit?—"make enquiries". Big cunts. But glitzy buildings in new Dog towers are future. They help us.'

Pam knew men like Dmitry treated information as commodities. She also knew they lacked any charitable shreds of decency. They gave nothing away for free. He wanted something.

'You must meet new Gods. Show human face for business. Take lunches on "Isle of Dogs".'

'How much does this new PR role pay?' she said, straightfaced and helping herself to a cigarette from his packet, a symbolic gesture combining the languages he was most familiar. The holy trinity of power, sex, and self-interest.

Smoke lifted from his lips, but his thick eyes never lessened in colour or intensity as the plume danced up his face. 'These arrogant "twats" is our future. No good to talk about you or me. Yours. Mine. This together. Ours. How say? "Partnership".'

His sleaze almost caused a self-laugh, but Dmitry never laughed at himself or allowed others to laugh at him. He knew her sass was a facade. Theatre for his benefit. She didn't want money. She wanted to be left alone. To do her job without micromanagement. It's why she'd risen. If she had to do a bit of PR to maintain the status quo, so be it. She would, and they both knew it. Her self-interest was part of the dance. No more. An appearance for the sake of his ego. But that wasn't what he wanted. Too insubstantial for a meeting.

Like a good girl, she remained actively passive, attentive to his monologues.

'Shops. All of them, together. Not take more than £100,000 cash profits without "enquiries". £100k Maximum. And is at maximum doner kebab and pretty nail shop. More not possible. Authorities know already too many. Many fake shops, but not too many for bad smell and "investigations". And other areas, too many big men already have shops,' Dmitry said, scowling at the mere thought of competition, let alone the physical reality of them dotted across the restaurant, holding their own dodgy meetings. He waved his hand dismissively at the other customers; to him, symbols of counter barrens saturating the market with their own money-laundering operations. 'Authorities are more knowing. Must have more careful. But is big problem because £100k is too small money in London now. Fuck!—' he said, slamming the table. '—Is fuck all money. Normal. Even you have two £100k cashes, at least. Is problem for us and must solve together if wanting more. As English say, must "move with time" and "victim of success".'

Pam had nearly 200k in her safe, and it was the first thing Dmitry said that unnerved her. Unlike him, it was everything she owned, and it had taken her ten years of frugality (save these unwelcome dinners) to gain it.

Other women her age had mortgages paid off, albeit with their husbands. They had jobs and pensions to see them into and through retirement. They had houses full of stuff. Sofas, tables, beds. Kitchens, bathrooms. Pam didn't. And she wouldn't until she left the country. She lived simply, owned little and would continue living that way until the day she could disappear forever. How can this filthy fat pig equate her life savings and day-to-day living with his yearly profits perpetually squandered away? Drinking Vodka. Eating Shit. Snorting Coke. And fucking girls, not that he paid for the fucking anymore. Pam covered that expense.

Again, she concealed her thoughts, but Dmitry knew he had rattled her. He could smell discomfort and taste resentment, even if confined to the brewing cauldron of the mind. That internal cave of curses. He penetrated it. It was his skill. He laughed nastily.

' "Look",' he said, opening his palms on the table, signalling the end of business. 'I bad man? No.' His palms shot up in mock, angry surrender. His demeanour hard and scary.

'I do "what needs to be done".'

The phrase muffled into itself. He hadn't pronounced it right; hadn't fully mastered it. But he didn't repeat himself, nor allow it to stumble his advance. 'People sometime not understand. But is ok. I make sure good people is looked after. You good, Pamela. To me. You good. To you. I good.'

He drank three more shots of vodka, giving Pam space to appreciate their fortunate, mutually beneficial relationship. She fake smiled at his benevolence, and willed her body to express deference; willed blood into her cheeks so they'd rouge, and he'd take it as a sign of gratitude. She hated him.

Her cheeks did rouge, and he ate it up, a tasty aside for him to enjoy alongside a disgustingly large rib-eye steak. The waitress placed it onto the white tablecloth and talked through the ingredients of the sauce it came with. Before she left, Dmitry began eating, slicing a sizeable chunk of fat from the steak and chewing on it with an open mouth. Pam forked her salad.

'Convince little Gods that girls are willing. Happy. That you treat them good. They looked after—'

'—They are!' Pam said, breaking her deferential performance. She thought of Ahmed bringing Lilly around earlier that day, and the cost of medical supplies deducted from her bottom line. If it was up to Dmitry, she would be six feet under. Far cheaper. The amount of girls they'd helped come back around over the years. She'd have enough money to leave for France now if she didn't pour money into them. She regretted interrupting him, but it was too insulting for her to hold back. He had riled her. But she would be damned if she allowed him to do it again. And so would he. She stilled herself, and he grinned. He'd give her one allowance. One instance of her speaking to him as an equal. An exception to prove the rule of subservience. They finished the course in silence. And the next two. Though Pam ate nothing for those. Only Dmitry had the taster menu.

'Little money Gods must know there is certain level of class to our "operations",' he said, the business term falling from his mouth with a mocking tone. 'These men think they do not have "idealism"—' Whereas the sociological term fell heavy and deadly serious, revealing the real man at Dmitry's core. The young boy, raised in deep-rooted suspicion and hatred, bathed among KGB spies, communist re-education camps, and neo-liberal gangsters, each parsing their own doctrines and self-appointed truths. '—These men are fools, deluded "tosser-pots". Blind. They have "Idealism", but is secret to them. They don't see who they are. I see. I know. They believe in money god. They are believers who do not know they believe—' he said, slamming his palms on the table and breaking into a laugh. '—All fuckers are believers!'

He shot several more glasses of vodka. Felt warm. 'Peoples in West are ignorant now. Not know their own religion. Rich men from money schools are big secret priest of their big secret religion. Of market, of "free exchange".'

This term did not fall into his sociological word bank. It made him howl with laughter. It was so ridiculously stupid a concept to him, for nothing in his world was free.

He continued with a biblical fervour. 'Your job is to convince—' he said, ignoring Pam's previous objection. '—To explain that brothel is good. Clean. Legitimate part of unfairly excommunicated church of "free exchange". You show brothel is a victim of Hippocratic—' For the first time, his inability to pronounce a word bothered him. He was trying to say hypocritical. Pam watched him struggle, abstaining from help, knowing he would receive it with hostility. Plus, she enjoyed his irritation. He moved on. '—Must show brothel as "progressive" part of modern world. Show restriction of brothel and drugs as unfair. Part of controlling state and bourgeois abuse of power. Too much privilege. Show brothel as freedom. What people want. Will be, as you say, "above board" soon, anyway. Make them feel like prophet; doing good for society. Make them feel big men.'

Pam nodded at his ranting. The vodka had kicked in and he was drunk. She knew what she had to do without his monologue. It was fairly simple. Parrot Thatcherite guff. She was more interested in what the bankers could do, that Dmitry couldn't himself.

'You think about what these banking devils do with cash?' He said, enjoying her intrigue for information he had.

'It had caught my curiosity,' she said openly. There was little point in disguising it once he'd sensed her mind wandering.

'I don't understand complete. But I tell because important not look idiot when meet them for lunch. You must be in know.'

His fat ugly grin cracked across his cheeks as he synced a smile to his words. He reeked of bullshit. Pam knew his real demand was coming.

'You must be in know. Show serious part of business. Have respect.'

Pam sipped the wine dispassionately, suggesting she was at ease. Comfortable being at the table watching him eat. Not wanting to be anywhere else.

'They take big cash. Up to one million profits per year. More big is problem. But low than one million is no problem because they can do "self-verification". No government checking for less than one million. They turn into "the shares" for offshore company. Plus, taxes on the shares much cheaper than taxes on kebab and nail shops.'

His teeth glistened. Not only was the city a route into larger volumes of money laundering, but it was also a route into paying lower taxes on the money already laundered.

'What are the risks?' she asked, demonstrating her competency in asking the right question at the right time. Something she would need to do with the young bankers; men, all young enough to be her children. Dmitry nodded, approving of her participation like a good play on a chessboard.

' "No risk." They will say. Men from big money school will say "responsibilities". No risks, but responsibility. Responsibility that we must extract only £1 of share back into legitimate UK account, for every £2 invested in company. How to say? For keeping fixed. £2 is example. Exact amount to store will change. Is what they will say.'

Pam realised why he was sending her. It wasn't as a reassuring face of the business, though she would be that. It was his way of telling her she needed to increase the quantity of business. They were making too much money for a small-scale money-laundering business, but not enough to move into the big leagues. The share scheme would only work with a much larger economy of scale, because half of the capital earnt would need to remain invested in long-term shares. Remain unusable. Dead money. They would function to stabilise the share price and give substance to an otherwise ghostly immaterial company. Dmitry took pleasure in smelling the cogs turn within her mind.

'Is good time for "apprentice", yes?'

'How much bigger?' she asked directly, showing she was keeping up in his cryptic reveal.

'Double.'

He took a long drag on his cigarette and stumped it out before exhaling.

'—By end of 1999. Triple by millennium.'

Her heart sank. Business couldn't grow that fast without the brothel suffering. Pam was a conservative businesswoman. She liked to grow slowly and securely, taking on clients and girls at a steady pace. Training them. Making them more resilient, so fewer ended up like Lilly. There was an art to challenging the men without offending their fragile egos, and it took time. Years of confidence building. Doubling the base rate by the end of the year was tantamount to turning the place into a sex factory. It would force her to delegate management; to abdicate control of recruitment, scheduling, daily operations. It opened up space for greater risks, fuckups, and worst of all, politics.

'Is promotion—' he said, his disgusting grin stretching again, one of the few parts of his body that regularly worked out. '—Polite for you give thanks to me, no?'

Pam mustered the strength to shift her lips and offer words of gratitude. Luckily, Dmitry filled both shot glasses, so she didn't have to hold the smile for long. She took the glass and tossed back the vodka, hissing at the burn.

'Cheers!' he said on behalf of them both, clinking his glass on hers. He refilled them and shot both.

After the meal, Dmitry left a wad of £20 notes for the waitress and cigarette girl to share. 'Cash not completely fucked,' he said to Pam, laughing. He stood, tossed the remaining drizzle of vodka into the glass, and knocked it back. 'Send Tatiana to my apartment.'

He checked his Rolex watch. '—for 2am, I will return by then. But afterward, I want a new girl. Fresh, innocent and virginal; somebody that knows what she's doing,' he said, snorting, knowing the contraction and impossibility of what he'd asked for. Pam knew he didn't expect or want a virgin, but rather a youngish girl, to play at it. To pretend whilst being very experienced.

'I will see what I can do.'

'No rush. I take Tatiana first. Then nice new girl after.'

Chapter 21 — Aunty June (1980s, Churchyard)

The image of tossing a stupid glass of water down the sink cycled through June's head for the unknown time. Why hadn't she simply tossed it away before running? It would have taken seconds. Seconds to avert the mess she'd created. She hadn't wanted to kill anybody. It was so easily avoidable, and that bothered her more than the death itself. Iris wouldn't die. The police wouldn't arrest Ma. She would go on sneaking into Ivan's bedroom. Taking his socks. His pants. His used tissues. Never again. She had screwed up. Well, and truly.

'Come on! Put your boots on,' Fran said, grabbing her coat. She had been in a foul mood since Ma's arrest, and June's sulking wasn't helping. Dejected, she sat on the bottom step of the staircase with her head wedged between her legs and her hair drooping to the ground. She looked like a soggy mop.

'What are we going to say to her?' June said from beneath her hair.

'It doesn't matter. Just put your boots on so we can go. She's alone. I can't believe how selfish you are.'

Fran yanked June's arm, pulling her out of the mental and physical bottom step cocoon. She stumbled forward onto the carpet. Fran threw a pair of boots down beside her. 'Put them on.'

June scowled at the boots and swapped them for the pair she wanted to wear. As she zipped up the first boot, she sighed dramatically. 'It wasn't Ma.'

'Of course, it wasn't Ma, you idiot,' Fran said, beyond irritated at her stupid comment. She didn't want to tell June a third time, but watching her put the boot on so slowly caused her to lose the little temper she had left. 'Hurry up and put your pissin' boots on June! For God's sake, Ma is waiting in a cell.'

June zipped up the other boot at the same speed. She didn't take a coat. It was too hot. 'You don't need a coat,' she said to Fran, who ignored her. She pushed her out the door and locked up.

Outside, they walked in silence until they reached the churchyard, which cut through to the police station. 'I can't see her again,' June said, halting on the narrow path. Tombstones stretched either side of them. It was a beautiful day and a clear blue sky hung over the steeple and church tower.

Fran didn't stop moving. She had too much rage inside her and she was boiling. If she stood still, it would have nowhere to go and she would explode. She couldn't handle June's pathetic narcissism in the heat. Her pace quickened. 'Then stay here, you selfish cow!'

June clutched her head with both hands, and tears mixed with sweat on her cheeks. She needed to confess. 'It was me!' she said, shouting across the churchyard.

Fran stilled a couple of yards before the main path beside the church. A woman pushing a pram approached in the opposite direction. Fran shifted off the path, making room for the pram to pass. The women avoided looking at her. Who was this crazy woman hovering on the grass in a thick winter coat on the hottest day of the year? The woman gripped the pram's handle and rushed past. Fran didn't care about looking crazy. Her heart pumped more fury than blood.

June didn't move out of the path. She stood weeping, her hands covering her face. The lady veered the pram onto the grass to pass around, eager to get away from the radioactive space between Fran and June, by whatever means, as quickly as possible. June's sobs became louder as the lady passed. The pram's wheels returned to the pavement, and the woman hurried away. June and Fran were alone.

'You have allowed them to keep her in a cell for two nights. Sat across her, broken, ashamed, and scared to death, without saying a word. You—'

Fran's mouth dried up. She couldn't believe it; had too many insults to hurl, her system crashed. Her face tensed like a boxer as she readied herself for punches. Fury burnt along an internal string attached to dynamite. Ticking. Like a clock, her muscles twitched to the beat of time, counting down to some arbitrary time. Once it arrived, she would blow. Would make June pay; would hold her to account. Bring repentance to her selfish, idiotic sister.

June continued to weep. The inside of her palms pressed against her face, leaving wet slime from the mixture of snot and tears. She was distraught; blanked out the world; made Fran disappear; muted her words. She put herself back into a mental cocoon. Left the real world, leaving her body in the churchyard.

Fran thought of Ma sat alone in the visiting room waiting for them. She tugged each of her coat sleeves, took three breaths without exhaling, and forced herself to walk on. Her legs did not feel her own. They carried her, not exactly against her will, but independently of it. She had to keep moving to avoid detonating on the spot. Like a devoted lieutenant or that friend that steps in to break up a fight, her legs removed her from the danger zone. Away from June. Away from the stupid woman, allowing their Ma to wrongfully sit in a cell.

Fran blitzed past the unstained glass windows of the post-reformation church. The non-saints watched her march beneath them, and prayed for the ease of her angry strides.

June remained in the same spot, pressing wet, gluey hands against her face, spending her last days of freedom in agonising self-pity and despair. She was going to prison.

Fran didn't turn back. She stormed through the gap in the stone wall, having cleared the church. She crossed the empty ring-road without looking for cars and rushed to the police station. At the entrance, she gripped the handrail beside the imperious Victorian lamps and stepped up to the platform beside the door. She paused, looked up the stiff posts supporting the lamps and imagined them saluting her actions. She had to do this. It was the right thing. There was no room for doubt. Just get on with it. Hesitation was too painful. It would allow the suffering awaiting June to pollute her conscience. Infect her with doubt. She felt a stab of terror as she pictured June still standing in the churchyard. Enough. Her hand stretched for the door handle. There was no question to Fran that June was going to prison. Indeed, that it was even right. But it was painful. No matter how right it was. She didn't want it.

Her legs motorised.

Fran stepped into the police station and clarified the situation, told the officers June had killed Iris. They already suspected June had done it. The arrest of Ma was a sneaky, underhand ploy to elicit June's confession. They didn't suspect Ma, but it worked. Fran, though, would forever believe she caused the police to know it was June.

Several officers flocked out of the station to collect June from the churchyard. As they approached, she remained in the frozen standing position, hands glued to face, tears trickling. The officers didn't cuff her. They shuffled her to the station with arms wrapped around her shoulders, guiding her past the church and across the ring-road without making her remove her hands from her face. She would go down without a fight.

Chapter 22 — Baby Summer (2000s, Harvester)

Scarlet pulled the pram off the train. The front wheels landed on the platform as a bloke squeezed himself beside the hood, too impatient to wait. The other wheels landed a second after. Arsehole.

Scarlet veered to the far side, allowing the other passengers to rush ahead. Nobody offered to help load or unload the pram on the tubes or trains, but she mostly preferred it that way; enjoyed feeling independent, even if it was exhausting.

Summer groaned, not enough for Scarlet to stop pushing the pram. She wheeled onward to the overpass, reversing the pram and pulling it up with each step. The bumps entertained Summer. She chuckled at each built up bounce. 'Ready? Steady? Go.' Chuckle. 'Ready? Stead? Go.' Chuckle.

At the top, Scarlet wiped her sweaty brows, wishing the nap on the train lasted longer than it did. Although Summer slept the entire journey, Scarlet wouldn't allow herself to switch off, setting her phone to vibrate every ten minutes in case she nodded off. It was a double-edged sword; Summer sleeping obviously made the journey easier, but it whacked them out of sync.

Going down was harder work. Scarlet lifted Summer out of the pram, gripped her, and angled it one wheel at a time down each step. Again, nobody offered to help. She was really sweating by the time she reached the ground. She rested Summer back in the pram, let her hold her finger for a minute, assuring her she was still there, then wheeled to the station exit.

She parked the pram beside the wall, took her handbag from the tray beneath the hood, and searched for her mobile phone. She activated the screen, morphing the digital clock into a pin request. Summer squirmed and began crying. Scarlet ignored her for the moment. She opened her texts to compose a message. 'Just arrived. On time! See you in 30mins X'.

The message sent and an old-fashioned swirling noise. It suctioned like the last drop of water draining through a plug hole. She waited thirty seconds, hoping Marc Cliff would reply. He didn't. She put the phone away and lifted Summer from the pram, acknowledging her need for attention. 'Hello, you little fuss pot. You knew Ma was sending a message to Daddy, didn't you? Yes, you did, and you didn't want to be left out. No, you didn't. But don't worry, my precious baby girl. No man will ever come before you. No, they will not because you are too gorgeous. Yes, you are. You are a little gorgeous pie. I could never love a man as much as you. No, I couldn't.'

Scarlet blew raspberries on Summer's cheeks, turning her cries into chuckles. She was in her rightful place. The centre of the world. Scarlet's world. Scarlet planted several kisses across her face, then rested Summer back into the pram, eager to get going. The walk would take her twenty-five-minutes.

But as soon as they set off, Summer began crying again. She must be hungry. Scarlet parked the pram once again, lifted Summer out, and rocked her lovingly against her chest as she searched her bag for a milk bottle.

Scarlet perched on the wall between Blockbuster videos and the train station, shuffling Summer from arm to arm and repeatedly offering her the bottle. She was reluctant to set back off until the bottle was empty, knowing Summer would stir again if she didn't drink it all. It took longer than usual. The more Scarlet worried and hurried Summer, the slower and longer she took. Fifteen minutes went by in the blistering heat.

'You are a little diva. Yes, you are,' she said, placing Summer back in the pram while telling herself she needed to pick up the pace in order to make it on time. She did. She paced along the streets, overtaking old and young alike with the pram.

At the restaurant carpark, sweat dripped down her forehead and though nobody else could see, her armpits were wet and uncomfortable. She checked the digital clock on her phone. Only five minutes late. Impressive.

She pushed the pram into the shade beside the building and gave herself a couple of minutes to cool off. Regain composure. She didn't want him seeing her sweaty and flustered, but had accepted she would never look her best. Even without the walk, she'd had a baby. He had to accept her body would be different, perhaps for a long time. Perhaps forever. 'I've given birth. Raised a child. Alone,' she said, armouring herself against potential criticism.

She pulled her handbag once again from the pram's tray and removed her phone. Marc had responded fifteen minutes ago. 'Brilliant. Am running a bit late. Will be there in half an hour. Can't wait to see you! X'

Against the backdrop of annoyance for having rushed unnecessarily, gratitude got the better, washing over her like a cool shower. His being late gave her a good ten minutes to catch her breath and freshen up. She gripped the pram and hurried into the restaurant, heading straight for the loo, where she could change Summer's nappy, splash some water on her face, and spray a bit of deodorant.

Summer was as good as gold in the bathroom. 'She's gorgeous,' an older woman said to Scarlet as she washed her hands.

'Thanks.'

The woman stroked Summer's cheek before leaving. 'Enjoy her before she becomes a teenager and makes your life a living hell.'

Scarlet placed Summer back in the pram and headed for the exit. She found it tricky manoeuvring the pram around the bend, but she had the foresight to pull, rather than push, and just about managed without breaking a sweat.

She asked the waitress for a table, glad she'd be there before Marc. Not the other way around. It was petty, but him coming to her was comforting, and she'd take comfort wherever she could get it. The waitress went to lead her to a large window table with plenty of room, but as they walked across the flowery carpet, Marc Cliff stood from an awkward table tucked into a narrow alcove. Perfect for a romantic couple. Totally inappropriate for a pram.

He waved them over, but Scarlet was three steps ahead. She scanned the space on instinct and knew the pram wouldn't fit. 'I'm sorry, is it alright if we take the window seat so there's enough room for the pram?' Scarlet said, directing the question somewhere between Marc and the waitress.

Marc over spoke the waitress—she agreed the pram would not fit. 'It'll fit,' he said, striding over to take control. Scarlet and the waitress knew with utter certainty it would not, but Scarlet gave the waitress a look that told her not to challenge him. She didn't want an argument before he'd even met his daughter.

Scarlet darted to lift Summer out of the pram before he grabbed it and started heaving. As predicted, it wouldn't go. He tried forcing it into the space, and Scarlet only intervened when she thought he was going to break it.

'Marc, it's not going to—'

He realised she was right and changed course before being backed into a corner. '—Yes. It's too narrow. Stupid putting a table here, really—' he said, giving the waitress a dirty look. '—We'll take the window table. It'll work better for us. You need to tell the manager to sort this out, though. We could have broken the pram trying to get it down there.'

He spoke in such a way that made it seem as if the window table had been his idea the entire time. And that the waitress had tried to push the smaller table on him, scamming him into a lower quality product for the same price.

Scarlet smiled at the waitress with pleading eyes that begged her to not react. It worked. The waitress took pity on Scarlet for having a child with such a rude, argumentative idiot. She smiled back at Scarlet and ignored Marc for her sake.

Scarlet stepped forward to reclaim the pram. She pulled it out of the wedge and followed the waitress toward the window table. Marc followed.

She parked the Pram neatly beside the wall, lifted Summer out and placed her onto Marc's lap before sitting down herself. He hadn't asked or offered to take her and looked awkward, as if he were handling a doll.

'Meet your daughter. Summer.'

He twisted her around and they stared at one another. Summer's legs dangled freely. Marc's face steeled, hard. Their eyes both examined the tiny reflection tucked away in the middle of one another's pupils.

Scarlet watched him handle their daughter. She arrived, having no desire for a relationship. Nick had convinced her to accept Marc's help; had encouraged her to allow him to play his part in Summer's upbringing if he was willing, which he was, at least in principle. But seeing him hold Summer made her skin prickle. Goosebumps and butterflies. She wanted him.

Marc inspected Summer like a Victorian schoolmaster would a pupil, or Bill Sikes would his dog. With interest and perhaps even attachment, but lacking in warmth. Unable to let go of himself. The reflection unnerved him. He disliked the thought of any aspect of himself as somehow outside. Shared. Or other. He was who he was. And that was it. He had other children, and they had failed to disturb his self-containment. Summer would be no different.

He continued examining her, weighing up her utility. She posed no immediate threat; indeed, she may even bring value to his life. His own children, now adults, were a disappointment. They barely visited and when they did, it usually involved wanting something. Money. He could have another go with Summer. She could be his fresh start. He glanced at Scarlet and smiled at her. 'I want to be a better man,' he said. Though she had played out the scenario of him wanting a relationship. Them together as a little family. He had sent text messages suggesting so. She had turned up, ready to let him down, ready to lower expectations.

His words brought a weight, the messages lacked. She brushed her hair behind her ears and rubbed the little scar behind her lobe. 'Marc, I want you to be as big a part of her life as you want—'

'—But?'

He lifted Summer higher into his chest, already putting her value to use. She was nothing to be afraid of. She could help him assert his own agenda; could help him convince Scarlet to be with him. He rubbed her cheek and squeezed her tight, using the sight of a loving father holding his daughter to paint the picture of the wholesome family they could be. Rightfully together.

Scarlet enjoyed seeing them together. Her stomach softened and her shoulders relaxed. She hadn't realised how good it would feel; how strong the pull would be to integrate him into their lives. Have him around to share the mothering. To share the care—the feeding, the cuddling, the nappy changes. The step-by-step mounting of the pram, up and down flights of stairs. The ability to pop to the shop alone for ten minutes. Somebody to split night duties with. Endorphins flooded her system. Chemicals of happiness, persuading her to go for it. But she was headstrong and knew her feelings weren't reliable in this situation; knew his interest would wane as soon as reality kicked in. Marc Cliff was an egoist. A child himself. Self-interest would not come close to the endless well of love required to raise a child. The utter devotion and sacrifice to something so vulnerable and needy. Then moody and churlish. At her core, she knew he would never be up to the job. That she'd end up like his wife, alone in the night, while he slipped out for a younger model to titillate his fancies. He wasn't a man or a father. Not in the way it matters.

Scarlet smiled with genuine affection. She didn't need Marc to be anything other than himself. Didn't need any man. She was prepared to do it alone. He wouldn't change, and she certainly had no intention of trying to make him. She put his domestic fantasy aside.

'This doesn't need to be about us. I'm not asking for anything, just offering a chance to be a part of her life—if that's something you want. We can figure out what we are later—again, if that's something you want,' she said, deceiving him with false hope. 'There's absolutely no pressure.'

She gave him control, suggesting a willingness for a relationship. It was all he needed. Possibility. Scarlet could one day become his new wife. He looked back into Summer's face and even cooed at her. He rubbed her cheek again.

'I'm taking her to visit my Ma afterward.'

Scarlet never spoke about her family. Their relationship was exotic and fantastical. Adventurous. Not realistic. Marc would take her on the Eurostar train to Paris, where they would dine out in expensive restaurants, sipping wine and eating food, pretending to enjoy it. They would tell one another their desires, brushing their legs together as they spoke. He would occasionally stroke her thigh, and she would always take an espresso at the end of the meal, energising herself for the rest of the evening. Reality was an infectious disease. Neither of them wanted to go near it.

Marc imagined himself as an award-winning crime novelist. He'd begin reading again, too, after losing the joy of it. He blamed it on teaching, but Scarlet doubted he'd ever really enjoyed books. Reading was a means to an end. Getting ahead. It wasn't about taking pleasure from spending time in other people's worlds. He didn't do vicarious life.

Scarlet dreamed of travelling to Egypt, seeing the sphinx and the Valley of the Kings. She fantasised about trekking through the red rocks and deserts of Petra; worshipping at the giant Buddhas on Lantau Island. She craved spiritual awe. Wonder.

Their relationship depended on red-wine and bistro chat. Pipe-dreaming. Flirtatious tit-for-tat and foreplay to idealised sex, which almost always failed to live up to expectations. Neither would acknowledge the disappointing end. The residual flatness left after the euphoria burst. Instead, they'd light a cigarette in bed, and share it while telling one another how amazing the evening had been. They'd wake up the next day and use the hangover as proof of just how great a time they'd had.

They'd return to their lives, not even knowing each other's full name. Well, Marc would. It began as role-play: on an early trip, they consciously pretended to be Parisians, Pierre Martin, a grand aristocrat, and Miss Pearl, a struggling artist. The names stuck. They called each other Pierre Martin and Miss Pearl on subsequent trips. Marc still had her saved in his phone as Miss Pearl. To him, her real name would never matter. What was a name compared to the smooth legs and body of a nineteen-year-old girl? Especially when that girl found his 50-year-old dad-bod attractive.

Scarlet could never forget who he was, though. His reality was already a fantasy to her: she was sleeping with a teacher from her old school. Mr Cliff. The authoritative, demanding Mr Cliff.

'You can come—if you want?' Scarlet said, inviting Marc to granny Finch's.

The waitress interrupted. She placed glasses of water on the table and let them know it was a buffet service so they could help themselves to food whenever they were ready. Scarlet nodded and thanked her. Marc asked for a beer. She went off to collect it.

'—If you want to be a serious part of Summer's life, then it makes sense for you to meet my family. It will make pickups and drop-offs easier. What do you think?'

He scrunched his nose at the idea of pickups and drop-offs. His head was still in the romantic image of them living together as a family. But equally, he liked she wasn't rushing him into commitments. They could change their living arrangements when it was convenient. It wasn't as if he was ready to pay for an additional apartment. He'd have to sell the house first. Have to tell his wife, they were getting divorced. The more he thought, the more attractive "pickups" and "drop-offs" became. He could take Summer off for the day. Do something fun. Keep her separate from the wife until it was time. Yes. Pickups, good idea.

'Meeting the family?' He said rhetorically, smiling at his daughter, then back at Scarlet. '—Why not? I can be charming.'

He did not mean it ironically or self-deprecatingly. She picked up he was going for 50% fact, 50% sexy and forced herself to swallow the impulse to laugh, knowing a snort would have irritated him at best; angered him at worst. The immediate yearning she felt for him was already wearing off. He was an idiot. How hadn't she seen it before? And with no drugs or wine in her system, she wasn't even sure she found him attractive. The allure for a partner remained strong, but it was increasingly clear Marc Cliff would never be it. Sobriety and motherhood had given her back judgment and taste.

But her not wanting him didn't stop her from letting him become part of Summer's life—if he wanted.

She saw the man in front of her; saw how immature and egoistically fragile he was beneath the dominance. A tragedy, really. Worthy of quiet pity, not derision, she thought, standing and gesturing that they head for the buffet. She was starving. Apart from a packet of crisps on the train, she hadn't eaten since last night. She leant over and stroked his arm, telling him what he wanted to hear. 'You charmed me. Now come on. Let's get some food.'

She came across sultry, unintentionally so. Her lips puckered, her chest lifted, and her shoulders drew back. He stood, and handed Summer over, needing his hands for the buffet, and in the short term, to place on her hip. She wiggled herself free as they walked to the counter. He didn't mind the resistance, interpreting it as coyness. 'Don't worry about feeling fat—' he said, whispering into her ear. '—More flesh for me to devour.'

He snorted in her ear, and Scarlet endured it without letting on as she bent down for a plate, gripping Summer with her arm and hand. They plated up, reminisced about their trips while eating, and then paid-up, eager to meet the family.

As they walked out, Scarlet asked about his divorce. It hadn't happened. Apparently, they settled on a separation instead. Kept the home and assets together and took their own bedrooms. He said it wasn't the right time to sell; and that there was no rush because his wife had taken it all really well. Scarlet suspected he was making two-thirds of it up, but it wasn't her business, and from her perspective, the less she knew, the better. She wasn't his secretary or therapist and didn't want to set any precedents for playing either role.

Marc wanted Scarlet to ask more questions about it, especially his wife; he got a kick out of talking about the real stuff and people in his life. It was fresh territory. Felt scandalous. Naughty. A nod to the old times.

When Scarlet changed the conversation, he sulked. She had graduated out of the fantasy stage of their relationship and couldn't play along earnestly. She was here for Scarlet. That was it. Marc didn't get it. To him, she could now be the ultimate cocktail: two parts fantasy. One part reality. The best of both. Wife and mistress. Why wasn't she up for it?

He also sensed it was a fight she wouldn't have right now, and rather than force it, he took comfort in savouring it for later. He banked his first guaranteed argument and would use it to propel them into a heated dispute, ending in passionate sex when the time was ready. Like a miser with coins in storage, his mood lifted.

Outside, they worked together to collapse the pram and get it into Marc's green Volvo. He ignited the engine and reversed the car, ready to visit granny Finch.

'So where does she live? No, wait. Let me guess,' he said, tapping the steering wheel as the car chugged in neutral in a parking bay facing the exit.

Scarlet held Summer on her lap and smugly awaited his condescension.

'Got to be in the catchment area for George Eliot school, obviously. But the fact you've never ended up in one of my classes means you must be from the better side. Whitestone?'

His reference to teaching lower sets was not self-deprecating. He saw it as a badge of honour that he had the power and fear to subdue unruly children. Only the best taught the worst was his philosophy. It also helped there were no expectations of his students to achieve results. Keeping them in the classroom, silenced, was a job well done. Whether they learnt anything was neither here nor there. He faced her expectantly, not liking to be wrong. She enjoyed twisting her head to reveal a smirk that told him he was wrong.

'Well, it must be Attleborough then, as you're definitely not a Hill Top girl.'

Scarlet kissed Summer on the head to prevent herself from reacting, let alone responding to his prejudice. She nodded, avoiding confrontation. She didn't want them arriving heated or moody. 'Marston Lane. The Green side,' she said, clarifying the address.

'On the edge there!' He said, shifting the car into first gear. They moved toward the exit as he pursued the conversation. 'I can't believe my daughter's Mom is an almost Hill-Top girl. You must have been an exception to the rule, to not end up in the bottom sets.'

Scarlet ignored him, nodding along, despite rejecting the premise of his statement. Her attention drifted to the outside. She wondered whether visiting her Ma was such a good idea. The romantic Marc in Paris getaways; the alluring out-of-bounds Mr Cliff from school; and the soppy man in the text messages gave way to the very real asshole sitting beside her.

It was one thing to develop a relationship for the sake of Summer, another to involve the entire family. What was her Ma going to think of him? She rubbed the scar at the back of her earlobe and felt anxious she had done the wrong thing. She never should have listened to Nick.

Summer woke, her bright blue eyes reminding Scarlet of a crisp, wintery day. Warm open fires against a clear blue sky. Her hesitation melted away. It was the right thing to do. He is her father. They would understand it wasn't about them. That it is about Summer. She had a right to know her father, something Scarlet, Lilly, Ma, June and Fran never had. It is the right thing. She told herself again.

Marc rammed the gearstick into fourth gear and forced the car into a dangerous speed along Eastborough way. Summer cried at the unfamiliar movements. The twists and turns of the fast-moving car. Scarlet whipped her nipple out to distract Summer from the turbulence, drawing her attention to something familiar and comforting. Warm milk. They'd be there in a few minutes. Just get through it, she told herself.

Chapter 23 — Nanny Evelyn, Part 1 (2000s, Gadsby Street)

Evelyn placed the shopping bags on the cobbled street, leaning them against the brick wall while she waited for Ma to answer the door. She still kept a key, but used it so rarely that it'd be at the bottom of her handbag by now. Much easier to wait. Ma used her walker to get to the door. She tried not to rely on it, but needed to more each year.

'Did you see Julie Anderson has got a new car?' Ma said, hobbling back along the hallway with its familiar musty wallpaper. She tilted the zimmer frame toward the living room and went in. The same wallpaper from thirty years ago. It was almost fashionable again. Evelyn took the shopping bags into the kitchen. The same worktops as forty years ago.

'I don't know where she's going to drive it,' Ma said, shouting from the living room.

Evelyn listened to her rant about Julie Anderson's new car while unpacking and putting away the shopping: a tub of margarine, two glass-bottles of milk, and a box of 6 eggs. All in the fridge.

Ma turned off the television and pottered into the kitchen. She filled the kettle on autopilot, taking two mugs from the cupboard as it hovered beneath the sink. After plonking the tea bags into each mug, she asked Evelyn if she wanted a drink. Not needing an answer.

'Have you seen Fran?' Evelyn said, closing the fridge and scrunching the carrier bags, ready to place in the bin.

'Don't throw those away,' Ma said, taking the scrunched bags and popping them in the cupboard among several hundred more she had stored. 'She's at Rachel's.'

Ma opened the fridge and pretended to search for something. She took out the milk, realising she did actually need it for the tea. Evelyn didn't challenge Ma's denial of Fran's relationship with Rachel. 'When did she last come round?'

'Popped in yesterday. She dropped off a birthday card for Rose. 92. Can you believe it?'

Evelyn shook her head. Though she didn't think about or appreciate the magnitude of Rose's age. It was just a number. She opened the backdoor and lit a cigarette, standing just outside to smoke it. 'Did she have much to say?'

'Not really.'

Ma poured boiling water into the mugs and took the fresh milk bottle to the fridge, exchanging it for the one already open. She stirred in the old milk and said to Evelyn, as if she'd only just remembered, '—she said something about their centre thing opening next month. Did she mention it?'

After inhaling, Evelyn squashed out the cigarette in the empty jar kept beside the back door. A pseudo-ashtray. The smoke fizzled out into the crisp air. She shut the door and took the tea. 'I haven't seen her this week.'

'—I don't know what good it'll do.'

Evelyn sipped the tea, ignoring Ma's negativity. She changed the subject away from Fran and Rachel. 'Scarlet's coming up today,' she said, still speaking to Ma like a child. Some things never changed.

'—Is she?' Ma said, turning into pop eye after a tin of spinach. Her energy and enthusiasm spiked. 'Why didn't you tell me earlier? Is Summer with her?'

'Yes.'

Evelyn prevented Ma's mood from souring like rotten milk. She took Ma's mug, and they shuffled back into the living room together.

'What time she's getting here?'

'She's already here.'

Evelyn sat on the sofa, and Ma lowered herself into her armchair. A new rose-petal three-piece suite. Technically, second-hand, and six years old, but it felt new to Ma.

'Where is she then?' Ma said, confused. If Scarlet was in town, why wasn't she here? She couldn't have anything more important to do than visit her own family. 'Is she coming straight here?'

'She's heading to mine after taking Summer to visit the dad.'

'He's from around here? I thought he was from London. Why's she in London if the dad's from around here? That doesn't make any sense.'

Evelyn shrugged. Ma could work out why Scarlet left if she wanted to know. The same way she did. But Ma wasn't interested in knowing the truth. Ma didn't do that, Evelyn thought as she shrugged off the questions. Easier to feign ignorance. Keep things on the surface. Depth only led to arguments.

'Who is he?' Ma asked.

'She didn't want to say until after she'd met him. I'm not sure if he wants to be involved.'

Ma huffed, the closest she'd come to outright derision. 'What man does?'

'I'll check to see if she's messaged.'

Evelyn fetched her handbag from the kitchen and sifted through for her mobile. She hadn't heard it go off, but she might have missed the bleep while walking back. She sat back down on the sofa and used both her hands to tap her pin code into the plastic buttons. A message from Scarlet appeared, sent ten minutes earlier.

'We're on our way now. Hope it's alright that Summer's dad is coming too X.'

Evelyn typed a response before telling Ma what the message said. *'Yes. At Ma's. But will leave now. See you in 10 mins X.'*

Ma asked three times what was happening. Evelyn murmured for her to hold on for a second while she ensured the message sent. It had. She put the phone in her handbag and stood, telling Ma that Scarlet and Summer were on their way, and that she had to get home quickly to meet them. Ma was irate.

'Tell her to come here! I want to see little Summer as well. It's very selfish not to bring her round, Lyn. I haven't seen her yet. Can't you ring and tell her? Go on, ring. Tell her to come straight here.'

The short sentences fired at Evelyn like pellet shots as her mobile bleeped again. Another message from Scarlet. Evelyn removed her phone to read it.

'Hi Ma. We've just arrived at yours, but we're in the car, so stay there. We might as well drive over to Nan's. X.'

'They're coming here instead,' Evelyn said to Ma, abbreviating the message.

Scarlet sent another text, which bleeped while the phone was still in Evelyn's hand.

See you in 5 mins. X.'

'What's she said now?' Ma asked.

'She's bringing the dad with her,' Evelyn said, not answering the question Ma asked, but telling her the information she needed. Ma sprung up quicker than she had in years. The house wasn't messy, but her immediate thought was to tidy something. It was one thing to disregard a man's worth in his absence; quite another to expose her home in his physical presence. She patted-down her trousers and cardigan.

'Do I look alright?' She asked, as the object of cleaning became herself.

'You look fine, Ma,' Evelyn said, standing and patting down her own trousers and top. With less conviction, though. 'Do I?'

Ma nodded, although she hadn't looked, and Evelyn wouldn't have noticed even if she did. Evelyn stopped caring about her appearance a long time ago, despite remaining well dressed. It'd become more of a habit to put on nice clothes. Instinct. Not concern for how she looked to others.

They moved into the kitchen. Ma shuffled, sorted and re-sorted the plethora of items on the small table: clingfilm'd bread rolls, a tin of biscuits, stacked birthday cards for Rose, a box of eclairs for Gran. Evelyn opened the backdoor and lit another cigarette. The table looked the same when she came back in. They heard the car pull up outside; heard the doors slam shut and the front door knock.

They expected a scruffy teenager. 18 or 19. Maybe even early twenties. Boyhood still visible in his facial features. Not a fifty-year-old bloke. When Marc Cliff bored back their stare, Ma crossed her cardigan in a dignified surprise. Scarlet's man was older than her children. For that, Ma gave him instinctual respect, regardless of who or what he was. Whereas Evelyn felt violated; stung by a thousand needles on the spot. His eyes jabbed at her like a pitchfork, pressing into her stomach. Yet she steeled her legs and summoned a defensive smile, forcing herself against the self-hatred and even stronger hatred for Marc Cliff to not make a scene.

Ma rushed to whip Summer from Marc's arms. She was cooing and blowing raspberries into her soft cheeks while reversing and tunnelling back into the living room. Scarlet introduced Marc and Evelyn to one another in the narrow corridor. Intimate. Scarlet pressed her back against the row of coats, creating the illusion of more space. Marc swept his arm out straight for Evelyn to shake like a solid piece of wood. 'Nice to meet you,' he said.

Evelyn was twenty years older than when Marc had last slept with her. But he recognised her intelligent blue eyes and caged soul. Scarlet made much more sense to him. He relived memories of touching Evelyn all those years ago; pictured gripping her palms and rubbing himself down her back. Suddenly, Scarlet made too much sense. Summer waterboarded him with sense. Now he felt violated. Truth stung him like ten thousand needles, bound his wrists and ankles to the staircase, and fucked him against his will.

Like Evelyn and the other girls, he learnt how it felt to lose voice; to have his own vocal cords abandon him when he needed them the most. Dryness throbbed his throat and soreness ached everywhere else.

Evelyn tore her hand from his, pivoting away as she spoke, 'I already know you, Mr Cliff. I was in your English class twenty years ago. Let's not pretend how unpleasant and intimidating you were. I'm not thrilled to learn you've become a part of the family.' Evelyn glanced over her shoulder to catch his reaction. '—But let's leave the past in the past.'

She, of course, did not mean it.

Scarlet's face turned lilac, somewhere between mortified embarrassment and pale sickliness. She ignored the awkward fact Marc was old enough to be her Ma's teacher. For Summer's sake. This is about Summer, she told herself. For Summer's sake, they needed to make this work. Regardless of the facts.

She clutched Marc's hand in solidarity. He resisted her affectionate touch impulsively, treating Scarlet like she was a burn. She winced. Hurt by his recoil. Noticing, Marc forced himself to take her hand and feign an apologetic smile. More than he could bear. But here he was, pushing himself, making new boundaries. Needs must.

Scarlet followed Evelyn into the living room, wondering about her and Marc together as student and teacher. Weird. More weird, though, was the way Evelyn spoke to him. So direct and bold. Lacking in self-consciousness. She'd barely seen her Ma like that with anybody, especially a man. But even stranger was Marc's timidness. Evelyn made him anxious. Nervous. She'd never seen him that way before.

And she wouldn't for much longer. Men like Marc Cliff don't exist long on the back foot. They fight back. Quickly.

He locked his grip around Scarlet's hand and pulled them into battle. Ma's living room swelled with testosterone. He remained standing in front of the gas fireplace, despite Ma's invitation to sit down. Scarlet unlocked her hand with a tug and bent down to fuss over Summer. She was in Ma's lap, and her tiny fingers reached out to prod Ma's wrists.

Scarlet pressed her shins into the carpet and rested her thighs on flattened calves, perching her bottom on her heels beside Ma's armchair. She smiled at Ma's adoration of Summer. It was warming to see somebody take the same delight as she did. It wasn't the same when Nick or Marc handled her.

'Hello beautiful,' Ma said, cooing at Summer. 'Yes. You are a little beautiful, Finch. Yes, you are. You are the most beautiful Finch. You are, aren't you? Yes. Yes. Yes.'

'Just like her, Grandma,' Marc Cliff said, lying and torpedoing Evelyn with his overconfident smugness. His way of letting her know he wasn't playing defence. She had as much to lose as he did. So might as well take back control. If she wants to call it out, that's her call. He readied himself to sort out the fuck-up. There is no way he would allow some hybrid, incestuous daughter-granddaughter monster tracing back to him, survive. It was too ugly. An abomination. His responsibility to relieve them of a wickedly inconvenient, disgusting future. He would kill it. Her. Start again with a fresh one. Marc Cliff had many flaws, but one thing he prided himself on was cleanliness. He'd clear up his own shit. Summer. No matter how messy the job was.

'Daughters don't necessarily take after the mother. They can turn out like their dad,' Evelyn said, mirroring Marc's tactics. All out offence. She allowed herself to speak on instinct; refused to think first. Let herself be guttural and dynamic. Dangerous if need be. 'Scarlet has nothing of her father in her. Luckily.'

Scarlet felt the comment as a back-handed compliment. Not to mention, inappropriate. She had asked about her father a few times; had a deep longing to know who he was. And the lack of information—Evelyn's lack of forthcoming—only intensified her desire. The longing had never drained or diluted. Why had Evelyn chosen this moment to bring him up? It felt cruel. It was one of the singularly few times, Scarlet genuinely didn't care to think about it. Today was about Summer. Not her unknown father. Scarlet frowned at Evelyn and said without saying it. That truth had remained buried for her entire life. Surely it could stay in its box for one more day?

'How about Summer?' Marc asked Evelyn with a twisted glare of evil glinting beside the white of his eyes.

Evelyn could smell as well as see his hatred. She remembered the taste of his fingers dipping into her mouth. Their spreading across her jaw, locking it into place. His dirty fingers placed in her against his garden shed, patio door, and back gate. She could now read the hatred for what it was. As a child she misunderstood, misidentified it for a thrill, danger, sex, fascination—even love. Now she knew. Hatred. Dominion. Power over something inferior and conquerable. He hated her. Hated most of his female conquests. Though Evelyn saw more. Saw what the others didn't. His dangerous indifference toward his own flesh. Toward Summer. Marc twisted his attention to her, glanced at her from his ridged position in front of the fireplace. He was going to kill her. Evelyn somehow knew. He didn't care she was his daughter. She was a problem. A weakness to eradicate.

'Too early to tell,' Evelyn said, lying about Summer's features. She had Marc's nose and his eyes. She would look just like him. Not Scarlet.

'Oh, she looks a lot like you, Mr Cliff,' Ma said, rubbing Summer's cheeks as she spoke to the authority figure towering in her living room. 'Hopefully, she'll have your brains, too. I say, a little teacher in the family!'

Ma chuckled. Scarlet winced, believing every woman in that room could run laps around Marc Cliff if they put their mind to it. As a teenager, Scarlet rallied against her nan's deference to men in a suit and tie, but she'd learned not to bite or argue. She psychoanalysed instead, concluding that an entire generation of women born before the 1960s had low self-worth and inferiority complexes. It allowed her to let their ignorant and offensive comments go, like the assumption she had no brains. No pointless arguments, she told herself. It's not their fault. She leant against the armchair, her thighs and shins still folded on the floor, smiling at Summer. Her brave warrior.

Marc swayed his hips in front of the fire and pressed his hands around his pelvis. 'Thank you, Mrs Finch. I'm sure Summer will have inherited some ambition from the mother's side of the family, too. Despite Evelyn's premature departure from school, she was quite bright, and Scarlet could have gone to college if she wanted—she had the brains. I believe it's all about ensuring children have the right opportunities in life, and I'll make sure our little Summer has plenty.'

His smirk disgusted Evelyn. She would have stabbed him there and then if she had a knife.

Ma, though, nodded along, hanging on every word the dickhead said. She also tolerated his incorrect title. Ma was Miss Finch. Not "Mrs". She'd not married.

'Actually, I am—have been—going to College. In London,' Scarlet said, confessional; repenting her sins to a priest. Ma, Evelyn, and Marc were all surprised.

'Well, there's no need to go back now you've a baby and a man,' Ma said.

"Low self-worth and an inferiority complex", Scarlet repeated in her head, dismissing Ma's archaic views.

Evelyn smiled. She still felt sick to the bottom of her stomach, but she was glad beyond words that Scarlet had gone back to school. She didn't know why. It wasn't like she valued education, given her own experiences. Something just felt right.

The smile struggled to last as her attention returned to the paedophilic baby-killer, making himself comfortable in their family home. But the thought of her surviving daughter doing something with her life tapped into the core of goodness at the well of her soul. She didn't let him take the joy away from her. The love for her daughter and the hatred for Marc Cliff coexisted in equal strength.

Evelyn often struggled to accept the simple truth that she was a good person. That she was not only capable, but actively desired good for others. She wanted more than anything for her children to be happy. It was more important than her own happiness. She wanted them to have good long lives. It was a non-circumstantial truth she lived with since the day they were born. A timeless reality and unconditional fact. She also believed herself incapable of providing for them. She wasn't strong or clever enough, and they deserved better. It was the closest she came to piety; the religious like experience of having absolute certainty.

The pain and trauma of the aborted adoption never left her: it settled like a cloud of anxiety, blocking sunlight from the loving certainty at the core of her being. The day Scarlet returned home, she lost the ability to express herself. She struggled to embrace the truth within: dry and thirsty like the ancient mariner, with water, water everywhere, but not a drop to drink. Evelyn raised her children with a heart locked away, a heart that could only hug and love through the bars of a prison cell. She lost her freedom too young; sacrificed before she had learnt how to replenish herself. Gave everything before she was ready. Before she should have. She tried—willed—herself to love her children unconditionally, but the emptiness had weeded, rooted. She couldn't undo knowing it, couldn't hide her time in the darkness. In hell. Her children saw—Lilly saw. Scarlet saw. Nick saw—saw she was never fully there. Never fully present. A demon gnawed her always. Always there.

They never fully had her. A little part, always with him; trapped behind—some place—some void. They didn't know where that place was—she was. Just waited for her to come back.

They'd wait on the staircase. The back porch. The kitchen table. For her to return. Scarlet, sitting on the floor beside the armchair, saw her Ma smile at the revelation of her attending college alone in London, whilst pregnant, and she felt it was one of those miracle moments where her Ma was there. That her love was strong enough to pierce the clouds and solder the iron bars to shine and burn through. She was there. Her soul was present; one of the few moments that the cage unclipped and her Ma flew free. Where they coexisted in the same—shared—reality.

Tears swelled in Scarlet, and she had to work hard to hold them back. She reciprocated the heartfelt smile to her Ma, acknowledging the inner journey she had made to the surface, like a great mama whale. A rare and beautiful sight.

Chapter 24 — Adult Summer (2020s, Cannes)

Summer fiddled with the envelope during take-off. She wasn't afraid of flying. She was worried about meeting the women who wrote the letters, their revealing a secret, perhaps better left buried. 'Hot towel Miss?' The attendant, tong in hand, shared steaming flannels while his colleague filled empty glasses of prosecco. She knew she had to give it a chance.

She bit her nails and thought about mother as Gatwick's grey drizzle turned into a white cloud and then blue emptiness. If she were here, her cuticles would be intact. Mother would have insisted she stop biting them. But alone, she chomped away, ignoring the health of her fingertips, let alone the gnawing guilt in her stomach. She wished mother knew about the letters, about the visit—was involved. Too late. Pull yourself together, Summer.

Three glasses of prosecco later and the plane began its descent into the French Riviera. 'Fasten seatbelts, please,' the attendants repeated while the plane windows lost the views of attractive countryside and tree hilltops. Madam Perez and Aunty Finch were out there. Summer folded the letters and stuffed them back into envelopes. No more reading. It was time to face reality.

She disembarked, climbing down the staircase of the BA plane in her turquoise heels, and breathing in the warm wind from the perfume town of Grasse. Her stilettos clacked on the aluminium frame. And against the spins, the swooshes of the blades cooling engines, Summer listened to the reverberations of her own steps with a sharp, meditative intent. She whizzed through passport control and caught a cab. No fuss. No drama.

'Merci, Madame,' the taxi driver said before speeding away from the small boutique hotel near Cannes. She wanted to meander the provincial streets, peppered with trellis and vine. Instead, she dropped her bags on the bed, threw tap water on her cheeks, and brushed her hair. It would have to do. Outside, she orientated herself using the square clock face of Saint Peter's Church and headed for the café to meet the ladies. Although it was only a short walk, she was glad of the eventual shelter from the sun, each alfresco table resting in the shade. 'De rien, Madame,' the waiter said, placing Summer's glass of Pinot. She finished most of the wine before they arrived.

Madam Perez strolled across the plaza in her ivory-coloured silk dress, a dramatic wedding hat, Louis Vuitton sunglasses, and a pair of Yves Saint Laurent heels. Aunty Finch bristled beside, lumbering in a flower print frock like some chintz obsessed pensioner. Her grey English hair hung heavy, and her flat sandals negated, rather than celebrated, her height. Chalk and cheese.

As they approached the café, both women towered over Summer, who was not short. Summer rose and stretched out a stiff hand. Madam Perez drew her own, and they shook, taking the edge off their first face-to-face meeting. Aunty Finch stood back and stared. She clutched a book at her chest, neither smiling nor frowning. Her eyes examined Summer, scanned her up and down like a X-ray machine.

Becoming rather awkward, Summer stepped away from the table. The unrestricted space allowed her to regain a sense of power. She moved forward, her arm stretching out for a handshake. But Aunty Finch spluttered to life and gushed like a river to wrap her gangly arms around Summer's slender shoulders, book still in hand. The manic acceleration unnerved Summer. She stiffened and though she returned the hug; it was a performative. Polite. Aunty withdrew, embarrassed she'd overstepped, given the lack of reciprocal affection.

Madam Perez broke the awkwardness by taking a seat, prompting Summer to follow. She removed her sunglasses and said in the thickest Mancunian accent, 'Good to meet you, Summer, love. We're glad you agreed—'

'—I'm sorry. I didn't mean to make you feel uncomfortable,' Aunty Finch said, interrupting her friend. She gripped the back of the chair and dragged it back.

Summer sipped the last drop of her Pinot, hiding her face and avoiding an immediate response. She wasn't sure what to say, and even if she did, her voice absconded. She wasn't in the forgiving mood—even as a gesture of politeness. Touching and speaking with her Aunty felt like a betrayal to mother. She held the glass close to her mouth and used it to evade Aunty's stares and expectations.

Madam Perez pulled back the empty chair. 'Sit down and give Summer some air. Hey, love?' She said, hoping to lower the intensity a notch.

'I'm sorry, Summer,' Aunty said again, stepping backward rather than sitting. She wasn't going anywhere, but she couldn't sit without first being transparent; couldn't beat around the bush and not acknowledge the reason for getting in touch. In her flower print frock, she jerked forward with the book and placed it on the table. 'Have you read it?'

Scarlet scanned the title. She was a keen reader but didn't consider herself literary. She'd studied Science at University. Very sensible. Exactly what the careers advisers and educators recommended if she wanted to get ahead, and secure a well-paid job. When she read, it was just for pleasure. Modern books. No stuffy curriculum rubbish. Nothing serious. Nothing that weird English teachers salivated over, and equated with the bible. She like the stuff on tables at the front of bookshops; novels with colourful snazzy covers she could read quickly and chat about with mother. 'I'm not a classics fan. More of a Colleen Hoover girl,' she said, glancing at the dark slab on the alfresco table.

'It's called *Daniel Deronda*. I want you to have it,' Aunty Finch said.

Summer refrained from inspecting the book. She packed light and didn't like feeling beholden for an unwanted gift. She could buy herself the book for ten quid in any bookshop in England.

'What's the girl want with that? Sit down, June. Let's order a bottle of wine and not scare anybody away,' Madam Perez said, lighting a cigarette and giving her friend a dagger'd stare. This wasn't part of the agreement. June was going off-piste. Far too intense.

'Many years ago, I did something terrible.'

'Not yet, love—' Madam Perez said, but Aunty June's voice strengthened against the resistance.

'—I served my sentence. Ten years in prison.'

Madam Perez rubbed her temple and sighed, but Aunty's enthusiasm escalated. Summer glanced at their jewellery and her heartbeat quickened. Was this some sort of swindle? Had two old jailbird cronies hoodwinked her into some scam? She almost left there and then, believing they would ask for money next. But something about Aunty June's zealous energy held her captive. She wasn't faking it.

'I cannot pay for what I did. The past is the past—I could spend my life in a cell, but it won't change what happened. I can't repair the damage. I killed her. That's it. But I can help others. Can do what I can to make the world a better place. To prevent suffering where it's possible. Even if it's got nothing to do with what I did.'

Summer twisted her neck and rubbed it. Aunty Finch was losing her with the mumbling tirade. In flat sandals and while sitting, June pushed her chair back, scraping it along the floor. She galvanised herself, sensing a moment. An opening. She lurched forward and prodded the book with her non-manicured fingernails. 'In the story, Daniel says, "feeling what it is to spoil one life may well make us long to save others from being spoiled." It's something that stuck to me. I spoiled a life—can never undo that. But I can help save yours; stop yours being spoiled.'

Summer's chair screeched backward. She rose, outraged. How dare these women prey on her? How dare they? She had a good life. Mother loved her; had paid for an excellent education, pushed her hard to make sure she was skilled and certified for a lucrative career that would ensure her independence. How had she allowed these spinsters to take advantage of her insecurities? To ruin and bring her down.

Madam Perez elbowed Aunty June. She glanced at her with told-you-so eyes, while flopping her hand to encourage her fifty-year-old companion to remain sitting down as she stood up to meet Summer, eye to eye. 'Reading a letter is one thing. Sharing a bottle of wine, something else. I get it. But please, Summer, love, I promise you, we don't want a thing.'

Madam Perez caught the waiter with her fingertips. He knew to bring the good bottle of Sauvignon without their asking. They were regulars.

Summer appeared trapped, unable to leave, having come this far, yet unable to stay, having no basis to trust either woman. Madam Perez took advantage of the delay. She clutched her fancy handbag and pulled out a fifty Euro note. She wedged it beneath the ashtray to stop it from blowing away. 'Look, finish your glass of wine and if you still feel uncomfortable, then we'll part and pretend this meeting never happened. You'll never hear from us again.'

Aunty June laid her palms flat on the table. She couldn't look at Summer in case her friend had failed to persuade her to stay. 'We've so much to tell you,' she said. Her voice hopeless. Not desperate. She expected Summer to leave. Madam Perez sat down and Summer, against her better judgement, did so, too.

'The waiter hasn't even brought a bottle over yet. Go easy on the girl,' she said, warning June to lessen the intensity. Pam Perez had not lost her accent since fleeing the country to live in France.

'I have a good life,' Summer said, owing mother due recognition. 'I'm not here because I'm worried about my life being spoiled.'

The phrase left a nasty taste in her mouth. Pam placed her hand on Aunty June's, less out of solidarity and more out of control. She didn't want her pumping up again. It worked. June contained her reaction and

Pam's willingness to take charge without being domineering or cruel, disarmed Summer's scepticism. It put her at sufficient ease to hear the ladies out. She wasn't the type to go weak at the knees without serious cause, and she didn't feign feelings. What did she have to lose from just listening? She was smart enough to leave if things turned shady.

'If you have something to tell me, I'll listen. But I'm not a fool—'

'—Of course you're not!' June said, looking and sounding hurt. Pam squeezed her hand, this time lovingly. It reminded them of why they were there. Calmed June. Allowed her to regain composure and apologise. 'Sorry—'

'—Love, it's almost time to tell her everything, just let her say her piece first,' Pam said, taking charge again. It stilled the emotions. June nodded and looked at Summer, apologetic and patient.

'I want to know what happened to her—to me,' Summer said. June didn't interrupt. 'I want to know what happened; why she did it—'

The waiter returned with a crisp Sauvignon Blanc and poured each of them a glass. After he walked away, Summer got the last question—the one she'd come for—off her chest. 'Did she love me?'

Chapter 25 — Nanny Evelyn, Part 2 (2000s, Gadsby Street)

Marc became irritated on three fronts: first, Scarlet going back to college. Second, her not telling him first. Third, her doing it in London. She was his sexy, rootless bohemian, not some trainee feminist, being brainwashed by a group of menopausal women, spouting commie liberal bollocks. 'Some back water college diploma dished out by discredited radicals is hardly going to help you achieve anything in the long run. Summer came along just in time. Just in time! I've seen these zealots get their claws into too many vulnerable and impressionable female minds. You won't be going back there.'

'Don't be silly. Bronwyn is lovely and—'

'—Bronwyn?' Marc said, scoffing at the name alone as if it proved everything. Arrogant as well as prejudiced. A drop of spit flicked into his beard. Everybody noticed straight away, except Marc. They looked away to give him a moment, in which he noticed, and rubbed it away with his fingers, believing none of them saw. 'So she's Welsh and a communist!' He elaborated, given nobody had responded to his first comment.

Scarlet didn't want a fight, but she owed the woman. 'Bronwyn,' she said, stressing each syllable of her name, making it sturdy. Dependable. '—is from Bristol. And she went above and beyond for me when our daughter was born. She stayed with me in the ambulance, called Nick, and didn't leave the hospital until the end.'

'—Generous, but hardly validation of her teaching competence!' he said, animatedly and without pause. 'In fact, it implies she's incapable. She clearly doesn't have the knowledge or expertise. The hard information. So she chums up to students, "winning them over", as people say. So vulgar. You deserve better than that, Scarlet. You deserve a serious, impartial educator. Somebody that knows what they're doing; appreciates the necessary distance between teacher and pupil. I could do a better job. You'd learn much more. Trust me on this one, darling.'

'You don't know what you're talking about,' Scarlet said, curt and direct. It sent Ma into a fit, but drew another affectionate smile from Evelyn. She was still present; in the room with Scarlet. And she didn't need to point out his hypocrisy, because her daughter had grown up smart enough to call it for herself.

'Don't be so rude, Scarlet! The man has just offered to help you,' Ma said, scooting Summer into her upper arms and twisting her upper body to look Scarlet in the face as she told her off.

'Thank you, Mrs Finch, but don't worry. If Scarlet wants to continue with a second-rate teacher, that's her choice. Stupid and ignorant. But she knows best. I'll be here when she changes her mind. I only want to help.'

'It's Miss Finch—Ma never married,' Evelyn said. She'd never asked Ma who their father was. Never asked about her love life. To them, Ma was practically a nun. Not in their entire life had they seen her with a man. It wasn't a topic ever up for discussion. Nothing. Ever. It took Ma's breath away. She felt deeply shamed, yet also alive. Human. She was the focus of a romantic enquiry—she was never that sort of focus. Unsure of what to do or say, she remained silent, gathered her composure. The room— even Marc—gave her time.

Eventually, she faced Marc and told him to call her Fae, and with an unusual tenderness, said, 'After all, we are family now.'

Ma had a secret type of hardness, and tenderness did not come easy. Bamboo-like, she appeared soft but wasn't. She seemed tolerant, but really got through life, not thinking about most things; didn't have a rooted opinion either way. She bent around reality. Snaked it. Adapted in her own quiet way. Tenderness was an illusion, except with the babies. That was honest. Ma lacked the intimate knowledge of life outside herself to be tender. A piece of bamboo. She held herself up; spent her life among others, but didn't intertwine.

Thus, she struggled to feel proper disgust. To abhor evil. To fight it. Ma was no warrior; could connect to no cause beyond platitudes. How could she? In her self-contained world, there was no evil. Could be no suffering. She could see none. Hear none. Know none. Life on the surface was easy. Unburdensome, lacking in messy tenderness. Ma lived there. She was not soft. Softness lives in depth.

Ma shot up as somebody knocked on the front door. A welcome disturbance. She handed Summer over to Scarlet and shuffled out of the living room, hoping to break the serious atmosphere. For God's sake, they were supposed to be talking about the baby, not communist teachers and absent fathers. Why did everybody have to become so serious?

'Sorry, I forgot my key,' Fran said, leaning in to kiss Ma on the cheek. Ma still hadn't become comfortable with the cosmopolitan physical exchange of affection, which felt a little forward and unnecessary. Why did she need her 45-year-old daughter to kiss her cheek every time she arrived on the doorstep? For God's sake. Rachel Evans followed behind and leant in for the double kiss too, taking pleasure in how much Ma hated it. Hated her. Ma resented Rachel's corruption of Fran. She never said so explicitly, but it bubbled beneath the surface, irritating Ma further because it forced her to acknowledge she had a "beneath the surface". Rachel loved that even more.

'Summer is here,' Ma said, ignoring her own irritation and shutting the door. Fran was already reaching out for Summer as Scarlet brought her through to the corridor. With her free hands, she gave Rachel a big hug—Scarlet idolised her.

'How's London?' Rachel asked, hugging her back.

'Great. You'd love it,' Scarlet said, pulling a teeth-grinding, apprehensive face as she pointed toward the living room, implying there was a surprise. Not a good one.

'This is Marc—Summer's father,' Scarlet said, gliding her arm out, encouraging a formal introduction. Something more adult and civilised than Ma and Evelyn's. They each shook hands. Fran first, then Rachel. They both had firm handshakes, which Marc disliked in women. Scarlet beamed with pride as they smiled and played the game. She knew they'd hate him, but wouldn't be rude for her sake. Fran clarified who everybody was.

'I'm Scarlet's Aunt, and Rachel is my partner—'

'—Partner?' Marc said, suspiciously. To him, lesbians only existed in pornography. Not real life. And they didn't look like Fran or Rachel. He was part disgusted, part intrigued, part mesmerised. He looked at the two women like sub-species of a kimono-dragon. They belonged in a carnival cage or sanitorium.

'They are opening a centre together,' Ma said, rushing to divert the conversation. Away from what they are. Away from them. Toward something noble. '—For troubled women. Isn't it, Fran?'

Though Ma was under a misapprehension. Charity did not impress Marc. He squirmed and wriggled on the spot, still uncomfortable with the open way they handled their sexuality and increasingly hostile to this project for helping "troubled women". More of the commie liberal crap. His suspicion upgraded to an intense dislike. They were offensive, and it'd only be a matter of time before they showed their true colours. Better guard up now.

Fran bubbled into a waltz around the coffee table to sit beside Evelyn on the sofa. She cooed at Summer, bouncing her on her lap, and smothering her with compliments and kisses. 'Oh my goodness, you are the prettiest little thing I've ever seen. Yes, you are! Yes. You. Are. You gorgeous little cherry pie.'

She blew raspberries into her cheeks the way she did Scarlet when she too was a baby. 'Yes. You are. Yes. You are.'

Over the years, Evelyn forgave Fran for reclaiming Scarlet, but she never stopped wondering how Scarlet's life could have turned out with a wealthy, loving set of adopted parents. Would they have paid for her to attend a posh school? Ballet lessons? Study Maths or Science? Go to college—even university? Get a fancy job? Not had a baby with her scummy piece of shit, dad. Ruin her life. The sadness rushed back into Evelyn. The drowning hopelessness. Her forgiveness evaporated. Fran was part responsible again for the mess everyone was ignoring.

Rachel helped channel Fran's self-righteous zeal into worthy causes, loosening her up to be much more tender at home. She rarely burnt up with them anymore. Rarely lost her temper. She'd grown-up. And that went beyond accepting her sexuality. It involved making peace with her own depth, and overcoming the urge to attack or become passive aggressive when around those lacking morality and gumption. Balls. She saw Ma; accepted the unlikeliness of her ever changing, and let it go. Didn't force it. She put her energy into helping women who wanted more. Who wanted to lose their gendered shackles. She put herself into Scarlet. Into Summer. Into the women at the centre, begging for somebody to help them.

'What do you do, love? I'm sure I recognise you from somewhere,' Rachel asked Marc.

'—Let me make some tea,' Ma said, standing up and hoping the conversation would change. She had a bad habit of leaving the room or busying herself whenever Rachel spoke.

'—He's a teacher,' Evelyn said, smirking. Her slip back into hopelessness gave her a combative edge: rob a woman of everything, she's no longer under anybody's power. She can become a ferocious opponent. Evelyn knew Rachel would soon figure out who he was, and so moved the conversation forward. 'He was the rude bastard arguing with you the day you pulled me out of class and gave me a home; said his love poetry lesson was more important.'

Ma gripped the tea towel in the kitchen and squirmed at Evelyn's language, let alone the tone of hostility directed at their guest. The kettle steamed. Not enough water in it. Ma listened to the ensuing silence, flattening the tea towel on the counter, buying time before she filled the kettle. She wanted to hear what they said next before turning on the tap.

Scarlet squinted, both curious and nervousness about Evelyn and Marc's relationship. She sat back in the folded floor-position beside Ma's now empty chair. 'You know each other as well?' She said, referring to Marc and Rachel, but leaving it open as to who should respond.

Rachel placed him immediately, but Marc couldn't remember the incident at all. He'd been rude and obnoxious to countless women over the years. Rachel Evans was not special. She wasn't the first woman he'd spoken down to in front of his classes. 'I don't remember,' he said, ending the discussion.

Rachel nodded and smiled at Evelyn, sensing she needed acknowledgment, but she chose not to elaborate much detail, which she also sensed frustrated Scarlet. 'We crossed paths not long after you were born. But don't know one another.'

Rachel placed her hands into her pockets, and lifted her chest, imitating Marc's commandeering posture without it feeling like she was challenging him. They were around the same age. Rachel turned her attention to Fran. 'It was the same day we met,' she said, proud and confident of their story. Plus, she enjoyed the fact that sharing it would irritate Marc, and also Ma, who she knew was eavesdropping from the kitchen. It would also compensate Scarlet for the disappointment of not hearing more about her connection to Marc. Win-win-win.

Fran accepted the open display of affection from Rachel in a way she never would a man. It still mesmerised Evelyn to see her big sister so intimate with another person, who wasn't a baby or one of them. She would never say so, but she liked it; made her feel a little closer to the sunshine.

'You were so feisty. Told me to piss off several times. I liked you straight away—'

'—You liked a young lady for swearing at you? Call me old-fashioned, but that makes no sense,' Marc said, churlish. Nobody reacted. They knew what Rachel meant. She saw and respected Fran's gumption; her willingness to fight and defend the family. Not a vulgar display of casual swearing, which Marc suggested.

Rachel ignored him and continued in her warm, soulful voice; a voice that put people at ease. 'You didn't trust or believe a word I said—' Rachel stretched her hands while still in her pockets, causing her trousers to expand. '—You kept firing questions and criticisms. Fearless. I loved it.'

'Not true, I was afraid.'

Ma listened to her daughter contribute to the conversation as the kettle boiled.

'—Well courageous then; because you didn't allow the fear stopping you doing what needed to be done.'

Marc bristled at that phrase. He put his own hands in his own pockets and lifted his own chest. Unlike Rachel, he meant it in a challenging way. He didn't like a woman taking his rightful and natural role as the alpha male among the group. 'So how do you know me?' He said, disrupting the gushing exchange of lesbian crap.

Ma poured boiling water into each mug. The steam blew off the row of them like a little steam train.

'I've dealt with many of your students, Mr Cliff. There's been a surprisingly large amount of girls that have ended up pregnant from your classes. Those love poems or the way you teach—'

'—I don't like what you're insinuating.'

'—Tea!' Ma said, almost sprinting from the kitchen with two cups in hand and moving into the space between Marc and troublemaker Rachel, dispersing the mounting radiation building between them. She handed Marc the first cup and turned to face Rachel, giving her the second, with a frowning, pack-it-in face. Rachel dismissed the scolding. Water off a duck's back. She took the cup and leant in to kiss Ma on her cheek. It was tantamount to kicking a wasp's nest. Ma inhaled aggressively. Through her nostrils. Her lungs opened wide, giving the insects space to sting and bruise her insides before they stormed out. She rushed to the kitchen for the teas but gave herself time to regain composure before returning.

Scarlet assumed Rachel was just playing with Marc, pushing his buttons because she could. She read nothing into the allegation he took offence at.

Fran, though, knew her Rachel wouldn't insinuate something serious without a great deal behind it. Her body language hardened. To others, Fran was about to be unquestioning loyal to her partner. But it was more than that. It was intelligence. She'd watched Rachel work hundreds of cases over the years and trusted her instincts; trusted the way she gathered evidence. Diligent. Unassuming until she was sure. When she switched mode and fought hard. Became a warrior, ready to die for the cause. Brave. Ambitious. Fran saw Rachel armouring-up. There had been a switch. Marc was no good. She knew by the way Rachel readied herself.

Warring energy circled the room like a baby tornado, worrying Scarlet; thrilling Evelyn. Ma returned with two more cups of tea. She walked into the centre of the storm and placed them on the coffee table, rather than deciding who to give them to. 'I'll get some biscuits too,' she said, facing Marc. '—Do you prefer custard creams or digestives?'

But before he could answer, she said she'd bring both. It'd be no bother. She scuttled back into the kitchen, leaving the storm to thicken.

Like the sound of thunder crashing in the background, a loud knock bashed the front door. 'Hurry-up Nan! I need the loo!' Nick said, shouting from the street. He travelled back last week to escape the press. Despite Matt's assurance they wouldn't bother him, they had. The hard-faced journalists lingering around the school gates at least encouraged the headteacher to make Nick take a few weeks off. He didn't want the school's reputation associated with the wretched affair, not even by loose association. 'Come on!'

Ma had given him a key, but he'd forgotten it. He brushed past her, pacing into the downstairs loo. As he relieved himself, his leg muscles slowly settled. Ten minutes of jogging on the spot and then sprinting home worked them up. 'Is that Scarlet in the living room? She said she was coming down this week.'

Ma nodded as she rushed back into the living room. Tea in hand. Nick could make his own. She needed to stay; stop things blowing out of control, which was bound to happen if she didn't placate people, distract them from getting deep into each other's business. It's what bothered her about Rachel Evans. She wore her depth as a badge of honour, even encouraged it. Dangerous woman.

'Is that Nick?' Scarlet said, wanting to break the awkwardness by saying anything. Even if it was redundant. It was obvious it was Nick.

Ma nodded again as she placed more tea on the coffee table. Nobody had taken the first two yet. The toilet flushed and Nick wandered into the living room, more able to sink back into his morose state now he had relieved himself. Rachel and Fran greeted him with big hugs and Marc Cliff stretched a hand for a more formal introduction.

'Good to meet you. Another man to even out the amount of oestrogen,' Marc said, impressed with his banter. He didn't remember Nick from school—he'd taught him, but only as a youngster. Nick was 11, but Marc hardly remembered students he'd taught for years. There was no chance he'd remember one kid he'd taught for only a year, especially given his age and gender. Perhaps a 14 or 15-year-old, striking girl might have stood a chance.

'Nice to see you, sir,' Nick said, defaulting to a respectful tone. Earnest too.

'Nick's got more oestrogen than the rest of us put together,' Scarlet said, snorting. She was glad to see her brother.

Ma tapped Scarlet's shoulder from the armchair she sunk back into—her version of a slap. 'Don't be rude, Scarlet.'

'—What's that supposed to mean?' Marc said, bristling at Scarlet's comment. 'Don't tell me you're a faggot.'

Scarlet pivoted up and exploded at her daughter's daddy. At her daddy. 'I think people stopped using the term faggot in the 90s, especially teachers. And if you ever say it to my brother again, you'll not see your daughter. Do you understand?'

'—Please can we not use that language,' Ma said, reprimanding everybody in the room. Collective punishment, though, an insinuation that Nick and Scarlet were the instigators—not Marc. Unjust, but effective in preventing Marc from feeling like a victim; validating the chip on his shoulder; that the world was out to get him. Despite him being the predator. Always the way.

Rachel stretched her hands, still in her trouser pockets, and fought past Ma's blockade. She wouldn't tolerate his abusive, controlling crap. She would also not allow Nick to feel bullied, or Scarlet to feel ashamed for standing up to a sick, old, homophobic bastard. Scarlet needed back up. Not a scolding. Ma needed to step up and sort her priorities.

' "Faggot" comes from the ancient Greek for bundle of sticks. It originated as an abusive term for the old biddies—the widows making a living from gathering firewood—"faggot-gathers". Then, some idiots belittled the more "effeminate" men with it; those who didn't take to fighting—not that I understand why not fighting was considered feminine. Plenty of women put up a good fight. Anyway, you get the drift. It became a term used to attack those who wouldn't bend into shape. Get with the program. Ironic really, when you think about it,' Rachel said, sipping her tea, and then continuing.

'I spent a bit of time with a traumatised woman. Her ex-husband was an academic. He used to give her these etymology lessons, right before he whacked her with a chunky hardback. A few slaps across the face and the odd kick in the groin. Poor dear—she's passed now. She used to tell me these brief stories as a way of loosening up to talk about the heavier stuff—'

'—Please Rachel. Let's not talk about battered women and fag—' Ma said, tutting beforehand. She couldn't pronounce the entire word. Too distasteful. Too controversial. She moved on. '—Everyone's got their own business, and that's their business. It's not for us to gossip,' she said, halting. Her speech felt unfinished. She stood up and deliberately changed the subject before anybody could rebut her. 'Oh! I forgot the custard creams! Let me get you some custard creams, Marc.'

He smiled at her hospitality, not because he was grateful or because he wanted a custard cream, but because he endorsed her behaviour. Wanted to give her a gold star. Naturally, he'd have much stronger words to say on the matter. Dirty faggots. But Ma had been the perfect, civilised woman. She'd closed down the conversation appropriately; relegated the topic to its shameful bin. Out of sight. Out of mind. Cleared the mess away beforehand, so it didn't need commenting on. She wasn't condemning it. Nor espousing tolerance. She was erasing it; erasing them. There was at least one well-behaved pupil in the family. One good girl. Hope.

Nick shifted around the coffee table and perched on the arm of the sofa beside Evelyn. Summer moaned. Fran rocked her side to side and squeezed her just a tad tighter to acknowledge her cries; to let her know somebody was listening. 'She might need feeding,' Scarlet said, reaching out her arms.

'—No. She's just letting us know she's here. Aren't you sweetheart? Yes, you are. You are letting us know you're here, too. My darling. Yes, you are. Yes, you are.'

The moaning faded. Fran was right.

'Do you have other children, Mr Cliff?' Evelyn asked, reigniting the tension. She already knew. Had sometimes watched them playing in the front garden while sitting across the street, watching his house. A long time had passed, but their faces burnt into her memory. At one point, she was so jealous of them; of their having him when her girls didn't; she could have murdered them all. Him. His children. His wife. Then herself. But she grew out of the madness.

Nick's father—John—helped. A good stepdad to the girls. Though never a full father. He loved Evelyn, but not the girls. Not in the same way. He wasn't theirs and Evelyn was incapable of being his. Like with the children, she was never fully present. Never fully with him. His love wasn't enough. Over time, it made the relationship lopsided. Resentment grew, entombed the tenderness—it was there. But buried. Inaccessible. Increasingly useless. Love locked away. He lacked the skills to help her through the trauma. He couldn't heal and unpack the hurt she'd suffered from the failed adoptions; from Marc Cliff; couldn't free her, so she could love him back. It made him angry. Angry he couldn't fix it for her; angry she couldn't love him; sad he couldn't make her happy. They'd fight. And over time, grow distant. He stuck around, but it did more harm than good. He became a gloomy mirror, a daily reminder of how much she'd failed those that loved her.

Evelyn drifted through twenty years, compartmentalising her soul. Chopping it into pieces like parts of a dead body rotting away inside her. No more. Her mind ripped like a tire, broke like a damn, ruptured like a torn air balloon. At once the air came out, the energy of holding herself together against this constant, internal fragmentation stopped. She stopped. Stopped trying. Stopped resisting. The demon slipped out of her body. Decades of sealed-away hatred, germinating through her entire system, left. Flooded out. Gone. The emptiness gave her back a wholeness she hadn't felt since childhood. She stared at Marc Cliff, standing against Ma's gas fire, smirking at her. She finally had him. And she, hand on heart, no longer wanted him. She saw the disgusting hairs creeping out of his ears. Saw his wiry nose. His bony shoulders. He was pathetic. Not even a monster. Just a cruel, self-pitying excuse for a man.

She sat quietly on the sofa, listening to the others argue about which words they could and couldn't use; about what biscuits to put out; about whether his love poems encouraged girls in his class to get themselves pregnant. It was all bullshit. Her mind was sharp. She thought clearly; deeper than any of them; could see beyond what they saw. He was vermin, in need of exterminating. And she'd do it. Properly this time. There'd be two killers in the family. At least one would mean it.

'What time is June coming home?' Ma said, asking another question to bury Evelyn's to Marc. His having children.

'When the library closes. She's obsessed; barely leaves to go to the toilet,' Nick said, sloping more comfortably on the chair-arm beside his Ma.

'What's she doing in the library?' Scarlet asked.

'Writing her book,' Fran said, answering before Ma could change the conversation she had accidentally started.

'—She's writing a book?' Scarlet said, a huge smile spreading across her face. Her thighs lifted upward and her heels lifted off the ground. June's writing a book made her ecstatic. 'What's it about?'

'It started about her time in prison—' Fran said, speaking openly on June's behalf in her absence. Ma hated them bringing it up. She's rather nobody ever mentioned June's stint in prison ever again. '—But she's spent almost every hour since leaving prison reading murder mysteries and anything to do with human trafficking. Very niche. But you know how Aunty June gets about things. Once she hooks onto something. That's it. Anyway, she's bent on tracking down this infamous woman, who's apparently spent years running some sort of underground brothel in London. She won't let it go. Won't stop until she gets the woman to talk; to tell her all about the lives of the working girls.'

Ma glanced at Marc Cliff to gage his reaction; to evaluate the damage of her reputation as evidenced by his eyes. Her daughter, a convict. It was only a glance, though. The shame was too overwhelming to look for longer than that. Unlike Fran, she was deeply ashamed and, with an authority figure in her living room, feared being chastised on the spot in front of her children, grandchildren, and great-grandchild.

'What did she go to prison for—stealing? drugs?' Marc said indifferently. He worked at the local comprehensive. Most of the children in his classes had at least one relative in prison. Ma thought him charitable for not scolding her with judgement, but then grew irritated and further embarrassed as she came to recognise he had low expectations of her and the family. That is why he didn't scold. Evelyn read Ma's thoughts; watched her catch-up.

'Of course not,' Ma said, pulling her cardigan tight across her stomach. It came out as close as she could come to a snap, but lacking experience in having a spine, she folded quickly, regretting her tone. She'd never spoken to any authority figure like that in her life. She remembered her teachers threatening to break the neck of girls speaking in that way to superiors, and Ma stupidly believing them. Her face flushed and her arms stiffened, as she instinctively prepared herself for penitence. No more sass. Not that Ma would ever even think about the word sass, let alone use it.

Rachel, Scarlet and Fran rolled their eyes and mostly ignored Ma's melodrama. Fran answered Marc's question about why June went to prison. 'Through sheer stupidity, she killed our neighbour. A long time ago—nearly twenty years. She served ten years inside, and that's the end. No drugs. No stealing. She's not a bad person. Just made a stupid mistake.'

'Have you ever committed a crime?' Evelyn asked Marc.

Ma's worry that somebody might think she had raised a drug-addict stealing child didn't affect Evelyn. She had raised two drug-addict daughters and one had died from an overdose. Though the police never knew for sure. They refused to investigate the case properly because she was an addict and had been involved in prostitution. Though they, of course, didn't put that down on the paperwork. Lilly wasn't worth the resources. Easier to say it was drugs, even if it wasn't. They would have got her, eventually.

Evelyn had nothing to worry about. She already knew what people thought about her and her daughters. She was beyond shame. And there was perverse freedom in it. For the first time, she felt unrestricted. In her state of disgrace, she had no reputation to protect. Her attention sharpened on the world around her; on the people around her; the person. On his transgressions. His crimes. She examined and dissected Marc Cliff, split and diced up his dirty, corrupted soul instead of her own.

Ma flew the white flag. Gave up policing her daughters. She became despondent and sat back; stopped preventing them from fighting. Evelyn had an unquenchable fire Ma had never seen or felt. Her heat was too much. She couldn't, and wouldn't, control it.

'Of course not,' Marc answered Evelyn, still smirking. Certainty still charging his words with an inhuman, domineering arrogance. No flexibility or doubt. No hint of repentance. He had been nothing but perfect for life eternal. He was a God. 'Normal people don't go around committing crimes.'

'How about something that wasn't illegal, but still wrong? Something you did before you grew up?' Evelyn said, dancing with him.

'If it were wrong, then it'd be illegal.'

Nick felt sick again. The talk of prison and crime sent his thoughts back to Matt's involvement in the money laundering for the sick Belarussian guy. He'd wined and dined on the dirty money; on the pimping out of his dead sister's once alive body. Not that he knew that yet—June was yet to find Pam Perez, who'd reveal all.

Nick had done nothing illegal, but he had done something wrong. He felt wrong. Criminal. Criminal and wrong, he'd spent so many years living with a man he didn't know. A man he hadn't worked hard enough to know and leave. He felt responsible; felt dirty for taking the easy-route. Felt he'd sold his soul. He had. A little.

'Calling me a faggot is wrong, but it's not illegal,' Nick said, drawing more clouds away from his mother as he spoke in plain words, showing he could be honest in front of his Ma. Could overcome fear and do what's right. She rarely saw his light, rarely heard him express his true feelings. He was like her. The type of person who allowed clouds into the mind; allowed themselves to become insulated from the world and its people. The type of person who withdrew. Ran inward, rather than sweated through the discomfort. His backbone made her happy. His courage to go against himself strengthened her own resolve to do the same.

'It wasn't illegal to deny my daughters the right to know who their father is, but it was wrong,' Evelyn declared, staring flatly at Marc Cliff, who was strategizing a response to Nick's faggot comment. But it wasn't coming easily. He was sweating. Baking. His mind working overtime to take control. But the truth was too hot an iron rod for him to handle. He was stuck. For now. Evelyn and Nick watched him suffer. They took no pleasure. But equally, felt no sympathy. It was right for him to squirm. He was a devil.

Rachel Evans kept her breath steady. She already suspected the impossible, unspeakable truth; that, as a lady of truth, was causing her one of the first existential crises of her life. She removed her hands from her pockets and clutched them together, making sure she avoided Fran's eyesight without it being obvious.

Scarlet was speechless. Rachel looked at her astonished face, unclutched her hands, and placed her palm flat on Scarlet's shoulder, deciding that she should try to end the conversation somehow. It was the closest she had ever come to feeling like Ma; that a bit of surface living wasn't completely without merit.

'Shall we take little Summer for some fresh air, darling?' Rachel said. She wanted to get Scarlet outside. Away from the firing line. It shouldn't happen in the heat of the moment like this.

Scarlet placed her own hand on top of Rachel's, acknowledging her good intent, but there was no way she was leaving. She needed to know what everybody else seemed to have clocked.

'Nice to see you still know how to make it about you, Evelyn,' Marc said, committing to offense as the best form of defence. 'We're supposed to be here for Summer. Not stoke up history.'

Rachel concealed the daggers she wanted to throw at the dirty bastard. He was one manipulative cunt. His comment seemed to elicit the old shame that kept Evelyn and Nick in their boxes. Kept them from their roads to Damascus. Their shoulders slumped. Their heads bowed. Hands withered inwards as they fell back into their storms, surrendering.

'I think you're right, aunty Rachel. I'll take you up on the walk,' Scarlet said, pulling herself up to her feet and crossing the room to take Summer from Fran.

'He's your father, Scarlet. I'm sorry, but Marc is your father.'

And that's when I finally arrived.

When everybody forgot about the hole at the centre of every tornado.

When the room turned to ice.

When in I came.

Freezing.

Numbing.

A kick from within.

An internal stab.

Terminal illness.

Day nightmares.

Motion sickness standing still.

An abomination.

An unfixable tear.

Ugly.

Wretched.

Evil.

Dirty.

Impossible.

Ma tightened her cardigan; Fran shivered and squeezed her legs; Rachel covered her mouth; Nick covered his face; Scarlet simply turned blue. But it did no good. The truth was out. I was out. My identity revealed. My fate sealed. The Lost Finch. I had to go. How couldn't I?

While I was there, it would be forever cold. Joyless. My nature prevented life from going on. They couldn't keep me. Even Fran knew it.

I destroyed them. I was the end. Am the end. Even Pa looked like he saw a ghost when the bomb finally dropped; when he realised it was over. That she had caught him. Had won. Game over.

Evelyn gave me life. She brought me into the world. But alienated me too. Despite her clouds. Her disgrace. The uncertainty of what would happen next. She told them. She told them who he was and, by implication, who I was. Who my Ma was. A father-fucker.

I became the hideous monster-baby they could not look at without seeing him, a reminder of the most hideous parts of themselves. Their years of deceit. And lies. Their waste. I became Summer Finch—the Lost Finch. A castaway. Sent away. The baby that finally left the nest of shit.

The baby that got adopted and had the better life Evelyn dreamed of. The Ballet. Fancy schools. A good father.

But despite everything, I needed them. Need them. Need her.

I needed to know where I was from. My origin. Why my own Ma needed to abandon me. What went so wrong in her life? Why she gave me away?

I needed to know who she was, and why she couldn't be my Ma.

Now I know.

Love.

I needed a Ma. Somebody to look into my eyes and smile unconditionally. Year after year, even when I looked more like him: when my ears spiked like his; when my eyes tinted like his; when my lips curled like his; when I became stubborn like him; when I became bossy and domineering like him; when I became angry like him; when I became cruel like him; when I became selfish and manipulative like him.

For the times when I would fall, as all children do.

Scarlet knew I needed the unconditional love of a Ma that could pick me up. Could kiss my bad parts better, just like a bruised knee.

Knew I needed the love that thaws children. The love that transforms us into more than ourselves when the time comes. The love that makes us into women. Into men. Into adults.

Marc took that gift away from her. He took the most important thing she could give her child. Just as he had taken it from Evelyn. I understand now. She did the one thing we must all do. The thing we can not, not do. The thing that might break our hearts but which ensures our children's hearts grow strong.

She gave me that. And I will give it to my daughter.

I would love you to meet her, Scarlet. If you are reading this, please get in touch. I love you.

Yours forever,

Summer—The Found Finch.

Acknowledgements

Thank you to Arron for supporting and challenging me to produce this book with the love the story deserves. I would not have been able to create it without you. Thank you to Xavier, Mike, Keely, and Rebecca for always being champions of my work and agreeing most kindly to leave reviews on the cover! Thank you to Pat for proofreading. Spelling will forever be an Achilles heel. No matter how many books I produce. Thank you to Debbie for evening chats not about the book or its characters. Thank you to Sarah for our writerly catchups. Thank you to my parents, Jill and Mark, for raising me with love and giving me the ability to channel that into my work. And finally, thank you, reader, for sticking it out to the end. Please do leave a review on Amazon as it makes a tremendous difference to sales.

Please leave a 5-star review on Amazon. It makes a tremendous difference to sales. 4-star if you're mean. 3-star if you're an outright hater!

You can follow me on Instagram & Facebook @mjbirkett123
Thank you for reading *The Lost Finch*

Printed in Great Britain
by Amazon

15877418R00139